D0961152

SIX FEET BELOW ZERO

ENA JONES

HOLIDAY HOUSE · NEW YORK

Library of Congress Cataloging-in-Publication Data

Names: Jones, Ena, author.

Title: Six feet below zero / by Ena Jones.

Description: First edition. | New York : Holiday House, [2021] | Audience:
Ages 8–12. | Audience: Grades 4–6. | Summary: Rosie and Baker need to keep
up the illustion that their Great Grammy is alive before Grim Hesper takes away
the only home they have ever known.

Identifiers: LCCN 2020010384 | ISBN 9780823446223 (hardcover)

Subjects: CYAC: Grandmothers—Fiction. | Family life—Fiction. | Death—Fiction.

Classification: LCC PZ7.1.J68 Si 2021 | DDC [Fic]—dc23

LC record available at https://lccn.loc.gov/2020010384

ISBN: 978-0-8234-4622-3 (hardcover)

For Marie, who is remembered

ZERO°

Baker and I peeked between the curtains and watched our grand-mother's bright red sports car speed to the end of the driveway and turn left onto the road. When it disappeared behind the trees, we raced down the basement stairs and crawled underneath the table we'd walled off with jumbo cases of toilet paper: Disaster Headquarters.

Grim Hesper had said she'd be back after her celebration, so we needed to get to work. Baker squeezed beside me as I flipped my lap-top open, clicked Compose, and filled in the subject line.

I took a deep breath and began to type.

Dear Aunt Tilly,

We know you're working on your new project, and we're sorry for the kabillion phone messages and texts and emails, but the most terrible thing happened, and we need you home NOW.

Twelve days ago Great-Grammy keeled over—and died!

It started back in March, when she fainted in the yard.

Baker leaned into my shoulder. "Rosie, what are you doing, writing a book? Just hit Send already."

1

"I will," I said, nudging him off me.

"We have to search Grim Hesper's room for the lockbox! *Please*, don't make me go in there alone."

At this point I'd usually call him a baby, but I was trying not to do that anymore.

"Don't you get it?" I said instead. "We have to stay at the top of Aunt Tilly's inboxes so when she checks her messages she'll see ours first. I bet the email you sent yesterday is buried under a hundred more from people all over the world."

Baker rose onto his hands with a huff. "*You're* the one who told me to keep it simple. You said put EMERGENCY in the subject line, and then tell her Great-Grammy's sick and she needs to come home. '*That's it*,' you said. And what about never *ever* saying Great-Grammy's dead in actual writing? We're going to end up in jail. Again!"

"We were never in jail, Baker."

"I was six feet from a jail cell, Rosie, and there were handcuffed people everywhere. For eleven years old, that qualifies." Baker stabbed his finger at the screen. "At least take 'Great-Grammy's Dead!' out of the subject line."

I cranked my head and met his eyes. "She *is* DEAD!"

I didn't mean to shout. I'd been working very hard at *not* shouting, or calling names, or being difficult. The things that probably made Great-Grammy miserable—and disappointed—when she was alive.

I counted to five and started again in a lower voice. "Sick is not the same as dead. *Dead* gets a person's attention. That's what we're trying to do: get Aunt Tilly's attention!"

Baker rolled on his side to face me. "You know what happens when she goes underground to research her books."

"She promised Great-Grammy she would check her messages this time."

Baker shook his head. "Aunt Tilly doesn't visit places with phones and Internet. Remember when she went camping in Iceland? In *winter*? She disappeared for three months. Great-Grammy was worried sick."

"How else was she supposed to get those pictures of the northern lights?"

Baker might have been the brainy one in our family, but I was older, and I had a good reason for being bossy. Even if Aunt Tilly was living in some sort of laboratory base station at the bottom of the Atlantic Ocean, this email was our last chance.

We needed our aunt's help. Horrible Hesper was *her* mother, after all.

I hunched over the keyboard and kept writing.

Aunt Tilly, it's time to tell the truth. We've done something worse than bad, but we have a very good reason. See, Great-Grammy told us to do it. And she put it in writing! It was practically her last will and testament, and isn't it pretty much a commandment that you have to do what dead people want you to do? Especially with their bodies?

Baker mashed his face into the blanket underneath us and groaned. Then he got to his knees and heaved a frustrated sigh. "You're really going to tell her all of it? That Grim Hesper's living here and she's selling this place, and it's about three inches away from being bull-dozed? And about the money, and the will, and the reason those things are important: because Great-Grammy's—?"

I propped up on my elbows and glared straight into his eyeballs. "Yes. Because she's D-E-A-D, Baker. *Dead.*"

Baker cringed, then slowly backed out of our "office." For a second I felt guilty. Maybe I should have been helping Baker. But our aunt had to come home. Even *she* would be shocked by how despicable *dear* Grim Hesper had become.

I turned back to the keyboard. Letter by letter, I typed the impos-sible-to-believe words:

Aunt Tilly, I better get to the point:
We put Great-Grammy in the basement freezer, and we're pretending she's alive until you come home.
But like I said, we have a very good reason.

ONE°

Remember how I said the whole thing started in March?

It was a normal Saturday morning—the first official weekend of spring—sunny and cool, but warming fast. We'd just devoured an entire plate of Baker's sticky buns and the three of us were stuffed.

According to Great-Grammy—who might have been older than dirt, as she often joked, but was stronger than most men half her age—that meant we were ready for a day of yard work.

Great-Grammy and I dragged rakes and tarps from the garage to the middle of the front yard, next to her favorite seahorse birdbath. The winter had been long, with a ton of heavy, wet snow, and we had ten acres of mess to clean up. As usual, I was griping about it.

I spread a tarp on the ground and straightened the corners. "Where's Baker?"

"Oh, he disappeared thataway," said Great-Grammy, picking up a stick and waving it eastward. She brought the stick to the birdbath and began scraping the layers of slimy leaves, flicking pieces of muck into the air. "With the weather getting better, the birds will be looking for a place to shake off winter." She let the stick drop to the ground and squinted back at the house. "I need the hose to do this properly."

Next thing I knew she was galloping across the yard, over ground-hog humps and holes, and zigzagging around the wackadoo yard art you could probably see from outer space. When she got to the spigot by the front porch, she slung the first ten feet of hose over her shoulder and started the same maniac dance back to the birdbath, only this time she was dragging the longest garden hose in the history of online shopping.

I snuck a glimpse at the McMansions that straddled our property and cringed, imagining the neighbors watching through binoculars. At least the family graveyard was hidden back in the woods where nobody could see. No way I wanted people knowing about *that*. "Great-Grammy, *please,* walk like a normal person."

She harrumphed and kept going. "What is this 'normal' of which you speak, Rose Marigold?"

I swallowed my explanation that whatever normal was, her hole dance, her yard sculptures—including the eight-foot-tall alligator rock band and Home Sweet Home ornament shaped like a house that welcomed everybody to our long driveway—and almost everything about her, were the exact opposite. Especially here in suburban Maryland, on ten acres of land just 9.3 miles from the White House.

Home Sweet Home. *Please.*

The only sweet thing about our house was Baker's cookies.

I looked back at the closest McMansion. Karleen King, a neighbor who was a grade below me, had the perfect view of our past-its-peak house and most of our property, no binoculars necessary. The Kings moved in a year ago, and Karleen had been working overtime trying to be best friends.

At first I was polite, since Great-Grammy insisted I needed a friend. Karleen had a *the sun is shining every day* personality—maybe she'd tolerate my supposed moods.

Karleen's mom was a different story. Mrs. King was a well-known news anchor for a local television station in Washington, DC. Every time I saw her, my hair seemed to be full of brambles, my legs scratched and bug-bitten all the way to my bare feet, and my clothes shredded from jumping fences and climbing trees.

It was easy to imagine what Mrs. King thought of us. We were her "country" neighbors. Now, whenever she—or perfectly dressed Karleen—showed up, I hightailed it over the back fence and took a long walk through the woods. Great-Grammy was wrong. I *didn't* need a friend.

Great-Grammy caught me staring at the Kings' house and wagged her muddy finger. "I like his wife—she worries about her daughter the same way I worry about you—but that Ted King is just waiting for me to trip across one of these holes. Probably has six cameras pointed so he knows the very second I keel over. And you know who he'll call first?"

She'd told Baker and me a million times already. The worst relative in the history of relatives. The one who tried to send us away to separate boarding schools when Mom and Dad died in a car accident three years ago: Great-Grammy's daughter, Gram Hesper. Or *Grim Hesper*, as Baker and I secretly called her.

Great-Grammy reached the birdbath and yanked the hose hard. "Yes, sir," she said with a sorry laugh. "That daughter of mine would sell King Construction the whole kit and caboodle if she ever had the chance. They're hungry to cram a dozen mini-mansions on our piece of heaven." She clucked her tongue and squeezed her eyes shut, raising her fingers to her temples for a good rub. Opening her eyes again, she stretched her arms wide, the hose swinging. "All our land bulldozed. Can you imagine, Rosie? Our deer, rabbits, birds, even the groundhog...homeless, or worse."

I picked up my rake and began attacking the dead grass and leaves. I wasn't going to say so, but I *could* imagine it. I'd always wanted to live in a fancy new house—like Karleen's—and it made me feel like a traitor.

Ours was more than 130 years old, and the modern homes around us made it look even older and more rickety. Great-Grammy didn't see it that way, maybe because her great-great-great-great-somebody built it. "Stick by stick and brick by brick" was what she liked to say.

Great-Grammy pursed her lips, as if she'd read my mind. "One of these days, Rosie, you'll treasure what we have here the way I do."

I bent to pick up a large rock. As I tossed it on the tarp, I met her eyes. "I'd *treasure* a real shower instead of the bathtub contraption you rigged."

Great-Grammy snorted and pulled a bristle brush from somewhere in her jacket. "I'll have you know, Baker and I watched over thirty videos to come up with that design. I'm sorry you don't appreciate it." She began to scrub the birdbath, and her eyes lit with a strange mix of satisfaction and mischief. "Your grandmother Hesper doesn't like it, either," she said, chuckling.

I tried not to agree with Grim Hesper about anything, but this time she was 100 percent correct. I didn't blame my grandmother for hating the old house, or for running as far away as possible when she went to college so many years ago. I could see myself doing the exact same thing.

Unlike me, however, Grim Hesper looked out for one person and one person only. Like when she wanted to go to law school, and Great-Gramps and Great-Grammy said she'd be a good lawyer but would have to find a way to pay for it herself.

So that's what Grim Hesper did. Sort of.

She took out loans and put them in our great-grandparents' names—without telling them. A few years later, after Great-Gramps had died, and just about the time Grim Hesper graduated, found a good job, and got married, Great-Grammy began receiving bills.

Great-Grammy didn't pay them. Instead, she forwarded the bills to Grim Hesper every single month, without a word of explanation. Hesper was hopping mad that Great-Grammy didn't want to pick up the tab for her education. What kind of mother wasn't willing to help her only child attend one of the best law schools in the country? The two of them didn't speak for a long time.

Then my father was born, and Aunt Tilly, too, and Great-Grammy decided the argument wasn't worth it. She got herself on an airplane and made up with Grim Hesper. She'd always wanted to be a grand-mother, and she wasn't going to let a disagreement about money get in the way.

Everything was fine for a few years, until Grim Hesper's husband announced that he was moving to Australia. He hated the fancy house and cars, and he definitely didn't want to be forced to attend the business dinners Hesper dragged him to. He was more suited to living barefoot and carefree by the ocean. And that was that.

Grim Hesper drove three thousand miles from California to Maryland with Dad and Aunt Tilly, changed *all* their last names to her maiden name, Spreen, and began interviewing nannies. Great-Grammy thought Grim Hesper's heart was broken but never saw her shed one tear. Instead Grim Hesper found a new job and got to work.

And boy, did she. According to my dad, Grim Hesper worked constantly while they were growing up. The only sorts of things he remembered her saying to him and Aunt Tilly were "Good riddance to your father!" and "I work hard to give us the life we deserve, the best schools, and the nicest things for you two." Dad and Aunt Tilly never saw their dad again, even though they looked for him when they got older. So Baker and I never met our grandfather. It was as if he didn't just move to the other side of the world—he fell off the planet.

When Dad and Aunt Tilly were home from boarding school, they stayed with Great-Grammy. Everybody liked it that way. Dad, Aunt Tilly, Great-Grammy, and especially Grim Hesper.

I peered over my shoulder to my bedroom window on the second floor. I probably wouldn't be a lawyer when I grew up, and I wouldn't send my kids away to school or ignore them like Grim Hesper had, but I'd definitely earn lots of money so I could buy a brand-new house where my hair dryer wouldn't turn off because some pain-in-the-neck brother down the hall flipped a switch.

Great-Grammy was hunched over the birdbath, still vigorously scrubbing and going on about Grim Hesper, the way she did sometimes.

"...She never thought we gave her the childhood she deserved. I don't know how it happened, but that girl managed to come out of the womb in search of two things: diamonds and dollars." Great-Grammy's papery pink skin waggled under her chin. "Oh, but I know how to deal with my money-hungry daughter. I promise you, Rosie, I'll have the last laugh around here." She clutched the hose nozzle tightly with one hand and gripped the concrete birdbath with the other. I hurried over to help, mostly because I didn't want to spend Saturday afternoon in the emergency room for stitches or a broken toe.

Together we tilted it, and Great-Grammy smiled, her silver-blue eyes gleaming as she sprayed. "Yes, I came up with the perfect solution, even better than disowning her. Once Hesper finds out, *she'll* be the one who keels over."

I held the birdbath, bracing my whole body against it as she forced the muck out. "Great-Grammy, must you talk about keeling over so often?"

"Yes, I must," she said. "It motivates me."

I rolled my eyes and silently thanked the genetics gods that I wasn't as weird as she was.

We kept working, Great-Grammy filling the birdbath with fresh water, and me piling the remnants of winter onto the tarp. Everything boring and normal as usual.

When we heard screams, neither Great-Grammy nor I flinched, since *that* was normal, too. From the sound of it, Baker was in the middle of another standoff with some ferocious critter. Maybe a chipmunk. I dropped the rake, Great-Grammy flung the hose, and we headed his way. If we didn't, odds were good Baker would be stuck for hours, and I wasn't letting him get out of his fair share of work that easily.

Picture an impending catastrophe: the world is doomed unless someone calculates the speed of the spinning earth and coordinates that with the location of an approaching asteroid and the firing power of some superduper world-protecting laser weapon. In that situation, Baker would be the one to call. But if we need to relocate a harmless spider or wrestle a black snake out of the basement, Baker vanishes faster than a platter of his legendary peanut butter and raspberry jam squares.

As we crossed the widest part of the yard toward the greenhouse, Baker wailed again. "What's taaaaking so long?" Then he howled, "Huuurrry!" It sounded desperate, even for Baker.

We sped down the path between the storage shed and the greenhouse where Great-Grammy started seedlings for the garden every year. As we rounded the corner to the field on the east side of the property, we came to a sudden stop. There was my brother, statue-still, holding a tree limb that dangled from the gigantic oak—my favorite climbing tree.

I scanned the area around him. There wasn't a critter in sight.

"What's all the commotion?" said Great-Grammy, as confused as I was.

"Why didn't anybody warn me groundhogs could climb?" Baker's eyes slid our way. "I can't let go or he'll fall on me."

"I'll be," Great-Grammy said as she looked up at the tree and then at Baker. She chuckled and started for him, shaking her head.

I followed Great-Grammy's gaze from the limb in my brother's hands up to where the mini fur-monster swayed, its back paws twisted around a healthy tree limb and its front paws holding tight to the broken limb Baker had been trying to pull from the tree.

"Baker, seriously? Only you could get in a tug-of-war with a groundhog."

One false move and the groundhog would end up on top of him. Which was sort of funny—except, not. If it fell, Baker would die of fright, and then Great-Grammy would be mad at me.

"Poor thing's chattering his teeth," said Great-Grammy. "He's just as scared as you are."

"This has nothing to do with feelings," said Baker. "The problem is, if I let go, he's going to land teeth and claws first"—then he squealed—"on me!"

"You are *such* a baby," I said.

Great-Grammy put her hands on her hips. "Baker's only a year younger than you, my dear. You'll be thirteen this summer, old enough to realize you're on the same side. You two need each other."

Baker sobbed, clutching the branch with all his strength.

"I think *he* needs *me,* to be honest," I said with a shrug.

Carefully, I walked toward Baker. I put my hands beside his on the broken branch, keeping an eye on the groundhog above. "Super slow," I whispered. "Let go and back up."

Baker didn't waste time. He untwined his fingers, released the branch, and eased away.

When he was safely beside Great-Grammy, I locked eyes with the groundhog. "Steady, boy." I gripped harder and raised my end of the branch over my head so that it was almost level with the limb still connected to the tree.

It took a few seconds for the groundhog to figure out he needed to let go of the dead branch and grab the other one with his front paws.

13

Once he was on solid footing, I tugged hard on the broken branch and let it fall.

Great-Grammy, Baker, and I stood together and watched the groundhog waddle to the main trunk of the oak and disappear up the tree.

"Baker, perhaps you should thank your sister."

Red splotches crawled up Baker's freckled neck. "Thanks," he muttered as he turned and headed toward the garage.

Great-Grammy raised her eyebrows at me.

"You're welcome," I called after him, grateful she wasn't forcing us to hug like she usually did after we argued.

I started following Baker, but Great-Grammy touched my arm. "Just one second, Rosie."

I was probably going to get another lecture about how people held heartbreak and grief inside them and it came out in different ways. Yeah, yeah, I got it. Baker cried and I yelled.

Except, Great-Grammy didn't say anything. When I looked up, her eyes were the shadowy blue gray of a tall summer cloud, lit by sunshine on one side, heavy and aching to rain on the other.

"*What?*" It didn't come out like I meant it. Or maybe it did.

Her expression wasn't mad, or sad, but whatever it was annoyed me. "God really had a chuckle when he made Baker a firecracker red and you the mousy brown." She exhaled as she swiped wisps of her own white hair from her eyes. "That aside, my little hothead, you and Baker are more alike than you think."

"Ha!" I waved my hand at the oak tree. "Weren't you here a minute ago? Baker and I couldn't be more different."

"He wasn't always so afraid, Rosie. And you weren't always so—"

"So...so what?" I knew what she wanted to say: I wasn't always so awful. But she didn't. She abruptly pulled me close and wrapped her arms around me. "I love you, Rose Marigold Spreen."

Even though I didn't say I loved her, too, I think we both felt better—for a couple of minutes.

We headed back to the garage to restart our cleanup day, and I thought the drama was over. But just as we passed the greenhouse, the thing that started our whole six-feet-below-zero mess happened.

Right there in the middle of the early-spring lawn, still mixed with bare patches of dirt, Great-Grammy did the unthinkable: she sat down.

And then she keeled over—all the way to the ground.

TWO°

I didn't think much about Great-Grammy keeling over at the time. She popped right up, made a joke about needing more coffee, and everything went straight back to normal. Turns out, I should have paid more attention.

In the weeks that followed, there were plenty of clues. And I might have noticed them if I were as smart as I thought I was.

The first clue was that Great-Grammy never recruited us to help start the seedlings in the greenhouse—which also meant we didn't spend an entire weekend digging out the garden like we'd done every year since we were big enough to hold spades.

Then, about a week before Great-Grammy died, a clanging noise woke me up in the middle of the night. I went down to the kitchen to see what was going on, and there she sat, having her usual midnight snack: cherry pie filling over vanilla ice cream.

Only, it wasn't midnight. If we'd had a rooster it would have been crowing soon.

Great-Grammy had a spoon in her mouth as she shuffled through a jumble of envelopes and papers around her laptop. There was a metal box splayed open on the counter a few feet away and a stack of manila file folders beside it. She half stood and reached across the table to scribble something in a notebook.

"Great-Grammy, what are you doing? Why are you still awake?"

"Oh, I've been trying to get everything organized. The bills and whatnot," she mumbled, the spoon flapping as she spoke. "And hoping to hear back from your aunt Tilly." She took the spoon from her mouth as she sat back in the chair, giving me a queer look over her reading glasses. "You hungry?"

I glanced at the gloppy red-ribboned mess in her bowl. At 4 a.m. even canned cherry pie grossness looked delicious. So I got my own dish and brought it back to bed, not one bit curious about why she'd been up all night "organizing" bills, or waiting to hear from Aunt Tilly.

The next day should have been another clue. It was late Saturday morning, and I'd gone to my volunteer job at the animal shelter. Two or three times a week, I fed and watered the dogs and cats. This time, though, Great-Grammy forgot to pick me up. She wasn't answering the house phone, and for the hundredth time it peeved me that she refused to join the twenty-first century and buy herself—or us—a cell phone.

The worst part was Karleen King had picked that morning to volunteer at the shelter as a "junior helper." It was apparently her twelfth birthday, a chance to spread more sunshine in the world than she usually did. When she showed up, Mrs. Barnhouse patted her shoulder and proceeded to stick her with me.

Karleen's black hair was parted on the side, her tight curls spiraling to her shoulders. She wore white shorts, a white tank top, and white sneakers. If we were going to take selfies all morning, then sure, the white looked amazing against her brown skin. But she wasn't dressed for kennel work and I told her so.

"Karleen, you should have worn ratty clothes," I said. "We're going to get super dirty."

She smiled back at me, because what else would Karleen King do? "I'll be careful."

And she *was*. After a whole morning following me from kennel to kennel and doing everything I asked her to do, there wasn't a speck on her entire outfit.

It was maddening!

Because Great-Grammy didn't show or answer the phone, guess who smiled her sunshiny, perfect-house smile and offered me a ride home?

Mrs. King raised her right eyebrow as I opened the back door of her SUV and ducked inside.

"Mom, Rosie needs a ride. Is that okay?" said Karleen.

"Of course," said Mrs. King as she faced front again.

Mrs. King was one of the most beautiful people I'd ever seen up close. And the most prepared, because as soon as Karleen hopped into the front seat, Mrs. King handed her hand sanitizer and a lint roller to remove fur from her clothes.

After buckling up, I stared at my bitten-down fingernails, my knees scuffed with who-knows-what from the kennel floors, and my dark blue T-shirt carpeted with dog and cat hair. Karleen was blathering on about how hard math was this year and that she couldn't wait till summer. Before I could ask why she was in my pre-algebra class instead of regular sixth-grade math, she twisted in her seat and exclaimed, "I have an idea. We should do homework together!"

Then she handed me the lint roller.

By the time I stomped through our front door, I was steaming, and there was only one person to blame. Great-Grammy might have been right about a lot of things, like maybe I needed to scrub up better, but forgetting to pick me up was just plain wrong. I searched every room in the house and found her in the basement with a notebook, making a list of everything—and I mean everything—we owned.

Great-Grammy loved filling her shelves and cabinets with online "bargains." Normally, she stocked up on essentials to last through the winter. But it was May first, and the last time I'd been down to the basement, it hadn't looked like we were preparing to survive a pandemic—or a nuclear bomb.

Now it did. Every shelf was filled, stocked with canned fruits and vegetables and bags of rice. Even her two collapsible tables were set up and loaded with supplies. I opened the upright freezer and it was crammed with labeled storage containers: *Noodle Wiggle* and *Meatloaf* and *Lemon Cake*. More food than we could eat in a year.

I shut the freezer and looked to my far left, where Great-Grammy stood in front of a second, brand-new freezer. She lifted the lid and stared inside.

"Great-Grammy, *what* are you doing?" I might not have sounded very nice, but as usual, I didn't care.

I crossed the cracked concrete floor and looked over her shoulder. Deep as a tomb, the freezer was long and totally empty. From the determined expression on Great-Grammy's face, I could tell it wouldn't stay that way for long. I was about to ask what she was going to fill it with, when she let the lid drop and moved to the tables in the middle of the room.

I followed her, peering across the basement at the shadowy area on the other side of the stairs, the side that still had dirt floors, where the spooky Door to Nowhere was built into the ancient rock wall. Great-Grammy had done us a favor keeping her doomsday supplies on the less creepy side of the basement.

The first table was stacked with toilet paper, paper towels, and every other imaginable household product; bars of soap and jugs of laundry detergent. Farther down there were batteries, flashlights, and school supplies.

I stepped toward the second table while Great-Grammy continued to pencil in amounts in her notebook. There were two crate-sized boxes of medicine that appeared to cover any physical distress from diarrhea to colds and sore throats, and countless packages of snacks and candy bars. I looked over the supplies at my great-grandmother.

"What's going on, Great-Grammy? Are we expecting a blizzard this summer or something?" I'd mostly forgotten about Karleen and the unfortunate ride home.

Great-Grammy stayed focused on her notebook. "I'll explain everything later, Rosie."

Later would never come. But I didn't know that as I escaped up the stairs, leaving Great-Grammy and her supplies behind. I just thought her weird was getting weirder.

And boy was it! She kept doing strange stuff over the next week, and I should have been suspicious. Baker was weird, too. He never talked much, but he'd stopped talking altogether. And then he told his best geek-friend, Will, not to come over, that he'd work on their robot by himself.

I thought I was being a good sister when I asked Baker what was wrong, but when he stared back at me without answering, I lost my temper.

"It's an easy question," I said, instantly a bad sister again. "Just answer!"

He didn't, of course.

Then the thing that *should* have bonked me over the head and told me in a BIG FAT IMPOSSIBLE-TO-IGNORE voice happened:

Great-Grammy dragged Baker and me to the store and bought us the super-smartphones we'd been begging for since forever. And one for herself, too.

If that didn't scream "Your world is about to end!" I don't know what would have.

THREE°

Less than forty-eight hours later, I was sneaking looks at my new phone every chance I got, same as everyone else at school.

Mr. Kelly told us to get a head start on math homework while he graded our quizzes. Phones were supposed to be off, but there were only three weeks left till final exams, and my grades were fine. Maybe not fine by Baker's standards, but good enough for me.

When I felt the vibration in my pocket, I grinned. It was amazing to have a cell phone. Not just any cell phone. A smartphone. And not just *any* smartphone, it was the smartest phone in the whole wide world.

I nudged it from my pocket and peeked at the screen. A text! I'd received my very own text! I pushed the square icon and wasn't even disappointed that the message was from Great-Grammy.

I need to speak with you and Baker. Come straight home after school.

While I was reading, a second message popped up.

Important. Will explain when you get here.

I checked the time: 2:30. She expected me to call the shelter at the last minute to cancel? I could lose my shift.

"Rosie?"

I turned to find Karleen watching me with a questioning look.

"Is something wrong?" she whispered.

Oh, dang. I must have groaned out loud. "No."

I almost turned away, but something about her inquisitive dark brown eyes made me think. Maybe, *maybe*, my perfect neighbor could help, just this one time. "Karleen, my great-grandmother needs me at home, so I can't work at the shelter this afternoon. My shift starts at three-thirty. Do you think you—"

"Yes! My Board Game Club meeting was canceled because of the Risk tournament, so it's perfect."

"Risk? What's that?"

"It's a war game, but I don't play it. My favorite is Scrabble..."

Karleen was still talking, only I'd stopped listening. A memory of Baker and me and our parents sitting around the Scrabble board at our old kitchen table was trying to take over my brain. We used to play every Friday night.

Memories, especially the best ones, stunk. I shook the picture out of my head and forced myself to zero in on Karleen.

"...I can't wait to see those puppies! They were so precious last weekend. Maybe I could bring them—"

I held up my hand. "Sure you can." Then I dug deep for the manners

Great-Grammy harped about, because she *was* doing me a favor. "Thank you, Karleen."

I put my phone back in my pocket, bent over my math notebook, and pretended to work.

I'd have to hurry to catch the bus that dropped me off directly in front of our house.

Then I remembered the last time Great-Grammy had something important to tell us—almost three years earlier. It began with "There's been an accident..."

But it couldn't be anything like *that*. If it were, Great-Grammy would get in her car and come get us, like she did that day, when Mom and Dad—

A tingling feeling crept up my spine. I took a deep breath and checked to make sure Mr. Kelly was still grading our quizzes, then pulled my phone out again, typing fast.

Is anything wrong?

I slid the phone between the pages of my math notebook. I needed to escape my own brain, and math homework wasn't going to cut it. I snatched a worn copy of *Mockingjay* from my backpack and thought very, very hard about how Katniss was going to save Peeta.

Twenty minutes, three chapters, and zero problems later, the bell rang. I packed my things and headed into the hallway.

Somewhere between Mr. Kelly's room and the school bus, I realized Great-Grammy had never answered my text.

Baker was on my heels as we stepped off the bus and onto the asphalt. Because Great-Grammy would fuss if we didn't, I walked the extra fifteen feet to the corner of the property, around the flowery Home Sweet Home sign and between the heavy-metal-guitar-and-drum-playing gator-dudes, and grabbed the stack of rubber-banded mail from the box. Then Baker and I made our way up the long driveway, side by side.

The row of trees stretching across the middle of the property had recently exploded with leaves, hiding the house, which was set way back from the road. I loved it. Bright green was my favorite time of year.

"What do you think is so important we had to come right home?" I said.

Baker kept walking.

His staring into space and not answering questions was getting ridiculous.

"What's the matter with you?" I said.

He shrugged, then started jogging. By the time he got to the top of the driveway and onto the crumbling thousand-year-old brick walkway, he was sprinting.

My backpack was heavy, so I wasn't going to run after him, even though part of me wanted to. Baker took the front steps two by two and disappeared inside the house.

A minute later I'd made it to the porch and was reaching for the screen door when Baker appeared and pushed me back.

"Hey!" I said as I got my balance. "What are you doing?"

"Something's happened. And I need to tell you—" Rather than finish his sentence, Baker planted his feet wide and held out his hand like a crossing guard. "You need to stay here."

His strange tone made me hesitate, but only for a second. Since when was I going to listen to *him*? "Out of my way, Baker," I said, pushing past him. "I need to put my stuff down."

Just as my hand gripped the door handle and began to twist, Baker let out my name in a long painful wail.

I froze.

"Rosie," he said, this time in a whisper, which was even scarier. "I need to tell you something."

I turned and looked at him. Even his freckles looked pale.

I let go of the screen door. "Baker—what is it?"

He took a deep breath before he spoke. "Just listen, okay?"

He didn't want me to go inside.

"Baker, please. What's happening?"

He stared at the welcome mat, like the answer was down there. "You know how Great-Grammy wanted to talk?"

Baker was answering questions with questions. If I waited for him to fill me in, I'd be standing on the porch until breakfast tomorrow.

Before he could stop me again, I pulled the screen door open and barreled into the house.

I let my backpack drop onto the entry rug and kept moving. There was the faint smell of chocolate, and the sound of Baker's footsteps padding behind me as I crossed the living room.

Great-Grammy was dozing in her favorite chair in front of the fireplace, a notebook in her lap and the side table stacked with books. Everything was okay.

"Hi, Great-Grammy," I said as I got closer.

She didn't shudder awake the way she usually would at the sound of my voice.

Or take a deep breath as she woke.

Time felt woozy. I took another step.

Her head was slumped sideways.

Her mouth hung a little.

Her eyes were open—and glazed.

My stomach rolled up to the back of my throat and my heart throbbed in my chest as fear surged through my entire body.

I dropped the mail, fell to my knees, and shook her gently. "Great-Grammy?" I said, louder this time. She was the one who called this meeting, and she needed to wake up.

Baker was beside me in an instant. His hand slid down her arm and his fingers found her wrist. I heard a strange buzzing in my ears as my thoughts jumbled together. He'd practiced taking our pulses a zillion times last month because of his first aid rotation in PE. Was that what was happening now? Was Great-Grammy testing him?

He reached up and gripped my arm, tightly. "She's gone, Rosie."

Gone? What did he mean?

Part of me understood. Only, no—it couldn't be true.

Great-Grammy, the most important person in our entire world, *gone*?

"Check again, Baker." I said it, even though deep down I knew it wouldn't matter, no matter how many times he checked.

I laid my head on her arm. A sadness I hadn't felt in a long time overpowered me, dragging me like a rip current. I was crushed by a weight so heavy, I couldn't do *anything*.

I didn't want to do anything.

How could our great-grandmother be dead?

FOUR°

So there we were. Great-Grammy had just died when Baker told me the most insane thing ever.

I don't know how long we stayed quiet. The three of us...my head leaning on Great-Grammy, Baker's hand on mine.

After a while, Baker spoke, but there was no life in his voice.

"Rosie, there's something important we need to do."

I lifted my head and stared at him for a second before I understood.

"You're right. We need to call somebody."

Baker said, "That's not what I mean. Just listen, okay?"

His eyes flickered between Great-Grammy and me with an expression of sadness or guilt—I couldn't tell.

"All right, I'm listening."

He took a deep breath. "Great-Grammy was going to talk to us about what to do when she died."

I rewound what he'd said, not sure I'd heard correctly. "What?"

"She knew she was going to die, soon, and—"

"Wait. I mean—I don't understand."

It was as if he'd punched my brain. I was dizzy.

"It's in there." He pointed at the open notebook in her lap. "She had a plan, and it's going to sound crazy, especially now."

"Baker, you aren't making any sense. We have to call an ambulance, or something."

"We can't." Baker dropped to the rug beside me. "We need to hide her and pretend like she's still alive until Aunt Tilly comes home."

I shot off the floor like a rocket and backed away from him—from both of them. "You've got to be kidding! This is our *great-grandmother*, and you want us to hide her *body*? That's the creepiest, grossest thing I've ever heard. Are you insane?"

I stared at Baker. His lower lip was shaking and so was the rest of his body. He wasn't thinking clearly, and I didn't blame him. I wasn't, either.

I slowly counted to ten and then spoke as calmly as I could. "There are *laws*, Baker. Besides, it's not as if we can stick Great-Grammy in the closet and wait for Aunt Tilly to show up. That could be months from now."

"You're right," he agreed.

Good. I'd made him see sense.

I dug into my pocket for my phone, but before I could touch the screen, Baker was in my face. He took hold of my shoulders with both hands and looked me straight in the eyes. "That's why Great-Grammy ordered the new freezer."

And with that one sentence I knew, 100 percent and once again, our world had ended. Life as we'd known it was done.

I did the only practical thing. I screamed.

FIVE°

Great-Grammy always kidded that we should chuck her body into the nearest snowbank when she died, then wait till spring to bury her, like people did in the old days.

There were signs she wasn't kidding, though, and I'd missed them. Like the body outline I'd seen her and Baker tracing and measuring on the driveway, or the delivery truck that arrived with the extra-long freezer chest.

Yep, Great-Grammy was dead serious when she talked about keeling over, and how she'd lived a long and great life, and hoped she went fast, and that it was the most natural thing in the world to "pass on."

But put her body in a *freezer*?

I looked from Baker, my younger-by-fourteen-and-a-half-months brother, to our great-grandmother, slumped in her worn recliner, and then back to Baker.

"You've got to be joking. How long have you known about this idea?"

"Not that long."

I wanted to yell again, but it was like somebody was squeezing my throat and I could barely speak. "Why would she tell *you* and not *me*?"

31

Tears welled in Baker's eyes as he pointed to the notebook open in Great-Grammy's lap. "I swear, Rosie, she was about to. That's why she wanted us to come straight home."

"Answer the question, Baker."

He pressed his lips together. He was hiding something.

"*What?* Spit it out."

His head jerked the tiniest bit, and I knew I was onto something. He opened his mouth, but no words came out.

My voice got louder. "C'mon. Spill!"

"Okay, okay," he said. "It's just sometimes you make things—difficult."

Because I asked questions when things didn't make sense? How the heck else does a person get answers?

I stared at the notebook. The slightly crooked handwriting, the different-colored scribbles in the margins, the papers and Post-it notes marking pages. What had she been up to? Great-Grammy was crazy, but she wasn't *crazy*.

"You have sixty seconds."

"Sixty seconds?" He shuffled in place, like he wanted to run but couldn't. "For what?"

I threw my hands in the air, then stooped to pick up the notebook and waved it at him. "To explain why we're supposed to drag Great-Grammy downstairs, put her in the freezer, and pretend none of this ever happened."

Baker blinked, panic rising in his eyes again. "It's going to take longer than that."

No kidding. Must he always take everything so literally?

"Just start talking," I said.

Baker inhaled. "So, do you remember when Great-Grammy went to Baltimore to visit her sick friend Priscilla?"

I nodded. How could I forget living on pizza and cereal for three days straight, trying to keep rickety old Mrs. Knightly, the neighbor lady who was "taking care of us," from falling down the stairs?

Baker refused to look at me. "Well, she didn't go see Priscilla. She went to a hospital in Bethesda. For tests."

My heart dropped and a rotten kind of ugliness spread from my stomach to my shoulders. I felt myself sway, so I stepped back to the couch and sat. "*She* was sick."

"Yeah."

I closed my eyes, but I couldn't shut out the realization. "She was sick," I repeated. "And she never told *me*."

Baker cleared his throat. His confession wasn't over. "About two weeks ago she was on the phone talking to some salesperson about freezers, and she couldn't decide which one to order. A few minutes after she hung up, she handed me a piece of chalk and told me she needed my help."

I remembered that day. Great-Grammy was lying down on the driveway even though she was wearing a dress. Baker had the chalk in his hand and was drawing her outline. At the time, I thought it was weird because we hadn't played like that since we were young.

"I saw you," I said.

Baker nodded. "After I was done, she sent me inside to put the chalk away, and when I came back she was measuring the outline and writing everything down in that notebook."

"She told you then?"

"Nope," he said. "A few days later I had a fever and she kept me home from school. Remember that?"

"Yeah," I said, even though I didn't.

"Well, that's when I noticed a lot more. She cooked all day and put tons of stuff in the freezer. The doorbell kept ringing and deliveries arrived, one after the other. And the phone wouldn't stop ringing, either. Remember how she kept losing her voice? I think that's why—she was talking nonstop!"

"Then what happened?"

"The next day I went down to the basement." Baker raised his eyes to me. "Seriously, have you seen it?"

Seriously, I had.

"I came upstairs and I said I wasn't going to go to school until she told me what was going on."

"Where was I?"

"At the shelter."

"Oh." That made sense. "What did she say?"

"That she'd been to the doctor's and there was something in her brain that was 'inoperable' and it was going to burst. They told her it would happen anytime in the next six months, but she had her own feeling it would be sooner."

I looked down at my lap and opened the notebook. A receipt was paper-clipped to the inside cover: *$699.99 – 24.8 cu. ft. chest freezer.*

I unfolded the piece of paper tucked underneath the receipt. It was a photograph of the freezer, complete with measurements in our great-grandmother's crooked handwriting: *72 inches wide. 31.5 inches deep. 31.875 inches high (with door closed).* She'd drawn a stick figure beside it with up and down arrows and a 66" mark. And then a side-ways arrow marked: *24" give or take.*

"But I don't understand." As soon as the words were out of my mouth, it came to me. There was only one reason Great-Grammy would go to this much trouble. "It's because of Grim Hesper."

Baker nodded and sat beside me. "Great-Grammy knew what Grim Hesper would do the second she died. She didn't trust her to take care of us, or this property."

"Remember the day we cleaned up the yard?" I asked. "When the big bad groundhog attacked you?"

"Very funny. What about it?"

"That was when she said she'd figured out how to deal with Grim Hesper's money-hungry ways. Better than disowning her. Something about having the last laugh."

"Huh. Well, she told *me* she was meeting with people to make sure we'd be okay, and that's probably what she was going to tell us about today, only—"

"—only she died first."

And there she was, sitting in the chair. Waiting—for us to *do* something.

"Great-Grammy's plan was to make it so we could live here through high school."

"Without her? How?"

"Well, when she found out she was sick, she went straight to her law-yer and redid her will. And she officially made Aunt Tilly our guardian."

That was good news. Our aunt was amazing—so why were Baker's eyebrows knitted together?

Before I could ask, he continued.

"Aunt Tilly is the *first* choice, but the lawyer said she needed a backup, especially since Tilly travels so much. Grim Hesper is our only other living relative—"

I felt a quick burst of fear. "The lawyer *made* Great-Grammy pick a second choice? And she went with our very own Cruella De Vil?"

"No, of course she didn't do that. But since Mom didn't have any living relatives and there's nobody besides Aunt Tilly and Grim Hesper on Dad's side—well, Great-Grammy knew there'd be trouble." Baker paused and eyeballed me. "You remember why we started calling her Grim Hesper, right?"

How could I forget? We'd discovered how horrible Hesper could be—and how quickly she could make things happen—almost three years before, just hours after our parents' funeral.

A hundred of Mom and Dad's friends and coworkers were wandering around Great-Grammy's house carrying plates crammed with macaroni salad and sliced ham and biscuits, telling each other—and us—how terrible it was to lose both our parents at once, and how sad *they* were.

And then, in the middle of it all, Great-Grammy discovered that Grim Hesper had bought plane tickets and was sending us away the very next day. She'd enrolled Baker in a military school in Colorado, and me in a boarding school in New Hampshire, the same schools she'd sent our dad and Aunt Tilly to years before.

"You have no right to make such a decision without consulting me. I'm their guardian!" wailed Great-Grammy as she marched down the stairs and stood defiantly in the middle of the foyer, not caring that the house was full of guests.

It was the beginning of a huge fight: Grim Hesper insisted Great-Grammy was too old to take care of us and sending us away to school was the only logical thing to do. And Great-Grammy said the last thing we needed at such an important time in our lives was to be jettisoned a thousand miles away from her—and each other. She hadn't been able to prevent Grim Hesper from packing Aunt Tilly and Dad away to boarding schools, but she certainly could stop her this time.

And with Aunt Tilly's help, Great-Grammy won the argument.

That night Aunt Tilly hugged us goodbye, stepped inside a taxi, and went on her way to work on another book, this one about a tiny island in the South Pacific. Baker held my hand and we both sighed as we watched her taxi speed down the driveway.

Now, here we were, three years later. Baker squeezed my hand and sighed, same as he did that awful day. "If Great-Grammy could have trusted Grim Hesper to move in and actually take care of us—" He stopped and waited for me to picture such a thing.

"But she wouldn't," I said. "She'd have us on the first planes to those schools."

"Right," agreed Baker. "So Great-Grammy was trying to get in touch with Aunt Tilly. She hadn't yet, which is why she came up with the freezer plan—in case it happened before Aunt Tilly got back."

More than once Great-Grammy had told me she was trying to get in touch with Aunt Tilly. I never asked why.

"If she's our official guardian, that's protected by law—right?"

Baker shook his head. "She's not here. Technically, Grim Hesper is our grandmother. And what does she do for a living?"

Oh, yeah.

"She's a big-time attorney," said Baker, answering his own question. "Great-Grammy said Grim would find a way to finagle whatever she wants without Tilly here to get in the way."

I scowled. "But—"

"That's what she said. Grim Hesper knows every judge in the state, so nobody would stop her from taking control of us—or this place—because she's our closest relative."

Baker leapt to his feet, waving his hands like a conductor as he strode back and forth on the living room rug. "Did you know, Grim Hesper's been pushing her to sell the house for the last year?" He stopped and gestured at our great-grandmother. "Great-Grammy said Grim would put a For Sale sign out front in three seconds flat if she knew she was dead. That's why we need to follow the plan, Rosie."

I glanced at the empty foyer. This time there was nobody to protect us. Not Mom or Dad, or Great-Grammy, or Aunt Tilly.

I'd begun to see how big this was. If Grim Hesper sold Great-Grammy's place and sent us away to school, we'd have nowhere to call home. Even if I didn't particularly like this house, and even if Baker wasn't my favorite human, they were all I had.

I blinked as hard as I could. Crying wouldn't solve anything. What we needed was a miracle, and without Aunt Tilly there wasn't much chance of one.

An hour ago hiding Great-Grammy's body had been unthinkable. And *wrong*.

Now it was the only possible choice.

SIX°

There was only one thing to do.

"We need to move her, Rosie, and soon. Look." Baker pointed at the notebook. "She was very specific."

I stared at the list, written in large, impossible to ignore, bold letters. He was right.

#1: MOVE ME TO FREEZER.

I squeezed my eyes shut and heard Great-Grammy's voice from a few years ago, when we were talking about Dad and Mom's funeral. She didn't want to cremate their bodies. But she did it anyway, because that was what Mom and Dad wanted.

"We must respect your parents' final wishes" was what she'd said. "They asked that we scatter their ashes over our family plot, and they cared enough to put it in writing. So that's what we're going to do."

And we did.

The notebook held *Great-Grammy's* wishes, and the receipt for the freezer was clipped right on top.

"Fine, Baker, I'm in. But we have to be careful."

"What do you mean?"

"Even though we're doing this for the right reasons, nobody would understand…"

Baker nodded. "You're a thousand percent correct about that."

I held up the notebook. "The first thing we need to do is read this whole thing."

Baker stabbed his finger at #1 again. "That's not the first thing."

My eyes returned to #1 and I shuddered. Great-Grammy did what Mom and Dad wanted, even though she didn't want to, and that was what I had to do.

I set the notebook on the couch and stood. Slowly, I inched closer and knelt beside Great-Grammy.

Baker followed and knelt on the opposite side. As I put my hand on one arm, he did the same with the other. I stroked her gently.

"How are we going to get her—where she wants to go?"

Baker's mouth dropped open, and I realized he hadn't thought this far.

"Go open the basement door, okay?" I said.

He wagged his head and sprinted out of the room.

"Don't worry, Great-Grammy," I said. "We'll figure it out."

"It's open," called Baker as he appeared in the foyer. "What now?"

I Googled my own brain: How to move things. How to move *big* things. How to *carefully* move big things down *stairs*.

"You know how we clean up the yard and drag leaf piles and huge stacks of branches?"

"The tarps! I'll be right back." Baker disappeared again before I could tell him I meant a blanket, not a tarp.

I patted Great-Grammy's arm. "I promise, we've got things under control."

It was a lie, but if she were alive she'd understand.

Baker reappeared, dragging a gray tarp. He spread it on the floor and then stood behind the chair while I moved to her feet.

Baker bent over and gripped underneath her arms, then lifted his gaze. "Ready?"

I took a deep breath and squeezed her ankles. "Just be careful."

"Yeah, we might kill her."

I glared as we lifted and then lowered her body onto the tarp. "This is not the time to start experimenting with a sense of humor, Baker." I reached for my two corners of the tarp. "Pick up your end. She isn't going to move herself."

Baker pulled as I steered from behind. It was working pretty well. We'd made it out of the living room, through the foyer, and halfway down the hall, when the worst thing possible happened, if you're trying to hide a dead body.

The doorbell rang.

Baker and I locked eyes at the sound.

Then it rang again.

And again.

Whoever it was, they weren't going away.

Baker dropped the tarp. "What do we do?"

"How should I know?"

Baker was no help in situations like this. Maybe it was good that Great-Grammy had told him she was going to die before it happened, because my brother needed time to process information—especially bad-news information.

"Okay, just cover her." I flung both sides of the tarp over Great-Grammy's body like it was a tortilla.

Baker did the same. "You're going to answer it? I'm not sure if that's smart."

"If we don't, they'll come back," I said. "Can you try to get Great-Grammy to the kitchen by yourself while I get rid of whoever it is?"

Baker's eyes were wide, but he nodded. We secured the tarp so it was more like a burrito than a taco, and as Baker started dragging, I headed to the front door.

I tiptoed up to the peephole and squinted.

Great. What did *she* want?

I cracked the door open, stuck my head out, and widened my cheeks into the most authentic fake smile I could manage. "Hi, Karleen. I thought you were at the shelter?"

Karleen stepped forward with her own smile. "I was, but the shift was over at five o'clock."

It was after five o'clock already? "Oh, right," I said. "What's up?"

Karleen creased her eyebrows. "You know the puppies?"

I nodded. My cheeks were threatening to explode from friendliness, and I wasn't sure how much more they could take. I was about to inform her she was interrupting a private family gathering when she held her phone to my face.

It was a photo of the smallest puppy. She was curled up, eyes open but looking droopy. "The smallest one isn't doing very well," she said.

Darn. I knew that cutie pie.

I took a quick peek behind me. Baker and Great-Grammy, except for one navy-blue shoe, had disappeared from the hallway. I cracked the door and slipped outside onto the porch, making sure to shut the door behind me. Then I looked at the photo again. My heart couldn't take much more awfulness.

"Daisy."

Karleen nodded. "Mrs. Barnhouse said you'd named her. She's lost weight, and instead of getting stronger like the others, she's getting weaker." Karleen hesitated before she added, "Do you know what 'failure to thrive' means?"

Daisy was more than five weeks old. Usually puppies were out of the danger zone by then, but sometimes...I closed my eyes as I delivered the bad news. "They stop eating. And then the other puppies and the mom avoid them. Sometimes they're not very nice."

Karleen's hopeful expression told me she only partly understood what I was saying.

"So what do we do?"

After a second I put my hand on her arm. "Are you going in before school tomorrow?"

"Yes. Are you?"

I wasn't supposed to, but I had to see Daisy for myself.

"I'll meet you there. Maybe we can turn her around with some extra attention."

I backed against the door and gave Karleen my best *Sorry, I REALLY need to go now* look. "See you in the morning."

I watched her skip to our driveway, where her mom was waiting, and then, with a sigh of relief, I shut the door and turned the dead bolt. I picked up the blue shoe from the middle of the rug and headed to the kitchen.

Great-Grammy was on the floor, wrapped in the tarp with her face showing, as if she still needed air, while Baker sat at the table eating a sandwich, with carrots, chips, and a glass of milk on the side.

"Who was it?" he said.

"Karleen."

Baker stuffed a handful of chips in his mouth.

"How can you eat at a time like this?" I honestly didn't mean to screech.

Baker's eyes glistened as he swallowed.

"I'm *hungry*." He picked up the glass of milk, turning it so I could read a Post-it note with his name and a message in Great-Grammy's crooked handwriting: *HEARTS AND STOMACHS HAVE A DEAL. IF ONE'S EMPTY, THE OTHER SHOULD BE FULL.*

Baker put down the glass and slumped over his sandwich. "There's a plate for you, too."

I opened the fridge and looked at my plate before closing the door. Baker might be able to eat his way through awfulness, but not me.

I knelt beside Great-Grammy and put on her shoe. Then I scooted alongside her and lay down. Her face had a peaceful expression, as if she knew she was in the kitchen she loved and that Baker was horsing down the chicken cutlet sandwich she'd made him.

From the floor, I saw the open basement door. "I'm worried we're going to break her bones on the way down. This tarp won't protect her from the steps."

Baker chewed as he stared from me to Great-Grammy. "Well, she's dead, so we won't *hurt* her, but I get what you mean. What about the boxes in the garage? The ones from the deliveries? Remember the way we used to—"

I *did* remember. "—slide down the stairs when we were little?"

I got to my feet, and by the time I returned with the largest piece of cardboard I could find, Baker was putting his plate in the sink.

It wasn't pretty, but it worked, and within minutes the three of us were beside the freezer. Great-Grammy was still in one piece, but I was worn out. I considered the freezer as we huffed and puffed, catching our breath. It was a lot taller than I remembered—and it would take all our strength to lift her that high. Then what? We'd dump her inside? Part of me wanted to give up and call the police like we should have in the first place.

Baker lifted the lid. "Whoa," he breathed out.

I leaned over his shoulder.

"Whoa" was right. Our great-grandmother had thought of everything.

Somehow, she'd elevated the bottom and covered it with cushions and blankets. If we could lift her, it wouldn't take much to get her settled and comfortable.

Baker crouched over Great-Grammy and unfolded the tarp. "Are you ready?"

I wanted to say no, I wasn't ready, but it became clear he wasn't talking to me. So I squatted and held Great-Grammy's legs. "On three?"

The next thing I knew, we were looking down at her, stretched out in the freezer like she was asleep.

Neither of us moved. We needed to shut the freezer, but it felt more complicated than simply closing the lid.

"Should we say something? Like Aunt Tilly did at Mom and Dad's funeral?" said Baker.

"I don't know. Is this it? Are we finished?" I'd adjusted Great-Grammy's necklace, then folded her hands on each other and rested them on her stomach, and we'd laid her head on one of the pillows. She looked nice and comfortable.

But there was something we were forgetting.

After a few moments, Baker figured it out. "Rosie, ya know how Great-Grammy covered everything real good so it didn't get freezer burn?"

He had a point. I'd sometimes seen her scraping layers of furry frost off steaks. We didn't want to have to scrape Great-Grammy, but treat her like a piece of meat? The answer was no. "We can't cover her with plastic wrap."

"No, we can't."

"So what do we do?"

Baker raised his finger. "I've got an idea. Be right back!"

I leaned near Great-Grammy's ear as Baker bolted up the stairs. "Sorry this is taking so long."

Before long, Baker was back, his arms piled full. I looked closer as he triumphantly held up gloves, a scarf, and a ski mask with eye and nostril holes.

Duh. The winter clothes Great-Grammy kept in the hall closet. "You're a genius!"

By the time we were finished, Great-Grammy looked more like she might rob a bank than go to church, but she was ready for zero degrees.

"Okay, I think that's it." Baker looked at me. "Ready?"

This time he *was* talking to me.

I leaned over Great-Grammy and kissed her wool-covered cheek. "Thank you for being the best great-grandmother ever."

I stepped back and let Baker have his turn. He kept hugging her while he sniffed and his shoulders shook. For once I didn't mind Baker crying. He was kind of doing it for both of us.

I slid my arm across his back and waited.

When we lowered the freezer lid and walked up the basement steps, I knew nothing would ever be the same.

SEVEN°

Until we read her notebook that night, we had no idea how much thought Great-Grammy had put into her crazy plan. It even started to seem not-so-crazy.

"Sheesh, she's been busy," I said.

We'd been on the couch for hours, going through Great-Grammy's notebook and Post-its.

It was hard to take in everything she'd done. We'd probably survive a blizzard, or any number of back-to-back disasters, like World War Three and a continent-destroying asteroid. "We have cash, we have debit cards, a password book, passports, and she set up an account with Byron's Car Service so we can go anywhere we need. We have enough food for months. She even froze milk."

Baker nodded. "And the notes for school." He selected one from the shoe box we'd found by her chair and mimicked Great-Grammy's voice as he read aloud. "'Please excuse my grandson, Baker Spreen, from school today at two p.m. He has a dentist appointment.' And she wrote one for every possible time and type of appointment. Even if we catch the flu."

I looked at my brother. "We don't want the flu, Baker."

"I know," he said. "But if we *get* the flu, we're covered. Great-Grammy thought of everything."

"Sort of," I said, shaking my head. "They changed the rules, remember? A parent has to call *and* send a note. So unless you can figure out a way to get Great-Grammy to talk again, the answer is no appointments and no getting sick. If we mess up and somebody suspects anything, the vultures will start circling."

"It's kind of unbelievable she did this for us. She was a really *great* grandmother, don't you think?" he asked.

"Yeah," I said. "*Unbelievable* is the exact right word."

I turned back to the notebook. Great-Grammy wrote that technically her house wasn't as valuable as the houses around it, though the land was worth millions. The problem was, Grim Hesper knew that, and she didn't care about protecting the house or the family graveyard, or the memories and the history.

When I reached the last page, I read aloud.

"Your aunt Tilly is one of the only people you can trust, along with my attorney, Sherman Ashwick, and his secretary, Mrs. Rodriguez."

Baker was almost to the foyer, doing his typical pacing routine, so I raised my voice. "Sherman Ashwick is the lawyer she told you about?"

Baker spun around and nodded. "I guess. Keep going."

I bent my head and cleared my throat.

"As soon as Tilly returns, you must take my papers to them. Which brings me to the most embarrassing request. SEE #5 ON MY LIST: FIND LOCKBOX WITH WILL.

"I put my final will in a lockbox. I was afraid Hesper would find it if she had the chance to snoop, so I kept hiding the box in different places. The

problem is, the medicine the doctor gave me has made me forgetful, and I can't remember the last place I stashed it—or even the first. I only remember being very determined that Hesper not get her hands on it.

"I wrote myself a hint: Under the house.

"I've scoured the basement from end to end, and the attic, too, in case I wrote my hint in 'opposite code.' But there's a big black hole in my mind where that box is concerned. I promise, your great-grandmother has not lost her mind. Just a small piece of it. Unfortunately for you two, it's a very important piece. I am relying on you to find that lockbox—and don't worry. I lost the key, too, so it's unlocked."

"What should we do?" said Baker.

"Duh. *Find* the box," I said. "The hint was *Under the house,* so she thought she must have stashed it in the basement. Or maybe she did write it in some sort of code." I stared hard at my brother. "*You* should be able to figure that out."

"Even on her loopiest day, Great-Grammy was super smart. If she couldn't find it, how will we? She knew every nook and cranny in this old house."

"True," I said. "But as long as Aunt Tilly shows up to be our guardian, and as long as we're living here with her, the property can't be sold, right?"

"How should I know? Maybe we should ask the Mr. Sherman lawyer guy."

I shook my head. "We'd have to tell him Great-Grammy's dead. And since he's a lawyer, wouldn't he have to call the police?"

Baker's eyes grew wide. "The police would call Grim Hesper."

"We need Aunt Tilly," I said.

"We need Aunt Tilly, for sure," agreed Baker. "And the will."

I started counting days in my head. "We have two weeks until final exams begin. We can put up this act for that long, right? And then summer will be a lot easier."

Baker's mouth dropped open. "Summer? You don't think Aunt Tilly will come home sooner?"

I threw my hands in the air. "How would I know?"

Then I looked at the mantel clock. It was getting late, and Baker had a science test in the morning. "We can't worry about Aunt Tilly right now. How 'bout if I look at the other stuff Great-Grammy left while you study. The last thing either of us needs is to fail a test. We can't have anybody—especially a teacher—calling the house to talk to Great-Grammy."

"Yeah," Baker said. "I guess you're right."

I needed to go through the folder of household finances Great-Grammy had said was in her bedroom, just to double-check that the automatic bills were being paid and make sure her passwords to the bank accounts worked.

As I started for her room, though, my stomach growled and I realized I hadn't eaten anything since lunch.

Great-Grammy had left me a sandwich, and if I let it go to waste she'd probably rise like a zombie and come after me with a frozen lasagna or something. The thought of Great-Grammy beating me with one of her casseroles made me laugh, so I headed to the kitchen instead.

I opened the refrigerator and put my plate and glass of milk on the table. She'd used the smiley-face glass I loved. I picked it up to take a drink and felt something catch my fingers.

I turned it around. A yellow Post-it note was stuck to the glass, just like on Baker's.

Great-Grammy had drawn a heart and in big blue letters she'd written: *YOU'VE GOT THIS, ROSIE.*

It was the first lie my great-grandmother ever told me.

I sat at the kitchen table and cried until there were no tears left.

EIGHT°

In my head, I knew Great-Grammy was gone, but I didn't want her to be. My imagination worked overtime. We'd never slept in a house alone before and there were NOISES. Baker could sleep through anything—not me.

I bolted and chained all three doors and made sure the windows were closed and locked. Then I turned on every light in the house. If some terrifying thing *was* coming to get me, it would help if I could see it.

Or maybe not.

I turned the lights back off, closed my bedroom door, and buried myself under the covers, one eye peeking out just in case.

I'd read in a book that dead people's spirits hung around if they had things to finish on earth, especially right after they died. So a little after midnight I crawled into Great-Grammy's bed. If she was out there, she'd find me in her bedroom.

Then, after two more hours of not sleeping, I realized that if she *were* looking for me, it would be in my bedroom, not hers. I scrambled across the hall, back to my own bed. By 3 a.m. I wondered how the heck I would meet Karleen at the shelter at 6 a.m.

Somehow, I fell asleep and woke up on time. I showered, got dressed, and grabbed a banana on my way out, even though I'd never liked bananas. Great-Grammy had always handed one to me as I left the house, and before I could complain she'd say, "You need the potassium."

Right now, I wanted *her,* but potassium would have to do.

I got on my bike, and as I pedaled down the driveway the breeze felt good. Familiar.

But five minutes from the house the quiet of the morning road became even spookier than my bedroom in the middle of the night. The sun was up, just barely, and there were heavy clouds, as if it might rain. Even with my reflectors and the light between the handlebars, Great-Grammy wouldn't have wanted me out here alone.

I felt worse with every pedal. Silently, I swore that next time I'd call Byron's Car Service and I'd try not to do things Great-Grammy wouldn't like.

When I reached the shelter, I locked my bike to the rack and entered the key code to open the employee door on the side of the building. As it clicked I heaved a sigh of relief.

It wasn't that I'd made it without the boogeyman grabbing me. It was that every time I walked inside the shelter I forgot everything else. The animals needed me, and while I was there, I felt like a good person.

Other places, I didn't so much.

I walked down the gray corridor, with its concrete floors and cinder block walls. It wasn't a fancy place, but it was clean, and the animals were well taken care of whether they were there for three days, three weeks, or even three months.

I found Karleen filling bowls in row B. She gave a border collie a good rub as she backed out of its kennel, then closed the cage. "I was waiting for you. I'm done with rows A and B. Somebody else is taking care of the cats on C, so we can go see Daisy now."

Wow, she must have gotten here before 5 a.m.

She kept talking as we walked, reaching out so eager dogs could sniff her hand as we passed. I did the same on the other side of the aisle.

"Mrs. Barnhouse said you usually do both by yourself. I wanted to get here early so we'd have time to help Daisy."

"Yeah, I've been worried," I said. As we got to the end of the row, I hung back and trailed behind Karleen, wondering how I'd missed what she was all about. She was nice—and good-hearted.

And today she was dressed in a worn pair of sweatpants and a T-shirt, and her hair was tightly braided in long smooth rows. Perfect for the kennel.

"You changed your hair," I said, taking a closer look.

Her hand swept over her head and she glanced back at me, smiling. "My mom spent hours doing it last night. She said it would be better if I'm going to be working here."

Even though Karleen was in sixth grade with Baker, and even though she was annoying, I could be nicer to her. Especially since she liked animals the way I did. "Thanks for taking my shift yesterday. It's been an awful week and that was a big help."

She opened the door that led to row A, letting me enter first. "Is your grandmother okay?"

My heart raced. How did she know? *What* did she know? "Uh, what do you mean?"

"You said she needed you yesterday, so you couldn't work."

Oh. *Oh.*

I chose my words carefully. What was that illness in the notebook? The one that would keep people away?

"She's sick with shingles. So we sort of have to, er, do more things around the house to help her."

"That's terrible!" said Karleen. "My grandmother had those and she was miserable."

"Yeah, I biked over here, so let's hurry. I gotta get back home as soon as I can." I wondered if that made any sense, so I added, "To catch the bus."

"Don't worry. My dad's coming to pick me up. He'll give you a ride. And we can help with anything you need while she's sick."

Curse words. How did I end up in this conversation? I had to learn to keep my big mouth shut.

"That's okay, we're—"

Karleen put her hand on my arm as we approached the puppy kennel. "Dad won't mind. He loves your grandmother. He's always watching her work on your property and says if there were more people like her this world would be a better place."

"Your *dad* says that? About Great-Grammy?"

"Yep," she said.

I didn't understand how that could be true. I mean, Great-Grammy and Karleen's mom got along. But Karleen's dad? Great-Grammy always said he wanted to snatch up her property.

I unlatched the kennel and changed the subject, which turned out to be an easy thing to do. Our furry girl was curled up in a ball resting against the backside of her mom. "They're all feeding except Daisy," I said, worried.

"What do we do?" said Karleen.

There was a special formula they kept for times like this. I had a feeling Mrs. Barnhouse and the others had already tried, but maybe we'd have better luck. "I'll be right back," I said to Karleen. "Why don't you pick her up and snuggle her in that blanket?"

Then I ran from the kennel to the kitchen.

I returned to find Karleen sitting against the wall, gently swaying Daisy in her arms and singing a lullaby I hadn't heard in a long time. I held up the bottle as I sat beside her and whispered, "I warmed it up."

"Oh, good," said Karleen. "Do you want to feed her?"

"She looks too comfortable." I handed her the bottle. "You try."

Karleen took it and brushed Daisy's mouth with the nipple. Instantly, Daisy raised her head and began to suck.

I looked from the tiny puppy to Karleen. "She's eating!"

Karleen grinned. "She just needed some love."

I didn't want to get her hopes up. "Well, love, and food." Then I laughed. "She's sucking so hard. It's like she's starving."

"I think she *was* starving. But she'll be okay now, right?"

"We just have to wait and see," I said. "But this is good."

"Yes," agreed Karleen. "This is really, really, good."

And the two of us sat side by side and watched Daisy start to come back to life.

NINE°

I started worrying about almost everything and everybody, and then it got worse. There was a lot to worry about!

Karleen's father lifted my bike from the back of his truck and waited till I had it steady. "Thank you, Mr. King."

"Not a problem," he said. "You let us know anytime you need a ride, okay? Tell your grandmother to feel better." He took a step nearer and peered at the house. "And whenever she's up to it, there's something I need to discuss with her. If she could give me a call?"

"Okay," I said. "Thank you again."

I watched him get back behind the wheel, practically hearing Great-Grammy screeching for him to get off her property. Because even if he *did* admire her, like Karleen said, I'd bet a hundred dollars that was what he wanted to discuss: buying her land.

Karleen leaned out the passenger-side window and waved. "Thanks for coming to help with Daisy, Rosie. I'll see you at school."

I waved back and walked my bike to the garage. Then I unlocked the side door and went straight to the kitchen, where I expected to see Baker finishing breakfast.

He wasn't there.

I looked at the clock on the microwave. It was 7:35.

I had a bad feeling as I ran up the stairs. "Baker? Are you almost ready? We can't miss the bus!"

He wasn't in his bedroom, either.

My heart raced as I sprinted from room to room with no luck. I raced downstairs to the dining room and then looped through the kitchen again.

Had he already left?

I checked the front door, but it was bolted and the chain was latched.

I forced myself to slow down and think. Where could he be?

The train room?

I walked through the living room, picking up steam as I approached the door on the far side. I was doubtful as I slid the pocket door open, but there he lay, sound asleep under Great-Grammy's favorite afghan, one of his locomotive controllers two inches from his outstretched hand.

"Baker!" I yelled.

Nothing.

"BAKER!"

His eyes popped open with a panicked *What's happening?* expression on his face.

"We have seven minutes till the bus comes," I said. *"Move!"*

He wrangled himself out of the blanket and leapt off the couch. "Why didn't you wake me?" he said as he flew from the room.

It was a miracle, but we made it. I just hoped we hadn't forgotten anything big. I dreaded the day ahead as I sat beside Baker on the bus and held out the granola bar I'd grabbed for him.

I leaned closer. "Remember, if anyone asks, Great-Grammy has shingles. Try not to talk to teachers or parents. We need to lay low."

Baker took the bar and shrugged me off his shoulder. "I *know*, Rosie."

Wow. Baker was the grumpy one. That was a first.

"I'm just making sure you understand how important—"

"How could I not get how important this is?" he interrupted. Then his expression softened. "I was thinking, even though Great-Grammy already left messages for Aunt Tilly, we can't just wait for her to show up. We've got to find her ourselves."

He was right. The problem was, how did you track down a famous author who changed her identity and went deep undercover to research her books? It wasn't like we could strap on backpacks and strike out into the wilderness.

"I guess we could email her and leave messages, too."

Baker nodded. "Okay. I put her contact info in my phone. I'll send her an email as soon as we get to school."

I don't know why, but Baker writing an email unsupervised made me nervous. "Just keep it simple, okay? Say Great-Grammy's sick and we need her to come home and help. Whatever you do, don't tell Aunt Tilly she's *you-know-what*."

I leaned back in my seat, my brain pinging between Aunt Tilly, Great-Grammy, Daisy, Karleen, and the assignment for my first class. Before I knew it, the bus had arrived at school and Baker was rushing out ahead of me.

I took a deep breath. It was time to focus for a few hours on problems that *did* have obvious solutions.

My first class was English. Mr. Davis had instructed us to arrive with a working title and synopsis sentence for our short story assignment. On the bus ride to school, I'd decided mine would be about a girl and her great-grandmother's ghost, who refused to leave her alone. We had the entire period to write "quietly," which was exactly what I needed.

The whole morning went the same way. Nobody asked questions, so I didn't have to give explanations. By lunchtime I was feeling good. Baker and I could definitely make it till summer vacation without people suspecting anything, as long as nothing screwy happened.

Then I swiped my card for the lunch lady.

"My." She looked up at me from her stool. Her eyes narrowed as she studied me. "That's quite a balance."

Uh-oh. I forgot lunch money. That was #4 on Great-Grammy's things to do: CHECK TO MAKE SURE THE PASSWORDS WORK AND THE ACCOUNTS ARE PAID EVERY MONTH.

"I'm sorry," I said. "I'll make sure my grandmother takes care of it tonight."

The lunch lady shook her head. "No, dear. Your grandmother is on top of things, don't worry. I think you have enough to see you through eighth-grade graduation."

I wondered how big the number on the screen was. Was it suspicious? "Uh, well, that makes sense, I guess." I thought of a saying Great-Grammy always used. "She said her ship came in."

The lunch lady chuckled. "It must have been a very big ship."

I pressed my lips together and hurried away with my tray. Great-Grammy's ship was big, all right. A whole six-by-three-by-two-and-a-half feet big.

TEN°

The rest of the school day went okay, and nothing much happened when I got home. Until the house phone rang.

After school, I walked up the driveway by myself. To keep things looking normal, Baker went to his Robotics Club meeting and wouldn't be home until five o'clock. I unlocked the front door and entered the house, but my feet stopped and I stood, unable to move, in the middle of the foyer.

I had no idea where to go.

Not the living room to my right, or the dining room to my left, or the kitchen ahead. Not even up the stairs to my bedroom. The fact was, no matter where I went, Great-Grammy wouldn't be there, her eyes lit up because she was happy to see me. She wasn't anywhere anymore.

Other than in the freezer.

I shook myself. There were plenty of things to distract me, like homework, and dinner, and the garbage bins that needed to be brought down to the main road for Friday pickup.

I started with dinner. Baker might be the better cook, but I could follow instructions, and Great-Grammy had left plenty of those.

After filling a salad bowl with greens, carrots, cucumbers, and celery, I turned on the oven and stuck a creamed chicken casserole Great-Grammy had left in the refrigerator inside. Then I opened the pantry and read the directions on the side of a box of wild rice, instantly relieved. Even I could measure water and a cut a tablespoon of butter.

While I waited for the water to boil, I unpacked my backpack and sat at the kitchen table, feeling proud of myself. Baker would be shocked to arrive home to a real dinner. Maybe I'd thaw some brownies for dessert.

It didn't take long for the saucepan of water to boil. I turned down the flame and dumped the rice and flavor powder into the pot, and got back to homework.

Three problems into math, the house phone rang. For a second I couldn't decide whether to answer it, but it wasn't like we could ignore the phone forever. After the fourth ring I took a deep breath and grabbed the phone from the charger. The display showed a local number.

"Hello?"

"Hey, there." It was a man's voice. "This is Matt Grooms. Can I speak with Ms. Spreen, please?"

"She's not available right now, Mr. Grooms," I said. "Can I take a message?"

"Sure," he said. "Tell her I'm sorry I couldn't make it over on Tuesday. I got real behind. But I can take care of that tree tomorrow or sometime next week. Just let me know when's good for her. She can leave a message on my cell and I'll get it done."

"The tree?"

"Yeah, she's got a tree she wants taken down," he said. "I'll give you my number again in case she needs it. Got a pen?"

The fact that I had a pencil—not a pen—wasn't important enough to share. Great-Grammy would never call him back anyway. I turned my math notebook to a blank page. "Yep."

"301-555-1222. Got it?"

"Yes, sir." I copied down the number. "I'll give her the message."

Why did Great-Grammy want to cut down a tree? I didn't remember anything about it in her notebook. I regretted hanging up before asking which tree Mr. Grooms meant, but then the phone rang again.

This time I didn't hesitate. I picked up the receiver and looked at the caller ID. Then I slammed the phone back in the holder.

There wasn't a chance in heck I was going to talk to Grim Hesper right now.

I tried to concentrate on math but kept glancing at the phone. Before long, the message light began to blink. There was only one thing to do: ignore it. I shifted my chair so I faced the opposite direction.

Three, two, one—

The doorbell rang.

At this rate I'd never to get to problem five, much less finish my math homework.

I headed through the dining room to the front of the house, wishing I could ignore the doorbell the way I'd ignored Grim Hesper's phone call. But something told me I should find out who was at the door.

Until I saw Karleen through the peephole, I hadn't realized I was afraid it was going to be Grim Hesper standing on the porch.

I opened the door and stepped outside. "Hey, Karleen."

She held out a casserole dish covered in aluminum foil. "My dad told my mom your grandmother was sick, so she came home early from work and made pork enchiladas for you guys."

I reached for the casserole dish, not sure how to react. "Oh, well, tell her thanks."

Karleen smiled and backed down the stairs. "Gotta go," she said. "I'm going to the shelter to feed Daisy."

I watched as she ran down the walkway, and then waited. It seemed to take forever before her mom's SUV pulled down the driveway, something I wanted to make sure happened.

When I returned to the kitchen there was a distinct smidgen-past-done smell, and steam shooting out of the silver pot. I set Mrs. King's enchiladas on the counter and hurried to the stove, quickly turning off the burner and lifting the lid with a pot holder. From the top it looked like regular rice, but when I stirred the grains I found a crusty bottom.

I re-covered the pot, set the fork on the stove, and padded across the kitchen floor to the back hallway. Then I opened the door to the basement and hollered as loudly as I could, "Great-Grammy, you forgot to add cooking lessons to this plan of yours!"

I stood there for a second, almost expecting her to answer. She didn't, but just in case she was listening, I added, "And Mr. Grooms called about the tree. He says to call him back and let him know when he can take it down."

I closed the basement door, returned to the kitchen, and finished my pre-algebra homework. For the first time I sort of understood why Baker liked math so much: you can't think of anything else while you do it.

ELEVEN°

After dinner I informed Baker that since he knew how to cook, he should be in charge of cooking. He told me the rice wasn't so bad and the chicken was just right. I said there were brownies but he'd better finish his salad. He ate every speck.

Then there were the dishes.

We got up from the table and Baker headed out of the room. "Hey!" I said. "Where are you going?"

He turned. "It's been a long day, and I need to chill. Plus, I've got homework."

Since when did Baker use the word *chill* when he wasn't talking about pastry cream or mousse? "You think I'm going to clean up this mess?"

Baker looked from the table to the stove to the sink. "We can just leave it till tomorrow."

This was not my brother talking. Thanks to Aunt Tilly, Baker was neurotic about cleaning—down to the last teaspoon or measuring cup when he made a batch of cookies. Aunt Tilly taught him that the summer she returned from some small village in France, where she'd spent a whole year learning how food gets from the farm to the kitchen and how to prepare delicious meals and bake breads and pastries.

Baker was seven years old at the time. He'd always liked to bake with our mom and Great-Grammy, but that summer Aunt Tilly rented a house nearby and took over my parents' kitchen. She taught Baker everything she could. The first lesson: "Clean as you go!"

Baker was so proud the first time they made hamburger buns, and I'll never forget when they made lamb with potatoes and fresh-picked peas, biscuits, and chocolate soufflé for dessert. My mom walked into the kitchen after working all day and inhaled deeply. "Please move in with us, Tilly. You can write here!" she said. "We eat so well when you're around, and our kitchen has never been more organized—or as clean!"

And that was true. Aunt Tilly had gotten the neat-and-precise gene from Grim Hesper, while my parents were more like Great-Grammy. They would tidy up every now and then, but mostly, fussy and formal didn't live at our house—and neither did four-course meals. We ordered a ton of takeout, but Baker and I never minded, because even though Mom and Dad both had important jobs, they were home for dinner every night and never missed anything that had to do with us. Once there was a huge computer disaster at work and Dad had to stay, so Mom sent him food and put an iPad where his plate usually went, and he Facetimed us so we wouldn't miss dinner together.

I looked from the mess back to Baker. My heart rate was rising—a lot faster than any of his bread doughs. "The pots, and the chicken pan, and the salad bowl? And our plates and stuff? Are you insane? There will be *more* dishes tomorrow."

"Great-Grammy was right. You need to simmer down."

I kept glaring. "What would Aunt Tilly say?"

Baker picked up his plate. "Fine. But we've got a thousand paper plates and bowls downstairs, and who knows how many boxes of plastic forks. I vote we start using them."

Logic! He was back! "Good point. For now, get to work. Just because I'm a woman doesn't mean—"

"You're not a woman."

"You know what I mean."

I handed him the rice pot with the black crust on the bottom, and because Baker was still there somewhere under his grump, he took it.

Just as we finished the dishes, I noticed the phone's blinking light. Dinner wasn't the only mess we needed to deal with. I gestured to the phone. "Grim Hesper called earlier, and she left a message."

Baker stared. "The last thing I want to think about is *her*."

"Me neither," I said. "Besides, there's plenty else to do. First we have to email Aunt Tilly again and tell her Great-Grammy is getting sicker. Remember the sticky note on the first page of Great-Grammy's notebook? There were four things after . . . the freezer."

Baker sighed. "What was number two again?"

"Go through the stuff she put by her dresser."

"*Tonight?*"

I narrowed my eyebrows accusingly. "Baker, you're the one who talked *me* into this."

Baker hesitated before he nodded. "Okay. But can you stop being so bossy?"

I couldn't promise that, and my brother knew it, so we stared at each other until Baker gave up and walked out of the room. "Oh, all right. C'mon."

He stomped up the stairs to Great-Grammy's bedroom and stood in front of the three crate-sized baskets lined up beside her dresser. One had a few binders, some loose papers, and different-sized envelopes; another had her laptop and office supplies like a calculator, pens, and paper clips; and the last was filled with file folders crammed tight together.

He glanced back at me. "Maybe the lockbox is buried somewhere in this stuff."

"That would be too easy." I remembered seeing the same files a couple of weeks before, when Great-Grammy had stayed up late "organizing bills." There had been a metal box on the counter. Had that been the lockbox Great-Grammy hid from everybody, including herself?

I scanned her bedroom for anything else she might have left us. Nothing seemed out of place. It was the same as always, except for the messy bedcovers, and those were my fault.

I smoothed the covers, but just as Baker was about to set one of the baskets on the bed, he stood rod-straight.

"I don't want to be in here." His eyes were glassy and ready to spill over. "Let's move this stuff to the train room."

I liked the feeling of Great-Grammy in her bedroom, but I also didn't want to start Baker's waterworks. "Okay," I said.

I picked up one of the other baskets and headed downstairs.

The train room used to be an old porch, just off the living room. Years before, our great-grandfather converted it to a place where he could run his train sets. After Great-Gramps died, Great-Grammy saved the trains and one Christmas she gave them to our dad. When he died, they went to Baker and returned to the train room.

The room's entrance was a small pocket door that slid into the wall on the far left side. There were a cozy seating area, a game table, and tons of books that lined shelves built into one of the walls. Baker's trains were everywhere you looked: there were two different platforms, a larger one with a hole in the middle, a smaller one, and a single track that looped the entire room at different heights. You needed a ladder to reach where it traveled over the bookshelves.

Because the pocket door seemed like part of the paneled living room wall, most people forgot the room was there. Including Grim Hesper.

We sat at the table, and while I got the baskets organized, Baker opened his laptop and started another email to Aunt Tilly. I kept peeking over his shoulder, making sure he didn't mention anything that could get us in trouble with the FBI. Like the truth.

In the subject line he wrote: PLEASE COME HOME, AUNT TILLY!!!! He kept the rest of it short and said Great-Grammy wasn't doing well so we needed her here as soon as possible.

It was perfect.

Once Baker hit Send, I opened Great-Grammy's notebook.

"We need to decide who's responsible for what," I said. "The garbage and recycling, the cooking and washing dishes, and vacuuming...stuff like that."

"All right." Baker was scooting his chair closer when he abruptly jumped up and charged out of the room. "Be right back."

A couple of minutes later he returned with a large foam board and a package of markers.

"Great-Grammy bought enough school supplies to last till college." He set the board on a chair so it stood on the seat like an easel. "We might as well use them."

I opened the package and handed him a black marker. "Okay, you're the neat one, so you make the chart."

Box by box, we divided jobs, memorized our "story," and learned what our great-grandmother had been up to for the past month.

And instead of me yelling at Baker, we argued back and forth. Which was sort of a good change.

TWELVE°

We divided jobs and solved problems. Baker said he'd take the garbage out every Friday morning, and to make up for the plastic and paper plates we'd be using, he was going to figure out how to recycle them into fabrics to make T-shirts and bags. I said I'd keep track of the bills and start using the timer when I cooked.

We didn't discuss Grim Hesper's message, so at breakfast on Friday the kitchen phone was still flashing, like a lighthouse warning us away from a dangerous shoreline.

We used our new cell phones to distract us. There were games to learn, apps to download, selfies to take, and friends' numbers to add. This last one took Baker a long time. Me, not one second.

Even though we didn't live far from Great-Grammy when our parents were alive, our old house was in a different school district. So when the accident happened, we had to change schools—and leave our friends behind.

Most of the kids at our new school already had best friends. Great-Grammy said somebody nice was sure to pop up, but nobody ever did. I guess that was why she constantly tried to push Karleen and me together.

It was different for Baker. He got involved in Chess Club and robotics and within two weeks he was running with his brainy-bud posse. They spoke the same language. Plus, he'd won them over with his malted chocolate chip cookies, which nobody on earth could resist.

There was also Great-Grammy's cell phone to deal with, which happened to be #3 on her Most Important To-Do List: START COMMU-NICATING AS ME.

She explained that that would keep her friends away from us for a while. Great-Grammy had prewritten a bunch of texts, and all we had to do was send one to a different friend every day or so. Baker said he'd be in charge of that, which was fine with me.

I knew we couldn't avoid Grim Hesper forever, though, so when I left for the shelter Saturday morning, I silently swore I would listen to her message when I got home.

Karleen and her father had insisted on picking me up for our morning shift. I was learning that nice people are pushy with their nice, and Karleen's dad was turning out to be a lot nicer—and funnier—than I'd thought. He joked with us the entire drive to the shelter, pretending he was our nosy chauffeur.

Karleen and I were still laughing when we checked in with Mrs. Barnhouse, but she wasn't. Something was up.

"Girls," said Mrs. Barnhouse grimly. "I know you've been taking extra care of the puppy that's struggling, so I need to tell you something."

My stomach tightened. "Daisy?"

Karleen clutched my arm. "What's the matter? She's not—"

Mrs. Barnhouse shook her head. "No. The bottle supplements haven't helped as much as we hoped. Her siblings will be ready for adoption next week, but she's continued to get weaker. I had the vet look at her, and we've started treating her for an infection."

Karleen turned to me. "Is there anything else we can do?"

"Maybe some extra attention?" I looked from Karleen to Mrs. Barnhouse. "Karleen can try to feed Daisy in the nursery while I take care of both rows. I'm fast."

"That's fine, but I don't want you two to get your hopes up. We'll just have to see." There was a warning in Mrs. Barnhouse's tone, though I wasn't sure Karleen heard it.

Karleen ran toward the nursery. "Don't worry," she said, reaching for the doorknob. "I fed her yesterday and she perked right up."

We watched Karleen disappear, and then Mrs. Barnhouse turned to me. "I'm very sorry to hear about Ida."

At Great-Grammy's name, my heart raced as my brain scrambled for a way to respond. How did she *know*?

"I made macaroni and cheese. It's in the refrigerator, so remember to take it home with you. And please, please, please, tell me if there's anything else I can do to help. My goodness, shingles is horrible. Let her know we understand she can't see anyone right now."

That was the understatement of the century. But macaroni and cheese sounded pretty good.

Mrs. Barnhouse paused and gave me one of those troubled grown-up looks.

I kept my mouth shut and nodded, afraid I'd say the wrong thing. I needed to practice for times like this—maybe in front of a mirror so I could see how my face looked when I lied.

There were a few seconds of silence before Mrs. Barnhouse changed the subject. "I think you know this, but I'm concerned about Karleen. It's sometimes difficult to turn a puppy around."

"I know," I said.

And Mrs. Barnhouse knew I knew. My first week at the shelter, three puppies died. One of them stopped breathing in my arms. I wanted to say it was the saddest thing in the world, but I knew that wasn't true.

"Okay," said Mrs. Barnhouse. "We'd better get to work. There's a lot to do this morning. The county shelter is full, so Animal Control is bringing three new dogs and a litter of abandoned kittens." She pulled out a file and started writing, but as I was walking away she called out, "Rosie, I'll check on you two in an hour or so, but let me know if you need me before then."

"Is that your way of telling me to keep an eye on Karleen?"

She smiled and returned her attention to the file. "That's exactly what I'm telling you."

I went straight to row A and got to work. I moved dogs to separate outdoor pens while I cleaned their cages and filled bowls with food and fresh water. I gave each one a hug, or a big pet, and told them they were good pups and someone would adopt them soon. Most of them loved a nice ear rub, but there were always some who didn't.

When I was halfway done with the dogs on row B, I hurried to the nursery to check on Karleen. I found her sitting on the floor of the kitchen, leaning against a wall with Daisy snuggled in a blanket on her lap.

I sat beside them and watched Daisy suck from the bottle Karleen was holding. After a couple of minutes I said, "What do you think?"

Karleen shrugged. "She was balled up in the corner of the kennel while her brothers and sisters played. It took me a while to wake her up enough to eat."

I stood, opened the refrigerator, and found the container of puppy mush Mrs. Barnhouse had shown me. I dug into it with a spoon and sat back down, holding the spoon out to Karleen. "Put some on your finger and let her lick it."

Karleen put the bottle down and dipped her finger in the mushy food. She held it out to Daisy, who sniffed and then stuck her tongue out.

"She likes it!"

"Yeah," I sighed. Even though she was eating, I couldn't help feeling sad.

Daisy should be wobble-running and pouncing-and-tumbling with her brothers and sisters, but she'd gotten so weak she could barely stand. Mrs. Barnhouse was right…the poor girl was at a crossroad. I hoped the medicine would work. She was going to go one way or the other very soon. The time to do something was now. Only, what could we do? She was one of many, many animals.

I had to explain the facts of shelter life to Karleen. "She needs more than the medicine. She needs attention and to be fed like this a few times a day until she catches up. But there aren't enough people here to do that." I paused and then added, "There aren't any foster families available right now, or she might have a chance."

"You don't think she has a chance?" Then Karleen planted her face in front of mine, her eyes bulging. "What do you mean, 'foster family'?"

"People who take in animals temporarily. Either because they need some sort of special care, like Daisy, or because there's no room at a shelter and they'll be put down otherwise."

I suddenly remembered the other dogs—the ones I was supposed to be taking care of—and leapt to my feet. "I'll be back after I finish row B. Come find me if there's trouble."

For the next hour I went from one kennel to the next, feeding, watering, and petting, thinking how each animal ended up at the shelter lost, afraid, and wanting a home. I imagined the dogs as they once were, puppies like Daisy. Ready to give love, but with nowhere for their love to go.

After my parents died, Great-Grammy always said life was fair to some people and not to others. I guessed the same was true for dogs, and cats, and all animals, really.

Later that morning, after I was done with row B, Mrs. Barnhouse sent me to C room to change the cats' litter boxes. I checked in on Karleen every chance I got. Daisy stood by herself a few times, then immediately collapsed, exhausted from the effort. I hoped the medicine would start working soon, even though Mrs. Barnhouse had told me many times that medicine wasn't always enough.

But by the time I finished with the cats, Daisy looked like a different puppy than the one that could barely open her eyes two hours before. "You're a miracle worker," I told Karleen.

Karleen smiled back at me as she picked up Daisy. "I don't want to leave her."

I knew the feeling, except we didn't have a choice. There were rules, and unless—

I stared at Karleen. I couldn't take Daisy home for the rest of the weekend. Even if Great-Grammy would have allowed it, she was in no position to sign papers for Mrs. Barnhouse. But *Karleen* was a different story. "Do you think your parents would let you take care of Daisy for the weekend, just to try to get her caught up and healthy?"

Karleen gasped. "That's a great idea." She handed me Daisy, who had fallen asleep. "My mom always says no pets, but maybe since it's just a couple of days... My dad's outside. Wait here and I'll ask!"

Thirty minutes and a few signed papers later, we were on our way home with Daisy snuggled in a small, blanketed box on Karleen's lap, and Mrs. Barnhouse's macaroni and cheese casserole on mine. Between us was a large bag filled with a heating pad, a container of medicine, an eyedropper, bottles of puppy formula, special mush food, and a list of instructions.

I thought things were looking up, but I was wrong. Grim Hesper was about to swoop in on us.

And it was our own fault.

THIRTEEN°

We learned a big lesson: DO NOT send a group text to every single contact in a cell phone to save time. Ever.

I didn't feel like going inside, so I stood on the front porch and waved to Karleen and her dad as they drove away. Then I balanced the casserole dish on the railing and dug into my pocket for the house key.

I opened the door, but as I stepped inside, I hesitated at a familiar sound. Disaster.

Slamming the door shut with my shoe, I shouted, "Baker! Come here quick!"

I ran to the dining room and put the casserole on the table, then rushed to the window, parting the curtain with my finger to peek outside.

"What is it?" Baker said as he barreled down the stairs like a tumbling elephant.

A bright red sports car zoomed around the bend and I gestured with my free hand for him to hurry. "She's here!"

"Grim Hesper?" His voice squeaked over my shoulder.

I nodded and watched her accelerate up the driveway. There was a long screech as her car skidded to a stop behind the garage, out of our view.

We stepped back from the curtain and gaped at each other.

"Shoot, shoot, shoot! We never listened to her message."

"It's too late now," said Baker. "What do we do?"

We didn't dare let her inside, so there was only one thing to do. "Convince her to go away."

"How the heck do we do that?"

I raced through the foyer and cranked my head toward Baker as I opened the door. "I have no idea. But get ready to think fast."

We were halfway down the walkway when Grim Hesper, her tall, thin frame looking like a checkered racing flag in a top-to-bottom black-and-white pantsuit, appeared around the corner of the house. She bulleted toward us, her snakeskin briefcase in one hand and her cell phone in the other. "Where is Mother? And how in the world did she get *shingles*?"

First Mrs. Barnhouse and now Grim Hesper? How did they know?

I glanced at Baker, then back at our grandmother. "She told you?"

Grim Hesper slowed her approach, her laser-sharp eyes taking us in. It was obvious she wanted to go around us, but she'd have to step on the grass—an absolute NO in her fancy stiletto heels.

A piece of bleached-blond hair fell across her face and she jerked her head to send it back where it belonged. "She sent me a text. A text! That's another thing. When did my mother get a cell phone?"

That question was the easiest to answer, so I did. "Last week."

"It's about time she joined this century, but somebody should teach that woman to write a coherent sentence." Grim Hesper twisted her lips and narrowed her eyes. "And if she has a phone, she needs to use it. I keep calling, but she refuses to pick up." She looked past us toward the house, then swept her eyes from the front yard to the greenhouse, down the line of trees, all the way to the driveway behind her. "Is she here?"

"No," I said.

"Well, *where is she?*" said Grim Hesper.

I'd been trying to come up with places a person with shingles might go, especially on a Saturday when doctors' offices were closed, but there weren't many.

"Her doctor called in a prescription and she went to pick it up," said Baker.

Oh, that was good.

"She went out? I thought she was ill." Grim Hesper raised an eyebrow. "And her car's in the garage, so—"

Baker interrupted her. "She called Byron. He's the man who takes us places when Great-Grammy doesn't feel like driving. She hasn't been out much lately and said she was stir-crazy."

I caught on to what Baker was doing and laughed as if Great-Grammy's excursion were funny. "Yeah, she said she was going to hit as many drive-thrus as possible. The pharmacy, Starbucks, even the grocery store will let you pick up groceries if you order online. And boy, she ordered a ton of stuff!"

"She'll be gone a while," said Baker.

I pictured the "shingles" photos Great-Grammy had tucked inside her notebook. "Trust us, Gram Hesper. She's miserable. You don't want to see her. She has oozy, gooey sores all over her face and neck."

I scrunched up my nose, puckered my lips, and shuddered. "It's so gross."

I scratched my head and then remembered something else from the notebook. I switched on my most sugary-sweet tone of voice. "Have you had chicken pox?"

Grim Hesper stared back at me. "I don't remember. Why?"

Baker choked, but he'd better be keeping a straight face. We had to convince Grim Hesper that this was the last place she wanted to be. "Shingles can give a person chicken pox. That's why she's being so careful about exposing anybody. She even made sure Byron had it when he was a kid."

Grim Hesper eyed me and stepped back. "What about you two?"

"Oh, we've had our shots." I smiled as pleasantly as I could manage.

Grim Hesper stepped back again and lifted a large envelope from the side pocket of her briefcase. "Give this to Mother and tell her to call me. Hopefully now that she's come down with this dreadful disease, she realizes she's not competent to take care of this house—or you two. It's far past time to make changes around here."

She swiveled in place, then click-clacked down the walkway and disappeared behind the garage.

I held my breath at the *vroooom* of her car's engine and waited until she sped down the driveway, a blur of red. I turned to Baker and let out a long moan. I'd figured out how Mrs. Barnhouse and Grim Hesper knew about Great-Grammy's fake disease.

"What?" he said.

I raised my fists to the sky. "Why on earth did you text Grim Hesper?"

"It's worse than that." Baker winced as if he expected me to punch him. "Remember last night when I was writing a text to a couple of Great-Grammy's friends?"

"Yeah," I said. "What happened?"

"There's so much to do around here, so I thought it would be more efficient to send it to everyone in Great-Grammy's phone."

"You're supposed to be the tech wizard in this operation, Baker!" Great-Grammy always made me to count to ten when I was mad, but this level of bad was going to require counting past a hundred. "What did the text say?"

"I copied it word for word like she wrote it. It went something like: *This is Ida and this is my new cell phone number. I have shingles and will be indisposed for the next few weeks.*"

Even if Grim Hesper and the whole world got that text, it wasn't so bad. "Well, you're a dope for sending it to everybody, especially Grim Hesper, but at least they know now. If we're lucky, maybe it will keep people away."

Baker cringed. "Um, I said that's what I *wrote*, but that's not what they *got*."

"What do you mean?"

"Autocorrect."

"You've got to be kidding, Baker. What did it say?"

He slid Great-Grammy's phone from his pocket and hit the screen a couple of times. Then he cleared his throat.

"*This is Ida, and this is my new cell phone number. I have shingles and will be starving for putrid cheeks.*"

Baker raised his eyes to meet mine. "Oops."

I stared back at him. "You think?"

FOURTEEN°

Baker sent a "Sorry, I'm not the best texter yet. Here's what I meant to say..." text to the same group AFTER we double-triple-checked it. But that didn't change the fact that Grim Hesper wanted to speak with Great-Grammy. We had no idea how to pull that off. Plus, there were other problems. Apparently phones ring even when nobody's around to hear them.

After Grim Hesper left, we made a pact to keep the doors bolted day and night.

Between the food Great-Grammy left us, Karleen's enchiladas, and the mac & cheese, we were eating pretty well. Or, Baker was. He devoured everything, while I nibbled. Upsetness didn't equal hunger for me like it did for Baker. I was perfectly happy to be plain old grumpy when the world was wrong.

We left Grim Hesper's official-looking envelope on the dining room table while we ate, and tried to forget it for the rest of the afternoon. Baker worked on his robotics project and I caught up on homework, but that envelope nagged at me. Whenever my brain paused, its evil energy pulled me like a magnet.

At some point I gave up. We'd ignored our grandmother's message on the house phone—and that had worked out beautifully. *Not.* I marched out of the kitchen, picked up the envelope, ripped it open, and took a deep breath as I pulled out a thick booklet. The cover page had big block letters spelling out PROPERTY APPRAISAL across the top, a picture of our house in the middle, and our address at the bottom.

"Baker!" I didn't mean to screech as if I were dying, but it looked like Grim Hesper was doing something with Great-Grammy's house. Without even knowing she was dead!

If Great-Grammy were here she would handle it, and if Aunt Tilly were here she *might* be able to handle it, but Baker and I absolutely *could not handle this*.

I was flipping through pages when Baker appeared, his eyes wide, probably expecting to find me with a knife stuck in my heart.

"What's the matter with you?" he said.

"You know what Grim Hesper dropped off?" I didn't wait for him to answer. "An appraisal. It says how much the house is worth."

"What does that mean? She's going to sell it?" said Baker, coming closer.

I shrugged. "It means she's going to try. Even though she thinks Great-Grammy is alive. You heard her spouting off about how Great-Grammy can't take care of this place—or us. This is bad, Baker. What if she finds out what's really going on?"

"She'll send me to that military school Dad hated."

"And me to that school Aunt Tilly couldn't stand."

Baker's lip quivered. "And we won't have a home ever again."

"*Somebody* has got to know how to reach Aunt Tilly," I said. "The problem is she never tells anybody where she's going until she gets back."

"I sent emails to everybody Great-Grammy listed who might know how to reach her, but nobody responded. And her agent is on vacation, not that she'd help. Why does Grim Hesper want Great-Grammy to sell, anyway? It's not her house." Baker reached for the appraisal and thumbed through it. "How much is this place worth?"

"A lot."

Baker's eyes traveled down the columns. The second he landed on the final number, his eyes bugged out. "Holy guacamole!"

"Yeah. With that much money Grim Hesper could put us in boarding schools, buy a yacht, an airplane, and her own island, and never see us again."

Baker let out a long sigh. "This is a mess. And Grim Hesper keeps calling Great-Grammy." He took her phone from his pocket and swiped the screen. "I had to put it on silent, 'cause now that she has this number she's called five times, and sent a bunch of texts that say 'CALL ASAP!' You know what that means."

"Yeah, it means she's acting even more obnoxious than usual."

"Great-Grammy won't let her boss her around," said Baker defiantly. As soon as he said it, the corners of his mouth drooped. "I mean *wouldn't have* let her."

It was depressing to learn the difference between past and present tense—*really* learn—this way. "We need to act for her," I said. "Come on."

I hurried to the kitchen.

"What are we going to do?" said Baker from behind me.

"First, we're going to check that message Grim Hesper left." I picked up the kitchen phone. "We need to figure out what she's up to."

I put the phone to my ear, hit the message key, and listened. The robotic lady voice started her spiel:

"You have seven new messages..."

What? *SEVEN* new messages?

I hit Speaker and followed Robot Lady's instructions: "Press two to listen..."

Message #1: Wednesday, May 12.

Dead air.

"Save or delete?" I asked Baker.

"Delete."

Message #2: Thursday, May 13.

Long impatient sigh that could only be Grim Hesper. And then a loud click.

I raised my eyes in a question.

Baker shivered. "Delete."

Message #3: Thursday, May 13.

"Call me, Mother. I just received the appraisal. Even you would be impressed."

Old news. "Delete," I said.

Message #4: Thursday, May 13.

"Hello, Mrs. Spreen. My name is Harry Mudd and I'm with the National Association of Graveyard Preservation. I'm searching for a historic gravesite and believe it might be located on your property. Would it be possible to come take a look? My number is 212-555-1776. Call anytime."

"That's weird," I said. "What do we do?"

"We don't need somebody creeping around here, even if they *are* only looking at the family graveyard."

"Yeah, we have enough problems. Delete."

Message #5: Friday, May 14.

We both grimaced when we heard the next voice: Grim Hesper again.

"We need to talk, Mother. You can't ignore me forever. And you can't ignore the fact that you are too old to take care of that dump of a house or those children. I toured a wonderful condo you'll adore, and I've found schools that will guarantee Baker's and Rosie's entrance to the most prestigious universities. They deserve to be properly educated. Think of their futures! Listen to me, Mother, the real estate market is booming right now, and this opportunity is too good to pass up. Call me."

Baker squeezed his hand into a fist and shook it at the phone. "I knew it! Boarding schools again. Why does she want us to go away so badly?"

I hit Save harder than I needed to.

Message #6: Friday, May 14.

"Hello, Mrs. Spreen. Matt Grooms here again. Just checking on when you want me to take care of your tree. Please call me as soon as possible. My schedule for next week is filling up. 301-555-1222."

Baker folded his arms. "Nope. No grave people and no tree people. I vote delete."

He was right. Besides, I'd already written Tree Guy's number—somewhere.

Message #7: Saturday, May 15.

It was *her* again.

"*Mother, I realize we aren't on the best of terms, and we don't always see eye to eye, but you usually return my calls. Is this because of the group I brought by to walk the grounds last week? I promise you I rang the bell. You didn't answer, so I had no choice. I showed them around myself.*" There was a pause and then the noisy shuffling of papers before Grim Hesper continued. "*Anyway, this isn't like your neighbor, Ted King, who can't afford what the land is worth. The person I'm thinking of has deep pockets and can pay top dollar, all cash. I'm dropping the appraisal by today for you to see. This is the chance of a lifetime, Mother. I don't want to take you to court, but if I must, I must. You are proving you are not competent. If you force me, I will take control.*"

Baker pressed Save.

And that time when I screamed like I was dying, I meant to.

FIFTEEN°

Great-Grammy always said she loved Grim Hesper but raising her was like raising the Queen of Hearts. Right now I could totally imagine our grandmother pointing at me and Baker and screaming, "Off with their heads!"

"Baker," I said, after I'd calmed down. "Did you hear her?"

"Who?" His eyebrows scrunched.

I had to be very specific when I spoke to my brother.

"Grim Hesper. The only *her* who called!"

I opened the kitchen junk drawer and pulled out a pad of paper and a pen while Baker hovered behind me. "I meant what she—*Grim Hesper*—said about Great-Grammy. I mean, I get it about the house. It's ancient and creaky and needs to be put out of its misery. But how can she threaten Great-Grammy like that? Just because she's old?"

I sat down at the kitchen table and wrote #1.

Baker sat beside me. "What are you doing?"

"I'm writing down the messages before we forget. There were three that matter, right? Grim Hesper, Mr. Grooms, and that grave guy."

"We need to—"

Before Baker finished his sentence, the doorbell rang. We locked eyes, and I knew we were both thinking the same thing: *Please don't let it be Grim Hesper again.*

We raced through the dining room together, but Baker got his eye on the peephole first. "Did you fail a test or something?"

I punched his arm as I tiptoed up and peered through the tiny hole.

It wasn't Grim Hesper. It was Ms. Pinkleton, my history teacher.

"Why's she here?" said Baker.

"I have no idea. What should we do?"

Baker unchained and unbolted the door. "Duh. We see what she wants."

He pulled the door open, and there was a long awkward silence until Ms. Pinkleton spoke.

"Hello, Rosie. Hi, Baker. I'm sorry to intrude on your Saturday, but I heard that your grandmother's not well." She lifted a bright blue shopping bag in the air. "I made you something for dinner. There's a salad and casserole and cookies for dessert."

I opened the screen door and took the bag. "That's so nice of you, Ms. Pinkleton. You didn't have to do that, but we appreciate it."

"Yeah, Great-Grammy's not doing much cooking lately," Baker blurted.

I stabbed him with my elbow. "She's sleeping right now, so she can't—"

Ms. Pinkleton fluttered her hands and backed away, taking a step down the stairs. "No, no, I don't want to bother her. I just wanted you to know I'm thinking about you, and please tell Ida that I'm here if she needs help."

"Thank you," I said again.

"You're welcome. I'll see you two at school on Monday." Ms. Pinkleton twirled around and walked down the steps. "And remember, you can call me anytime, day or night."

We waved as she disappeared around the garage. Then I shut the door and headed to the kitchen with the shopping bag while Baker locked up.

In a second he was on my heels, poking at the bag. "What did she make?"

"Baker, we ate lunch an hour ago!"

"But she said cookies!"

Everything was labeled in Ms. Pinkleton's blocky teacher handwriting. There was Bruschetta Chicken Bake, Caesar salad with dressing and grated Parmesan cheese on the side, and a tin of homemade oatmeal raisin cookies.

"Baker, did you accidentally text our teachers, too?"

Baker pried the plastic lid off the cookie container. "Nope. Great-Grammy didn't get around to adding teachers to her phone. But it's weird, right? I wonder how Ms. Pinkleton found out Great-Grammy's sick."

I watched him sniff a cookie and take a bite.

"Baker, you know Great-Grammy's not *sick*, right?"

He didn't answer. He just kept chewing.

I put the Bruschetta Chicken and the salad in the refrigerator. We could have that for dinner tomorrow night. I wondered how long the cookies would last, since Baker had already scarfed down two. Not that it was a big deal. Our regular, everyday, didn't-have-a-dead-grandmother-lying-in-it freezer was full of cookies, brownies, and cakes from Great-Grammy's baking extravaganza. And if we ever ran out, Baker was great at baking, or he was before all this started. Now it seemed like he just wanted to eat.

I returned to the kitchen table and picked up the pen. "Where were we?"

Baker was on to cookie number three, so I was about to answer my own question when the doorbell rang—again.

"I'll get it!" said Baker, sputtering crumbs everywhere.

I wrote down Mr. Grooms's name after *#1*, adding a dash and the word *TREE*. I thought for a minute. Maybe we should call him just to make sure he didn't drop by, along with the rest of the world.

From the front door, I heard a giggle that could only mean one person. I headed in Baker's direction, hoping he'd remembered we had to keep *everybody* outside.

Somehow, he'd forgotten.

There in the foyer were Baker and Karleen, and between them sat a box that held Daisy, snoozing on top of her blanket. The bag of supplies was beside the box.

Baker shot me a warning look. "Mrs. King is allergic."

"She started sneezing the minute Daisy came in the house," said Karleen.

"Oh, no," I said.

"I don't know what to do." Karleen frowned. "I left a message for Mrs. Barnhouse, but she hasn't gotten back to me. We can't take poor Daisy back to the shelter, especially on the weekend, when there are fewer workers around."

I picked up Daisy and snuggled her into the crook of my neck. "Have you fed her?"

"Not yet." Karleen reached for a piece of paper tucked inside the bag. "I have her schedule," she said, unfolding the instructions. "She gets a dose of medicine in an hour. And she eats again in two hours."

Lately I hadn't been so great at predicting things, but I saw what was coming next.

I put Daisy back on the fuzzy blanket and watched her sway in place, her eyelids creased and heavy. She plopped onto her side and fell sound asleep again. She really *was* cute.

"I know your grandmother's sick, but do you think she'd let you take care of Daisy, just for a couple of days?" said Karleen.

I felt Baker's eyes drilling into me. His whole being, except his mouth, was shouting *NO!*

But this was an emergency! If we sent Daisy back to the shelter, she probably wouldn't make it to Monday morning. She needed regular doses of medicine and food and cuddling.

I kept my eyes on Daisy and Karleen.

"Sure," I said. "Why not?"

SIXTEEN°

Baker had his _over my dead body_ body language down, that's for sure.

The three of us surrounded Daisy's box, Baker with his arms folded and the corners of his mouth turned south. "I'll tell you why not. _I'm_ allergic."

I rolled my eyes. "You are not. It's just a couple of days, Baker."

"Yes! Just a couple of days!" Karleen parroted. "I'll come over first thing Monday morning and take her back to the shelter."

I beamed my bossiest face at my brother. "Then we're good, right, Baker?"

"Um…" Karleen looked behind us, at the stairs leading to the second floor. "Shouldn't you ask your grandmother?"

"_Great_-grandmother," corrected Baker. "She's too sick to have a dog around."

I narrowed my eyebrows at him. "Great-Grammy will barely know Daisy's here."

"What if I ask my parents if I can stay and help, and you ask your _great_-grandmother if it's okay?" Karleen smiled brightly at Baker. "I won't let Daisy near you, if that's what you want. Plus, I'm good at laundry and stuff if you guys need help." She jumped to her feet. "If my parents say yes, I'll be right back with my pajamas!"

Baker and I stared at each other with open mouths. Had Karleen just invited herself to stay for the rest of the weekend? We watched the door close behind her.

"We *could* use some help. I'm running out of clean clothes," said Baker. "Oh, I forgot to tell you, Will's coming over so we can work on our robot, and since we have so much food I told him he could stay for dinner."

"We agreed, Baker. Nobody inside the house!"

"What about Karleen? If she's going to be here—"

"I didn't invite her. And no, she can't do your laundry. The washing machine is in the *basement*, remember?"

"Okay, well, except for when we eat, Will and I are going to be in the garage, not anywhere near the basement. We have to finish our robot for the competition."

"Fine," I said. "Just make sure everybody stays on the first floor. No upstairs, where Great-Grammy's supposed to be, and no down in the basement, where she actually *is*." There was a swishing feeling in my stomach, but it was different than the usual upset swishy feeling. Baker's friend was coming over, and even though we weren't officially friends, Karleen was coming back to help, maybe even to sleep over.

Baker shot me a weird look. "What's with you?"

"What do you mean?" I said.

"You never smile like that."

"C'mon." I clamped my lips together and swirled in place. "We have to figure out what to serve for dinner. And dessert, since you've already eaten every single cookie that's not frozen."

Baker bounced beside me as we entered the kitchen. "We're having a party!"

I grabbed the refrigerator door and glared at him. "Whatever this is, it's not a party. You're working on your robot, and Karleen and I are taking care of Daisy. That's it!"

A whining sound came from the front hall. "Well, you better *start* taking care of her," said Baker. "Remember, I don't do animals."

"How could I forget? Just go watch her for a second while I figure this out, since you seem to want to invite the entire world over." I opened the refrigerator and stared inside. The chicken casserole and salad looked like enough for four people. Then I remembered the iced tea Great-Grammy used to make. We could have that, too.

When I caught up with Baker, he was standing in the living room staring at Daisy, who was in the box a good ten feet away, whimpering with her eyes closed.

"She's too small to hurt you," I said.

"I'm *not* afraid." Baker looked from Daisy to me. "It's just that Will texted and he's on his way over, and I have to get the garage ready. I've been working on my recycling project, too, so it's sort of a mess."

I'd seen his mess. "Okay, go. But we're not using paper plates or plastic utensils this time. And if Karleen and I get dinner ready, then you and Will are doing the dishes."

Baker accepted the deal with a shrug and an "Okay," then booked through the dining room and out the side door.

I picked up Daisy's box and returned to the kitchen. My homework was on the table from earlier, so I gathered my books and returned them to my backpack, then looked at the oven display. It was three o'clock.

I stroked Daisy's ears, and a nervous thrill prickled my spine as I pictured the hours ahead. Karleen was coming over to help take care of Daisy and maybe spend the night—like the sleepovers I used to have a long time ago. We'd feed Daisy, then set her on the puppy pads Mrs. Barnhouse had packed and wait for her to do her business. Maybe we'd make popcorn and watch a movie. And maybe we'd pour a can of cherry pie filling over bowls of vanilla ice cream at midnight.

I was light-headed just thinking about it. This time I let myself smile, because I remembered having this strange, tingly feeling. It was forever ago when *everyone* I loved was still alive, and I had friends.

I sped from room to room on the first floor, straightening cushions and tidying up. It had only been three days since Great-Grammy died, but Baker had left enough empty water bottles around to make a dozen bags or T-shirts. If he was going to suck down this much water, he'd have to start drinking from an actual glass.

Daisy whined whenever I left her, so I unloaded my backpack and put it on backward, meaning frontward, then zipped it halfway. I stuffed a small towel in the bottom and tucked her inside. She snuggled in safely, and I could see her, like a baby in a pouch.

Like magic, she stopped whining.

I figured Karleen and I would sleep in the train room, so I carried pillows and blankets from the linen closet, careful not to squish Daisy, and dumped them beside the couch. I hid all Great-Grammy's baskets under the table, then realized: a game table was for games.

I found our old Scrabble box and set it on top of the table, just in case we felt like playing.

Next was the iced tea, so I sprinted to the kitchen, and as I was about to scoop the powder into a pitcher, the doorbell rang.

I told myself there was no reason to be nervous and opened the front door. Karleen stood on the porch holding a purple duffel bag in each hand, with her father directly behind her, hugging a large paper grocery bag.

Karleen scooted inside and put her bags down. "I brought nail polish and beauty scrubs and masks and everything I could think of. I even made a playlist." She took the grocery bag from her dad and set it on the rug. "And my mom sent a few snacks, and a bag of baby carrots even though she thinks we won't eat them."

"I love carrots," I said.

Karleen's mouth dropped open. "Honest? Me too!"

Mr. King looked up the stairs toward the second floor. "Rosie, are you sure your grandmother is okay with this?"

"Dad," said Karleen, "Mrs. Spreen is her *great*-grandmother, remember?"

"Don't worry, Mr. King," I said. "She just wants to be left alone, and with Karleen here we won't bother her as much."

"All right," he said. "You girls call if there's a problem, or if Karleen needs to come home." Then he put his dad face on. "Keep any antics to a minimum. Rosie's *great*-grandmother needs her rest."

"Oh, we will," I assured him as he backed into the screen door. I felt a paw poke my stomach, reminding me of why we were having this sleepover. "Thank you for letting Karleen come over to help take care of Daisy."

Mr. King smiled, and with a wave he was gone. We were on our own. Now what?

SEVENTEEN°

I stared at Karleen's smiling face, hoping she had an idea.

"We don't have to make dinner for a while. What do you want to do?"

Karleen's eyes scanned the floor. "Where's Daisy?"

I grinned and patted the backpack. "In here."

Karleen was at my side—or my front—in an instant. I unzipped the backpack and Karleen lifted Daisy out.

She cradled the drowsy ball of puppy fur and began to sway. "First, let's give her the medicine. Then we can take her outside. You guys always look like you're having so much fun running around your yard. We can bring the carrots and my mom's dip. Daisy will love it."

"Like a picnic," I said, grabbing the grocery bag. "I'll get a blanket!"

It was a sunny day, and we found a grassy spot in the shade of the giant oak tree where Baker had played tug-of-war with our resident groundhog a couple of months before.

Once I spread the blanket and arranged our snacks, Karleen handed me Daisy and sprinted back to the house. "Be right back!" she shouted.

After a few minutes she returned holding a portable speaker. She plunked down on the blanket and swiped her phone screen. "What music do you like?"

Karleen selected her playlist and turned on the speaker, and that's how the most-perfect-afternoon-since-forever began.

We opened the bags of chips and carrots and uncovered Mrs. King's creamy concoction, then proceeded to feast on every chip, carrot, and dip combo we could think of. The fresh breeze woke Daisy, and we watched her tumble from one corner of the blanket to the other as we snacked. After a while she found her courage and took a running leap off the blanket to attack blades of grass and pounce on sprouted balls of white clover.

Karleen laughed as Daisy chased a bumblebee. "She's so much better than she was this morning. It's almost a miracle!"

"Great-Grammy always said, er, says, that being outside on a nice day makes everybody feel better." I used to think that idea was ridiculous. "I guess she's right."

Karleen grinned and dropped onto her elbows. "She's definitely right. This is awesome, and it's even better with you and Daisy." Then she turned over and gazed at the oak. "I wish we had a tree like that in our yard. My dad said they had to bulldoze all the good trees to make room for our house."

"It's my favorite." I pointed at the branches that climbed the tree trunk. They stuck out like long rough arms, randomly stretching and twisting every direction, a haphazard sort of ladder. "Sometimes I take a book up to that thick bumpy one and read for a while."

"That high?" Karleen gasped, obviously picturing me in the tree.

"I'd be scared." After a few seconds she hopped up and put her hands on her hips. "Rosie, I've never climbed a tree. Will you show me how?"

I peered up at the tree and back at Karleen. "Are you sure? Baker gets stuck a lot."

"I'm sure," she said. "I want to try."

Daisy toddled onto the blanket and collapsed. "Okay," I said, lifting the puppy and getting to my feet. "Let's do it."

I stood at the bottom and talked Karleen up about three branches, which was pretty good considering how much her arms were shaking. She balanced on the joint of a branch, one hand pressed against the trunk and the other holding the limb above her. A wide-eyed smile spread across her face as she took in the view. "This is amazing!"

A few minutes later, she was ready to return to earth. I should have warned her that getting back down was the hardest part, especially for a beginner.

"That was scary, but so much fun," she said when she was on the ground again, still beaming. She spread her arms. "You're so lucky to have all this!"

I spun in place and looked. Really looked. A strange feeling came over me as I remembered how much Great-Grammy had loved her land—and that if somebody bought this place, there would be nothing but perfectly mowed grass, just like at Karleen's house.

"Yeah," I said. "I guess you're right."

Karleen bounced around me. "What's next?"

Daisy was napping, so I tucked her inside the backpack and led the way around the house, through the gate, and across the backyard. I showed Karleen how to hop the fence and then we hiked the years-worn path through the woods to our family graveyard. It was in a small clearing surrounded by a short rock wall that leaned slightly inward, and a circle of trees that seemed to get closer and closer to the wall every year.

The trees canopied over us, bits of sunlight speckling the gravestones as I led Karleen around and told her about each person, the same way Great-Grammy had told Baker and me. Twenty grave markers stuck out of the ground in no particular order, some big and others small, and I had a story for each and every family member.

Karleen's eyebrows knitted together. "But where are your parents?"

A feeling flooded through me, like taking a swallow of hot cocoa on a snowy day. For the first time, the mention of my parents didn't feel awful. "They're here," I said. "They wanted to be cremated and have their ashes scattered inside the rock wall."

"Oh," said Karleen. "So they're part of the whole family, not just in their own spot." I stared at the small graveyard. I'd never thought about it that way: Mom and Dad wanted to be part of the land and the family they loved. Dad always said Great-Grammy's home was his favorite place in the entire world, and my mom felt the same way. The trees, the birds, the chattering squirrels, the chipmunks, the groundhogs, the raccoons, the foxes, the deer, the bees, the wind, the sun, the rain—and the family. For them, this was where life started, and where it ended.

"Yeah, like that." I faced Karleen. "Where's your family?"

She gave a small shrug and ran her hand across the giant tombstone my great-great-great-grandparents shared. "We don't have anyplace like this. But I have loads of family stories, too."

A peaceful feeling overcame me. "Let's go make dinner, and you can tell me some."

"Okay," said Karleen. "I was just thinking, my grandfather taught me how to make lanterns out of newspaper, and then after it was dark we'd fly—"

"—them up in the air like glowing hot-air balloons!" I finished her sentence. "Us too! Great-Grammy has a big stack of newspaper in the garage—"

"I could get my dad to help, since your great-grammy can't."

"Good idea. And we can make popcorn—"

"And paint our nails!" Karleen took a running leap over the rock wall. "Let's go!"

I followed Karleen, carefully cradling the backpack as we raced through the wooded area, hopped the fence again, and skipped across the backyard. When we got inside, I reached into the pouch for Daisy. "Isn't it time to feed her?"

Karleen took charge of Daisy while I grabbed the chicken casserole from the fridge and turned the oven on. Then I went to the basement freezer for Great-Grammy's lemon cake, since the sleepover was sort of a special occasion.

When I returned with the cake, Daisy had finished eating and her eyes were droopy. Karleen moved her to the box and tucked her into her blanket, and we both watched as she curled up and fell asleep.

"Okay," said Karleen, "we need to make a list of everything we want to do, so we don't forget anything." She rummaged through Great-Grammy's junk drawer and found a pen and pad of paper, then sat on the floor beside Daisy while I unwrapped the casserole and the cake.

By the time we called Baker and Will for dinner an hour later, the table was set, the food was ready, and we'd planned every minute of the night ahead.

Each bite of the chicken casserole and salad was delicious, and, except for Will, who was on his third helping, we were finished eating. I'd opened the freezer to get vanilla ice cream when Baker signaled for me to meet him in the dining room.

He kept his eyes on the door to the kitchen and his voice low. "I know you wanted us to do the dishes, but we've been working all afternoon and Will's mom is coming to get him in an hour. And we want to play some Xbox—"

My mouth opened, ready to argue that he was nuts if he thought he was getting off the hook, especially when he and Will hadn't done a single thing to help put dinner on the table. The "No way" was on its way from wherever my moods came from, when the words came to a sudden stop at the top of my throat.

Karleen and I had been enjoying ourselves, even when we were setting the table, while Baker and Will had been working nonstop on their project in the garage. Plus, Will was going home, and Karleen was sleeping over.

Maybe there was a way to make us both happy.

I put my hand on Baker's shoulder. "What if we forget the dishes for now and you can do them after Will leaves. I don't even care if you leave them for the morning."

Baker's eyes widened. "Really?"

"Yes, really."

Baker launched forward and wrapped his arms around me. "You're the best sister ever!"

He disappeared into the kitchen with a loud whoop. "C'mon, Will. We can do some Minecraft in the—" Baker spun around, his eyes wide again. "Where's Karleen?"

I scanned the kitchen. Will was at the table, scraping up the last of his chicken casserole, but Karleen wasn't in sight. "The bathroom?"

Baker bolted from the kitchen to the back hall. A few seconds later he was back, shaking his head.

I ticked off places she could be that weren't where she shouldn't be—where she *couldn't* be.

"Rosie, I can't find your—"

I whirled around. Karleen was in the dining room, coming toward me with a tray loaded with food. When had she put that together?

"—great-grandmother. I thought she must be hungry, so I made her a plate and brought it upstairs, but she isn't there. Where could she be?"

I looked over my shoulder at Baker. Yes, *where* was Great-Grammy?

"Oh, yeah." Baker stood straighter and tilted his head to look at the ceiling. "I forgot. She left. While you guys were—um, she said she couldn't find you. But she got a call from a doctor in Baltimore and she had to go to the special hospital up there. For a test." Baker, who usually couldn't say anything on the fly, was getting pretty good at saving our necks. First Grim Hesper, and now this.

Will looked up from his plate, his forehead furrowed. "She did? Where was I?"

Baker glanced at Will. "In the bathroom," he said in a firm tone.

Will tilted his head, looking even more confused. "But I didn't—"

"Oh, yeah, I took Karleen to see the family plot," I said, purposely interrupting *that* conversation. "Did Great-Grammy say Mrs. Knightly was in charge again?"

Baker wagged his head. "Yeah, but she can't come till tomorrow morning sometime—and Great-Grammy will be back soon, so—"

"We're here by ourselves?" Karleen's eyes were wide, swirling like cinnamon rolls. "For real?"

I stepped toward her and took the tray. "Do you want to go home?"

Karleen stared at the floor for a second. "I don't want to leave. We're old enough to be alone, right? If something happens we can always call Mrs. Knightly, or my parents, and if there's an emergency we'll call 911."

"Right," I said. "Just like any adult would do."

"Besides, my dad said he'd help us with the newspaper lanterns at eight, right before it gets dark. So he'll be here part of the time."

I'd forgotten that. "Should we tell him Great-Grammy isn't here?"

"We can't lie," said Karleen. "But if he doesn't ask—"

If Mr. King asked and we told him, he'd probably make Karleen go home to sleep. That would be sad, but not the worst thing that could happen.

"Good idea. We won't lie, not one bit. We just won't mention it." I looked at Baker. "Not a word, right?"

Baker nodded. Then we stared at Will.

Will held up his hands. "Don't look at me. The only thing I'm interested in is dessert."

We cut the lemon cake and topped it with ice cream. Then we took our bowls into the train room, where, for the next hour, Baker and Will wandered around their Minecraft world and I taught Karleen how to operate two trains without crashing them into each other.

Will left, and while Baker cleaned the kitchen, Karleen's dad came over and helped us make lanterns. Later—after the lanterns sailed into the night sky, and Karleen's dad said goodbye and went home—we bolted the doors.

It wasn't hard to decide what to do next, since we were hungry again. We served ourselves more cake, and then Baker, Karleen, and I returned to the train room, where we played the most epic game of Scrabble ever.

I wished the night would never end.

EIGHTEEN°

Sunday morning might have been better if Baker had made waffles and bacon like he used to before we began our careers as criminal liars—but it was still pretty great.

Karleen and I toasted English muffins, then slathered them with butter and Great-Grammy's strawberry jam. The whole time we ate, Daisy stared at us from her box, whining, which was a good thing: she was hungry! After feeding her and giving her medicine, we took our picnic blanket outside, and while Daisy dashed around with more energy than the day before, Karleen and I painted each other's nails for the third time.

She bent over my foot, brushing a coat of clear sparkles over my Teal Dawn–colored toenails, then abruptly stopped chattering and squinted up at me. "I sure hope your great-grandmother's okay. Do you know when she'll be back?"

I didn't want to lie to Karleen again. Friends didn't do that. But what choice did I have? "Don't worry, she texted this morning and said she'd try to get home tonight." Then I took a deep breath and made it even worse. "If she isn't, Mrs. Knightly can stay over like she did last time Great-Grammy was away."

Karleen glanced at Daisy, who was digging her nose into the folds of the blanket. "What about Daisy? Will Mrs. Knightly mind that she's here?"

I smiled at the puppy. If she kept improving, she'd be even healthier than her brothers and sisters soon. "No, she won't mind. Besides, I think Daisy is strong enough to go back to the shelter." I was glad Daisy was doing so well, because leaving her home alone while we were at school could be a disaster.

"Yeah, that's what I was thinking. I'll come by before my shift to get her." Karleen sighed. "It would be so awesome if one of us could keep her—I mean, for always."

"I know." But that was impossible. I told Karleen what I thought Mrs. Barnhouse would say right now. "You saved her life by giving her the attention she needed. And puppies get adopted fast, especially when they're as cute as she is, so the most important thing is, Daisy will have a good life."

Karleen went back to painting my toes, but I felt a teardrop land on my foot. I reached out and patted her shoulder. She looked up again, her eyes glassy. "I'm okay. Sad for us, but happy that Daisy's better."

"I like that." I wiped my own cheek. "Happy-sad tears."

A while later Mrs. King texted Karleen and told her to head home to do her homework, which was just as well. Daisy needed a nap, and so did I.

Monday morning, Karleen and her dad pulled up our driveway just like she said they would. In the biggest shocker, Baker came out to say goodbye to Daisy. He even petted her! I hugged the puppy, then Karleen, and said I'd see *her* at school.

Though Daisy had lived with us for less than forty-eight hours, when Baker and I walked into the house, there was an empty feeling. Again.

Baker twisted his lips. "For a dog, Daisy wasn't so bad."

I stared. "You never got near her."

"Yes I did," he said. "Both nights when you were conked out she started howling. So I gave her one of the bottles in the fridge and held her till she went back to sleep." Then he smiled. "I think she likes me."

I rubbed his head and smiled back at him. "Everybody likes you, Baker."

We got ready for school and rode the bus as usual. But that week, nothing felt the same as before.

Karleen and I ate lunch together every single day, and once, her mom even let her ride the bus home from school with me and Baker. All week, the three of us did our homework together at our kitchen table while we snacked on leftover lemon cake, or cookies, or carrots and dip. Then we'd play as many rounds of Scrabble as we could before Mrs. King texted for Karleen to head home.

The only hard part was that Karleen asked about Great-Grammy a lot. "Why isn't the doctor letting her come home? Is she okay?"

My answer was always the same: "She's fine. She'll be home tomorrow for sure." By Thursday I couldn't repeat the same lie—it refused to come out of my mouth—so I told an even bigger one. "She's home! But she's resting, so we need to stay quiet."

Other than the big fat performance we were putting on for her, it was like Karleen, Baker, and I had become not only friends, but sort of like a family.

Then came Friday.

Baker and I stepped off the school bus, as usual. I walked to the mailbox to get the stack of rubber-banded envelopes, as usual. And we began our long walk up the driveway, where I expected to see Karleen—whose mom always beat the bus—running toward us, as usual.

She was running, but not *as usual*.

Karleen was hurtling down the driveway at top speed, flailing her arms and wailing, "Hurry! Hurry! *Hurrrryyy!*"

When she reached us, she grabbed our arms and tugged, urging us to move faster. "I'm so glad you weren't home. I was halfway across"—she signaled with her head at the open field between our house and hers—"when I heard a big crash and the ground shook like an earthquake. It sounded like it came from over there." She let go of my arm and waved in a half-moon motion, pointing clear across to the east side of the house, which was hidden from view. "It was like a bomb went off, so I ran as fast as I could."

Our feet started to move double-time, going from a jog to a sprint. There was the vague sound of sirens in the distance. "What are you saying, Karleen?" I shouted as we ran together. "A *bomb*?"

"No, a gigantic tree! It fell on your house and crushed the roof—the part that's one-story. That's the train room, right? I knocked and knocked and kept ringing the doorbell, but your great-grandmother didn't answer. I'm afraid she's hurt—"

Karleen was out of breath and began to slow down, but Baker and I kept going.

"It's a huge mess of leaves, it's hard to see how bad it is," Karleen called after us.

When we reached the far end of the house, we saw it: the uprooted trunk of a maple tree, its mass of green leaves flopped sideways over the old side porch that had been converted into the train room.

I put my hand on Baker's shoulder. The sirens were getting closer, and for a split second I wondered...

"C'mon! We need to get into the house!" called Karleen. She'd made it to the front porch and her hand was on the door handle, squeezing and twisting as if that would unlock it. "She got back yesterday, right?"

Baker and I snapped awake and raced for the porch. I knew we were thinking the same thing—we had to pull off the best acting job ever.

Karleen stepped back as we approached. "Oh, I hope she's okay!"

The sirens were louder, and as Baker inserted his key in the lock, I turned toward the road and saw emergency lights coming from both directions.

Whatever fear I'd felt three seconds ago was nothing. My heart raced a million beats a minute and my mouth fell open. Unable to speak, I faced Karleen and gestured to the road.

"It was an emergency!" Karleen hopped up and down behind Baker as he struggled with the key.

Baker pushed through the door, and as we crossed the threshold behind him, the earsplitting sirens and horns continued their cries, louder and louder.

I spun in place and watched a fire truck, an ambulance, and two police cars barrel up our long, but not long enough for this catastrophe, driveway.

This was not good.

NINETEEN°

So there we were, trapped in the police station. We thought it was the worst possible thing that could happen, but we were wrong. The worst thing hadn't even shown her face.

I didn't want to let Great-Grammy down, or Baker, but Karleen calling 911 might have ruined our lives.

Rotten tree. Silly Karleen.

Unfortunate me.

There had to be a way to fix things, but I wasn't sure how, considering where we were.

The officers took me and Baker to the police station, then separated us. For the past hour they'd tempted me with everything from pizza to burgers to ice cream to get me to relax and spill my guts. I hoped they were doing the same for Baker, because if I knew one thing for sure, it was that he couldn't talk and eat at the same time—meaning odds were decent he'd keep his mouth stuffed full, and shut.

The bad news was, I couldn't eat as much as Baker, so I was running out of options.

The seat of the steel-framed chair was cold. I shifted my legs, more to buy an extra few seconds than to get comfortable. Somehow, I had to convince Officer Payne to let us go home. We needed more time to reach Aunt Tilly.

I took a deep breath and stared back at the policewoman. Now that the cops were involved, there was only one choice: keep lying.

"Shingles. It's terrible."

"I see." Officer Payne's eyes flashed before she bent over her pad of paper and started scribbling. She thought this was a victory, as I'd answered one of her million questions. "How long has she been sick?"

Here was where I needed to be careful. "That's hard to say. It's been going on a long time."

"And she's been keeping to herself? No visitors?"

"Just me and my brother." I swallowed hard and said what I'd rehearsed with Baker. "It's been awful. Sores on her face and neck and even into her ear. Great-Grammy doesn't want anybody to see her. Sometimes it hurts so bad she cries."

Officer Payne looked up. "Is she taking something for the pain?"

I wagged my head. "Oh, yes. Her doctor prescribed medicine."

"Do you know the name of her doctor?"

I pictured page five of her notebook. Great-Grammy had been very specific: *YOUR FUTURE IS AT STAKE. YOU CAN'T TRUST ANYBODY EXCEPT TILLY. DO NOT GIVE PEOPLE DETAILS. SAY I'M SICK AND REFUSE TO SEE EVEN OUR CLOSEST FRIENDS. IF DISASTER STRIKES, THAT'S WHEN YOU SAY I LEFT TOWN THE DAY BEFORE. YOU MUST STALL UNTIL TILLY COMES HOME.*

"No."

"What pharmacy does she use?"

"I think it's cheaper to get medicine mailed from Canada."

Officer Payne looked doubtful. "You're sure?"

After I nodded, she printed big block letters on her pad: CANADA. Then she cleared her throat. "So, your great-grandmother decided to see a specialist somewhere, you don't know where. And she left you and Baker alone?"

"Of course not. She left us with Elise." Oh, boy, the lies were piling up faster than our recycling.

"Elise?"

"Yes." I pictured someone in her twenties. A very respectable, responsible young woman. I dressed her in a cute skirt with fashionable low-heeled boots. There was a canvas backpack hanging from her shoulders, and she was getting into her Prius. "She's a college student who's like our babysitter, but she hardly has to be around because Baker and I can take care of ourselves, pretty much. Plus, there's our neighbor Mrs. Knightly just in case."

"Just in case?"

"You know. In case of emergency."

Officer Payne squinted—more doubt in her eyes. "I'm afraid your neighbor Mrs. Knightly broke her hip and is recovering in a rehabilitation hospital." She paused as I held my breath, trying not to react.

When I didn't respond, Officer Payne returned her attention to the pad of paper. "When did your great-grandmother leave?"

"Yesterday." I said it like it was true, even though I hadn't set eyes on her for nine days, minus ten hours and twenty-two minutes.

Talk about Pants on Fire. And I'd have to come up with another doozy to tell Karleen, to explain the first twelve lies I'd told her, and then add this new one.

Officer Payne glanced at the green folder with my name on it on the table beside her: *Rose Marigold Spreen. 12 years old. Guardian: Ida M. Spreen.*

She drummed her fingers. "Well, we need to speak with Elise to be sure someone responsible is, er, handling things."

I knew the things she meant. The maple tree. The roof. And *us*. I also knew she wouldn't be able to speak with Elise, since she didn't exist.

"I can have her call you when—"

Before I finished, the door swung open. Direct from the underworld, our not-so-wonderful Grim Hesper swooped into the room, a black cape swirling behind her. She brushed a single streak of white-blond hair behind her ear, and when her eyes fell on me, the corner of her mouth rose in a satisfied smirk.

She dropped her snakeskin briefcase onto the table and presented Officer Payne with her hand and an official-looking piece of paper.

"Allow me to introduce myself, Officer," she said as they shook. "I am Hesper Spreen, and this"—she briefly nodded at me—"is my granddaughter. I am the senior partner at Spreen, Golden and Campbell and must sincerely apologize for my delay. I only heard the news of my mother's mysterious disappearance minutes ago."

I closed my eyes and wished I could plug my ears while Grim Hesper continued.

"As the children's closest relative, I'm happy to supervise them until we find my mother."

This couldn't be happening. Before I could stop myself, I was on my feet. "Aunt Tilly is supposed to take care of us. Not *you*!"

Officer Payne raised her eyebrows. "Aunt Tilly?"

Grim Hesper drew in her breath. "Tilly is my daughter. You might know her as D. A. Shaw."

"*The* D. A. Shaw? The one who writes those travel books?"

Grim Hesper's mouth grew wide, into what Officer Payne was probably mistaking for a proud smile. "The very one," she said, as if she were a regular sort of mother, even though she and Tilly had spoken once in the past two years, vowing never to speak to each other again. It was the only time I remembered them agreeing about something.

Grim Hesper continued, her voice iced with smooth confidence. "When dear Tilly's off on one of her secret assignments for months upon months—as she is now—no one, and I mean *no one*, is permitted to know where she is. So, despite whatever arrangement my mother put into place, at this moment, I am the only relative available to care for the poor darlings."

I collapsed back into the chair.

What on earth were Baker and I going to do now?

TWENTY°

Grim Hesper deserved an award for her my-poor-dear-grandchildren act. She assured Officer Payne she'd have the tree and the roof taken care of immediately, and that Baker and I would be in good hands until Ida returned.

We ended up side by side in the back of her law firm's limousine, Grim Hesper across from us. I'd never heard our grandmother speak in high-pitched, soothing tones before, words as sweet as syrup dripping from her lips. Yet there she was, telling us how everything was going to be fine and we shouldn't worry now that she was there to take care of us.

It felt like we'd entered another dimension. Baker clutched my arm and I pressed into him, but we didn't dare say a word the entire drive home.

By the time the limousine turned into our driveway, I felt like the tree might as well have fallen straight on *us*. Being dragged to the police station was one thing, but being dragged out of it by Grim Hesper was worse.

Grim Hesper's eyes were dark slits as she scowled at the far side of the house. "I'll need to get that dealt with right away." There was the tone we knew so well.

I followed her gaze. The tree was now lying across the lawn in three enormous pieces. The firefighters had called somebody from the county to take it off the house and cover the train room roof with plastic tarps until it could be repaired.

I wished I could disappear into the leather seat beneath me. Instead, I pulled out my cell phone and stared at the screen while the driver maneuvered the car into a spot at the end of the driveway. There were ten texts from Karleen.

I knew Karleen hadn't meant to mess up our lives, and for once I wasn't mad, or even annoyed at her. But why did she always have to do the right thing?

I glanced at my grandmother, who was staring at me with a strange, hard smile, and immediately put my phone away. I didn't dare read Karleen's messages with Grim Hesper watching, just in case she had some superpower like reading through aluminum and upside down.

The driver opened the door and Grim Hesper stepped out of the limo, waving for us to follow. "If memory serves, Mother keeps the suitcases in the back hall closet. I have a dinner appointment at seven-thirty, so we don't have much time for you two to get your things together. While you're doing that, I'll survey the damage and make some calls. Oh, and of course I need the spare key."

A key? My brain leapfrogged over the problems lining up in front of us. She wanted us to fill our suitcases . . . to go where? And she was going to inspect the train room. What if she didn't stop there? What if she decided to *really* look around? She probably wouldn't go near the basement freezer, since she had no interest in food that wasn't from a fancy restaurant. But that didn't mean she wouldn't find *something* that would ruin *everything*.

This. Could. Not. Happen.

I stayed seated as Baker climbed over me and out of the limo.

Grim Hesper snaked her head back inside the car. "What are you waiting for—dear?" Her whip-cracking once-over told me it was a demand, not a question.

I folded my arms. "Why do we need to pack our things?"

Grim Hesper sighed. "*Sweetheart. Rosie.* You must realize that you and your brother can't stay here. The tree, and my missing mother, make that impossible."

"Great-Grammy's not missing. She's seeing a doctor. And then staying with her friend for a few days."

"*Reeaaallly?*" Grim Hesper drew out the word like an evil cartoon stepmother. She raised an eyebrow and looked at the house. "A few days, you say?"

I took a deep breath. "Yeah," I said. "Maybe longer."

"The woman is insufferable. You know, she won't return my calls." She lifted her chin, and her lips slipped between her teeth, not quite hiding a smirk as she returned her attention to me. "And what about this Elise? How can I reach her?"

Elise who? Oh. *That* Elise. The one who was supposed to be watching us.

I had to think fast. College people were always getting ready for exams, so I bet that was what our fake babysitter was doing right now. "She's probably at the library studying."

"I need her number, so I can tell her she's no longer needed."

One thing I could do: make Elise disappear from our lies. "I'll text her."

Grim Hesper accepted this with a nod. "Good. Do that. Let's get moving, *dear,* or I'll be late for my dinner."

I had a vision of a trip to the airport and one-way tickets to New Hampshire and Colorado. "Where are you taking us?"

She stood upright and waved her hand as if she were shooing a fly. "Just come along, Rose Marigold. The police released you to my custody, so for now I'm taking you to my house."

This news jolted Baker out of his police station food coma, and his face appeared beside Grim Hesper's. "To Washington, DC? It's too far away from school! We have reports to do, and tests to take, and my robotics team is meeting tomorrow. It's two weeks till the regional competition!"

Grim Hesper clasped Baker's arm and guided him backward, away from the limo. I silently groaned as I scooted across the seat and stepped onto the driveway.

Baker and Grim Hesper were face-to-face, and she was using her sweet, cooing voice again. "Don't worry about anything. I'll enroll you both in the best private school in the area for the rest of this year. Everything will be fine." She snatched a quick look at me, then returned her attention to Baker. "Why, I'll bet your new robotics team will be national champions."

I cleared my throat. "*Gram* Hesper," I began, reaching for words to match the puzzle coming together in my head. "It's too late to move schools. Nobody would let us enroll with only two weeks left. Plus..."

I paused and looked as meaningfully as I could at the house and then at Baker.

"Plus," I repeated, "Great-Grammy knew the tree was a problem and arranged for a man to come take care of it. So when it fell I sent him a message, and I'm sure he's on his way. And Mr. King said he would get any damage fixed this weekend."

Grim Hesper twisted to see Karleen's house. It was as though something had just occurred to her. "Ted King?"

"Yeah," said Baker. "Karleen's dad."

"We're friends with Karleen. She comes over all the time," I said. "We can stay here, and I'm sure her parents wouldn't mind watching over us, since you're always so busy with work."

"No, I have a better idea." Grim Hesper met my eyes. "You say that the school year is almost over?"

I nodded. "Two more weeks."

"All right," she said. "Then you will stay here and finish."

Baker sighed his relief and started toward the house, but my grandmother wasn't finished.

"Yes, this may actually work." She strode across the driveway as she surveyed the property from end to end. "I'll take my old bedroom—it may be uncomfortable, but I can manage anything for two weeks, even this dilapidated old place. I'll make it my base of operations. By the time Mother returns I'll have buyers lined up the driveway fighting over it."

Baker and I locked eyes. She was going to live here with us?

Grim Hesper ignored our open mouths.

"Yes, *dears*, it is an absolutely perfect solution." She moved toward the limousine and stepped inside, snapping her fingers at the driver, who'd been waiting at the front of the car. As he approached the door, she stuck her head out and added, "I'll be back with my things after dinner. Don't forget to call that Elise and tell her she's no longer needed." Then she wiggled her fingers, and with a high-pitched "Ta-ta!" the door closed and she was off.

Baker and I backed away as the limousine carried Grim Hesper down the drive. We had no idea how long dinner meetings took, but this one couldn't possibly take long enough. The second her car turned onto the main road, we ran full steam with one goal: damage control.

It was the top, leafy part of the maple that had landed on the house. When it fell, most of the tree ended up on the ground, so, though the train room roof was damaged and the ceiling had three long cracks, and Baker's trains and tracks had scattered, along with the hundred Scrabble tiles from our last game, the room was intact. So were Great-Grammy's baskets. We'd been stashing them under the game table, making sure the notebook was buried and out of sight— the last thing we needed was for Karleen to pick *that* up and start reading.

While Baker gathered his trains and arranged them on the pieces of track that were still in place, I collected the Scrabble tiles and put the game box back together. Then I moved the baskets to the table and searched the files and folders. I'd written down Tree Man's name and number somewhere....

Duh. I'd been doing my homework when he'd called. I ran to get my backpack.

Sure enough, there it was, near the back of my math notebook:

Matt Grooms 301-555-1222

Mr. Grooms said he usually didn't work weekends, but as a favor to Great-Grammy he'd be over first thing in the morning to remove the tree. One problem solved.

Next, I texted Karleen and told her Great-Grammy had gone on a trip to see *another* doctor and that our grandmother, Hesper Spreen, would be staying with us until she got back. Did her father know somebody who could help get the side of our house back to normal?

Seconds later my phone rang. It was Karleen's dad, saying he'd be glad to help out and he'd be over to look at the damage as soon as he could.

It hadn't been so hard to turn the lies I told about the tree and fixing the roof into truths. I even pictured Elise dropping by to get her imaginary things. Maybe everything would be okay.

I looked at the baskets on the table. "Where are we going to stash Great-Grammy's stuff?"

Baker shrugged. "In your bedroom?"

"Grim Hesper's a snoop. We need the black hole of hiding places." Wishing Aunt Tilly would magically appear, I asked, "Have you been checking the emails and messages?"

"Yep," said Baker. "I even sent a text to Great-Grammy's friends telling them she's out of town."

Score one for Baker. "You're getting pretty good at this."

Baker half smiled. "Thanks."

"How are we going to deal with Grim Hesper living here? It's hard enough seeing her for five minutes." I looked at the damaged ceiling.

"Did you notice how she didn't bat even one of her fake eyelashes when I told her I'd already called Mr. Grooms about the tree?"

"And Mr. King about fixing the roof," said Baker. "You're right, it didn't faze her one bit."

"Baker," I said, thinking as I spoke. "She's used to having a bunch of assistants and junior lawyers do everything for her."

My brother added, "And a housekeeper and a driver."

"That's what I mean. This house has to run like one of your robots. Efficient. No late-bill notices, dinner on the table, the toilets cleaned. Everything. That way Grim Hesper doesn't have a reason to make phone calls, or look for the checkbook, or visit the bank."

Baker's eyebrows came together. "You want us to do all that?"

"We're basically doing it now. Well, except the toilets." I glared at him. "If you aimed better they wouldn't be so bad."

Baker flopped into a chair. "This is exhausting. Boarding school is starting to sound like a vacation."

"Seriously, Baker, you don't mean that."

"You're right. But I don't know how much longer I can keep this up. I got a B on my math test this week."

Only my brother would be upset by a B on a math test. The good news was, now if a teacher called because Mr. Brainiac was underperforming, they'd have a real adult to talk to.

"Focus, Baker. Grim Hesper's gone for dinner, not the weekend." I picked up a basket. "We need a place to keep these hidden. Somewhere we can access them."

Baker glanced toward the ceiling. "The attic?"

"Too empty. And she'd get nosy if we started disappearing up there."

"True." Baker stared at the stacks of files, papers, and baskets, and my open laptop. After a minute he tapped his chin. "Remember what you said earlier? That we need a black hole?"

"Yeah?"

"Well, the best hiding place is always in plain sight."

My heart skipped a beat. In plain sight so Grim Hesper could just plunk down and start going through Great-Grammy's private records? "We can't keep everything here."

"Not here. But you know the stuff piled in the basement?"

"Yeah."

"There's so much of it. Cases of paper towels and toilet paper and stuff. We could stack it around a table, like a wall. Grim Hesper would never know these baskets were underneath."

It just might work. "She hates everything about the basement: the dust, the crumbly floor, and especially the ghost Great-Grammy used to kid her about."

"Oh, yeah, right. The one behind the Door to Nowhere." Baker stood and picked up the other two baskets, and even managed to balance the Scrabble box on top. "I'm not worried about a fake ghost."

"And we'll always have an excuse to go to the basement because of the food and supplies."

Baker wagged his head. "We can make it like the forts we used to build," he said as he led the way out of the train room.

It took a few minutes to figure out which supply table we'd use, and another fifteen to arrange our fort. I spread a blanket on the floor while Baker stacked cases of toilet paper and paper towels around the most visible three sides. It was dark as a cave underneath, so I

127

snagged two of the camping lanterns. We arranged Great-Grammy's baskets on the left and stuffed the notebook inside one of the file folders. Then we leaned the Scrabble box against the baskets for camouflage. Even with the lanterns on either side, there was more than enough room for us and our laptops.

"Now what?" said Baker.

"I guess we should go through the last basket."

Baker dove underneath the table. I'd followed, scrunching beside him, when the click-clack of high heels sounded from above. "Oh, no! We forgot to bolt the door!"

We scrambled out from under the table. The last basket would have to wait.

Dear Grim Hesper was home.

TWENTY-ONE°

Grim Hesper had canceled her dinner meeting, now that she had her own operation going on: the takeover of Great-Grammy's house. And she wasn't wasting a second.

We rounded the corner into the dining room just as Grim Hesper's chauffeur wheeled two suitcases into the foyer. Right on his heels was a sour-looking woman lugging a vacuum, and another with an even more crotchety expression carrying a giant box filled with cleaning products.

Our grandmother stood in the living room dressed in ivory jeans and a silky blouse delicately layered with pastel fringe. She waved her arms to hurry her staff along, the fringe fluttering, and if she hadn't spoken, she could have been mistaken for an angel. "Why are you dawdling, Martin? Get those suitcases to my room. Up the stairs, turn right, and it's the first door you come to." She put her hands on her hips. "You two! Take one room at a time, top to bottom. Spotless, just like my house. Follow Martin. And start with my bedroom. Whatever's not finished by midnight, you can do tomorrow. Be here at seven a.m. Sharp!"

Martin clunked upstairs with the suitcases, and the housekeepers followed while Grim Hesper strode across the foyer to the dining room and back again, surveying everything in view, ceiling to rugs. Somehow we got in her way.

She stopped and took us in the way she'd been examining everything else—top to bottom—and frowned. "I cannot sleep in a house with so much dust." Her voice was snippy and accusing. "Mother has never cleaned this place properly, but that's about to change."

There was a noise, as if something was falling, and we turned to see Martin clomping down the stairs carrying one of the suitcases. "I hung your things in the wardrobe, ma'am. I'll store this empty case in my trunk so it's not in your way. Will there be anything else?"

"No," said Grim Hesper crisply. "I have a function tomorrow evening—I'm not sure I'll go yet, as we have a lot to do here, but make yourself available."

With one more "Yes, ma'am," Martin was out the door.

The whir of a vacuum sounded from above and Grim Hesper let out a happy *"Ahhhh."* She must have liked the sound of work being done without doing it herself. Returning her attention to Baker and me, she sounded more relaxed. "You, young man." She fluttered her fingers and smiled too brightly. "I'm sure you'd rather be playing video games."

As if that were that, she bent over and picked up her snakeskin briefcase from the nearest dining chair. Baker turned to me with a question on his face. I shrugged. I didn't love video games, but we might as well escape if she let us, so I grabbed Baker's arm and we headed for the train room.

"Not you, *dear*," Grim Hesper cooed.

I let go of Baker's arm and turned.

Grim Hesper floated across the floor and put her arm around my shoulders. "Let's you and me have a private chat while your brother is occupied," she said, guiding me into the kitchen.

She pulled two chairs from the table and sat, patting the one beside her. "Have a seat. I don't want you to worry, dear. Now that I'm here, everything will be all right."

"I'm not worried." My thousandth lie in the past nine days and six or so hours.

"Good. We're agreed." Her eyes flitted toward the doorway, like she thought we might be interrupted. "I've been concerned about my mother ever since, out of the goodness of her poor sweet heart, she took you two in, when she might otherwise have been able to sell this place and move somewhere more, er, comfortable and"—she paused briefly before continuing—"affordable."

I didn't understand what Grim Hesper was getting at. Whether Baker and I lived here or not, Great-Grammy *was* comfortable in her home. That was a fact. Besides, she never worried about money, except to track every single penny—which was annoying.

I stared into my grandmother's eyes. "What do you mean, affordable?"

Grim Hesper leaned back and angled her head. "You must know she's been struggling to keep up with this place financially, and with the two of you." Then she let out a long sigh. "I offered to help, of course, from the beginning." She shifted in her seat and lifted her eyebrow meaningfully. "You remember, don't you? I wanted to be your guardian. I had plans to bring you and your brother up properly, the way I wished I had been raised myself. But my mother wouldn't hear of it, no matter the cost to your future, or to hers."

I sort of understood what Grim Hesper meant. Great-Grammy was old-fashioned, down to her toes, and never shined things to a grand polish just to impress people. And she refused to grow out of her childhood, too. Even as an old lady she was always right beside Baker and me, no matter what we were doing. It was only last year that she stopped hopping fences.

Grim Hesper made it no secret that she would have preferred a fancier mother, a fancier house, and a fancier life. She'd get no argument from me about that—inside my head I'd always imagined trading houses and clothes with most of the kids at school.

There was something I didn't get, though. "Great-Grammy w—*is* very careful with her money. She always has enough."

Grim Hesper patted my arm as if I were three years old, not almost thirteen. "Yes, *dear,* of course you think that. She wants you to feel secure." Grim Hesper's face drooped with regret as she shuffled through her briefcase and pulled out a document. She leaned toward me and lowered her voice. "But to do that she took out a loan—well over one million dollars—against this property that *I* guaranteed. She doesn't know I'm involved, of course, but Lou Fontaine, the bank president, and I are old friends, and she called me because she wasn't sure Mother could—well, I'll be frank. Mother has missed four payments, so now I'm forced to act."

Grim Hesper flipped to the last page of the loan papers and pointed to the signature line. Sure enough, there was Great-Grammy's signature: *Ida M. Spreen.* And right beside it was my grandmother's: *Hesper M. Spreen.*

"So you see, *dear* Rosie, we need to pay this loan, and there's only one way to do that." Grim Hesper's mouth closed, then opened as if she had more to say, then closed again. She stood and bent over, awkwardly wrapping me in a hug.

"Let's keep this chat between us, *dear*? I need time to figure out how to deal with this predicament," she said into my ear as she clutched me.

"But..." I was confused. She didn't want me to tell Baker that Great-Grammy had money problems? I squirmed, but she only held me tighter.

"I need to find the house papers and get everything together before Mother returns. That way I'll have a solution before she even realizes how bad it's gotten. I'm sure you've noticed, she gets so confused lately. A woman her age shouldn't have to deal with such complicated matters. Do you see?"

It was as though Grim Hesper wasn't going to let me go until I *did* see. I gave her a short nod. Only then did she let me slip from her arms and escape to the foyer.

I climbed the stairs for the safety of my bedroom, replaying Grim Hesper's words in my head. By the time I turned over on my pillow for the tenth time, it was clear.

When Grim Hesper asked me to keep our conversation "between us," she hadn't been talking about Baker. It was Great-Grammy.

She didn't want me to mention anything to *Great-Grammy*.

Unfortunately, that wouldn't be a problem.

TWENTY-TWO°

Between the chain saws, the diesel engines grumbling across our front yard, and our dear Grim Hesper striding up and down the upstairs hallway speaking at full volume into her cell phone, who needed an alarm clock?

A half-awake Baker appeared in my bedroom doorway, looking like a Chia Pet having a bad hair day. "What the heck's going on?"

How could he not know? The tree people had arrived, and Grim Hesper was running her life—and ours—from this house. "What's going on is from this second forward, our full-time job is to keep you-know-who out of the basement and figure out what to do now that she's moved in."

"I say we get her to move right back out."

"Gee, thanks for that terrific idea. Do you have any others?"

Baker frowned. "I'm serious. We've got to get her out of here. She's up to something."

I looked at the hall beyond him where Grim Hesper was speaking, louder, then softer, then louder again. "What else is new? She's always up to something. But, Baker, there's more to her wanting to sell this place than we knew."

Baker glanced over his shoulder and stepped closer. "What do you mean?" he whispered.

"Not now," I whispered back. "Later."

Baker nodded. "You're right. Too risky. Besides, Will's mom is picking me up for the robotics meeting soon."

Shoot! Baker wasn't the only one who needed to be somewhere. I'd completely forgotten about the shelter. I jumped out of bed and pushed Baker out of my room, straight into a maniacally pacing Grim Hesper. She pointed to her phone and pressed her index finger to her lips in a shushing gesture.

"There are distractions everywhere around this house!" she shouted into the phone. "No, I've called my mother and left several messages, but she's saying she can't talk. First shingles and now a sore throat. As usual, she's avoiding the inevitable, so I'm taking matters into my own hands."

I shot Baker a questioning look. Grim Hesper had left messages on Great-Grammy's phone?

He signaled toward the stairs and jerked his head for me to follow.

We couldn't get to the basement fast enough. "I figured Great-Grammy wouldn't flat-out ignore Grim Hesper forever," he said as we ducked under the table, "so I sent some texts. If her throat's sore, that's a good excuse not to talk, right?"

"Maybe for a day or two," I said.

Baker smiled. I could tell he was pleased with himself.

He hit the voice mail icon and held the phone out so both of us could hear. Sure enough, there were three messages since yesterday afternoon, full of Grim Hesper ranting and raving, demanding that Great-Grammy call her back.

"I wish Great-Grammy *could* call Grim Hesper back," I said. "Even one message would help."

Baker's eyes grew wide. "Hmm. Maybe she can."

I stared at my brother. "What do you mean?"

"Remember you said something about bringing back Great-Grammy, you know, so she could talk? I found an app that might work."

"For real?"

Baker shrugged. "I need bits of her voice to work with, so I'm going through videos from the camera she gave me for my birthday last year. It's taking a lot of time."

Footsteps sounded on the floorboards above, reminding us we weren't alone.

The basement door creaked open. "Rosie? Baker? *Dears?* Are you down there?"

Baker shuddered. "What's with the *dears*?"

We scrambled from underneath the table. "We're getting something from the freezer for dinner tonight," I called.

Baker ran to the stairs as I opened the upright freezer and grabbed a mystery casserole and a storage bag full of cookies. I shut the door and looked across the room at the other freezer. I'd always known that my great-grandmother went out of her way to take us in, but I'd never understood how much it cost her.

"You didn't have to do it, Great-Grammy," I whispered. "We would have understood."

As I climbed the stairs I felt overloaded, and not by the casserole or the cookies. A huge helping of regret weighed me down.

Regret about what I hadn't said to Great-Grammy while she could have heard me, and, more than that, some of the things I had.

❄

Since Great-Grammy was "sick," Mr. or Mrs. King had begun driving me to and from the shelter if Karleen and I worked the same shift. Since Karleen's dad was spending Saturday at our house dealing with the damage from the tree, it was Mrs. King who drove us that morning.

At the shelter, Karleen and I hurried through our duties so we'd have extra time with the puppies, especially Daisy. She'd been back almost a week and we found her happily romping and rollicking with her brothers and sisters. They were days away from being old enough to be adopted. I knew Mrs. Barnhouse would make sure they went to good homes, but it still made me sad.

Daisy deserved a family who could take the very best care of her. That wasn't us, and it made my heart ache. Someday soon I'd never see her again.

When Mrs. King dropped me back home, she could only get halfway up the driveway. There was a trailer filled with long leafy branches blocking the way, and other vans and cars, too. I said goodbye to Karleen and her mom and walked the rest of the way to the house.

The noise of chain saws munching tree limbs drowned out the usual sounds of singing birds and reminded me that we'd left Grim Hesper alone the entire morning. There was a long list of things she could have done, or found.

It was hard to say if she would stay out of the basement, especially if she was looking for something. Or if she needed to show her house-keepers the washing machine. But what other options did we have? The house didn't have many hiding places that our nosy grandmother wouldn't find.

That's when I remembered the thing Baker and I were supposed to be looking for: Great-Grammy's will. The one Baker and I were supposed to give to Aunt Tilly and take to the lawyer.

It hadn't been such an emergency before—Aunt Tilly wasn't home yet, and until yesterday most everybody thought Great-Grammy was resting in bed with a bad case of shingles. Now people were looking for her, wanting to talk to her, and expecting her to come home. Even the police!

Grim Hesper moving in changed everything. If she started poking around and accidentally found the new will, it might disappear forever. Or she might find our hideout headquarters and read Great-Grammy's notebook. What would happen then?

Everything was becoming impossible, but the worst thing was the loan Grim Hesper had shown me. Great-Grammy must have borrowed that money to take care of us, and then got too forgetful to pay. Now the only way to pay the bank was to sell the house she loved so much. I couldn't think about it without feeling sick.

My heart fluttered as I approached the side door and twisted the doorknob. I burst inside and shot through the dining room, dodging something on the floor as I crossed the foyer and went into the living room, where I came to a sudden stop.

Grim Hesper was in a bent-head conversation with Mr. King. I cleared my throat and they both looked up.

Karleen's dad stepped away from Grim Hesper and mumbled a quick "Hi, Rosie."

Then he turned back to Grim Hesper. "I'll give it some thought, but I don't think I'm your man," he said, quickly adding, "Time to get back to work!" With that, he disappeared into the train room.

Grim Hesper beamed brightly as I stood gaping back at her, my brain registering what I'd almost tripped over.

I turned.

Our front hall chandelier was set square on the floor in the center of the area rug. I squinted and looked farther into the dining room, where the chandelier lay cupped in bubble wrap on the table.

I whirled in place and scanned the living room. Every single sconce had been taken down from the walls, too.

"What's happening?" I said.

Grim Hesper flashed her teeth and came toward me, her hands in the air. "Oh, *dear,* please don't panic. It's part of the process! If we're going to sell this property, everything must be in good order. The chandeliers and sconces must be sent out and the crystals polished so they sparkle like diamonds. The lighting fixtures in this house are over a hundred years old and extremely valuable, you know. I wouldn't even let my own housekeepers touch them."

In a way, it made sense. If we had to sell the house, it should look better than it did now. It was the sort of cleanup I'd always wished Great-Grammy would do, instead of the weekly sweeping that was more like bad weather, the way it kicked up clouds of dust that landed wherever they pleased.

Only, Grim Hesper was behaving like she owned the place. Since Great-Grammy wasn't here anymore, maybe she did, but Grim Hesper didn't know that.

She was still talking, and I realized I'd missed most of what she'd just said. I forced myself to pay attention.

"...so it will be very busy here and you'll want to stay out of the way. I suggest you start tidying your room. Fill garbage bags with things you no longer need so they're ready for the donation truck. The first pickup will be at five today, but not to worry if you don't finish. I have another truck scheduled to arrive on Monday."

Grim Hesper was like a bulldozer. Anything in her way was going to get scraped up and hauled off, either to some magical cleaning company, to the donation center, or to the county landfill—and that included me. The best place to hide *was* my room. For once I couldn't wait till Baker came home from robotics.

I missed my brother.

As much as anyone could miss Baker, anyway.

TWENTY-THREE°

It was obvious our grandmother was in a hurry to get everything done before Great-Grammy returned. I had a clear view of the driveway out my open window, and all afternoon, vans and trucks never seemed to stop coming or going.

Grim Hesper's too-bright voice sang through the house like a trumpet. A very loud trumpet. She'd tossed five garbage bags in my room with orders to "Reduce, reduce, reduce!"

Baker and I still had clothes and things from when we were younger. Great-Grammy never forced us to get rid of "memories" before we were ready, even if they were in the form of jeans our legs could no longer fit through, or jackets that started zipping at our belly buttons. I knew it was time to let most of them go, but it was hard to face the rainbow of colored fabrics that was now a mountain on my floor.

I was digging for the match to my favorite purple sock when Grim Hesper wheeled a two-piece set of flowered luggage into my room. "Look!" she exclaimed. "I express-ordered a set for you, and a set for Baker. Only the very best for my grandchildren!"

I looked up at Grim Hesper from the middle of the clothes pile. "Why do we need new suitcases?"

Grim Hesper's face froze the way it always did before she said something lawyer-y. My heart beat in heavy thuds as she stepped closer and her shoes disappeared into the foothills of my mountain.

Her eyelids wilted like the petals of a very sorry flower. "*Dear* Rose Marigold," she said. "Mother's disappeared off the face of the earth and refuses to answer her phone so we can have a frank conversation. She needs to regain a foothold on her finances, and I don't see how she can do that without selling this house, and the property. I have no choice but to manage this problem she's gotten herself—and you two children—into."

I inhaled, about to speak, but she held up a hand. "She may have abandoned us, but I am here now and will make sure you and your brother are taken care of, even if I have to dig into my own pockets to do it. You have my word."

If I'd ever felt comforted and terrified at the same time, it was at that moment. I wanted to believe somebody was going to take care of us, but trust Grim Hesper? None of this made any sense, so the answer to that was a big fat unfortunate NO. And even though she hadn't answered the question about the new suitcases, some-where down deep, I already knew the answer.

I let my gaze wander over my bedroom and took it in with fresh eyes. The heavy wooden door with the aged brass handle and the lock that didn't work; the lavender walls Great-Grammy had painted herself when I moved in; the wooden windows with wavy glass that didn't have to be cracked to let in a breeze; and the wide planks that creaked good morning when I stepped out of bed every day.

The not-exactly-fancy room that Great-Grammy had made mine. It *had* been polished, but until now, I hadn't known with what.

"Do you think...," I started, but then couldn't speak. I took a deep breath and began again. "Do you think that whoever buys this property will tear Great-Grammy's house down?"

Grim Hesper's lips drew together in a tight line and her eyes glistened. Was selling the house difficult for her, too? She *did* grow up here. Maybe she had feelings for this place and she truly *was* trying to help Great-Grammy—and us.

The phone in her hand vibrated. She glanced at it, then looked back at me. "I wish I could tell you, *dear* Rosie, but that would take a crystal ball." With an apologetic shake of her head, she slipped out of my room and brought the phone to her ear.

"I don't care if it's a Saturday!" she screamed as she made her way down the stairs. "If you want a job on Monday morning, you will put that document together and get it to me by three o'clock. *Today!*"

I felt tears escaping and furiously wiped my eyes with the orphan sock in my hand. Crying wasn't going to change anything. Nothing I did was going to change anything.

I buried my face in the mountain of clothes and pounded my fists. For the first time since Baker and I moved in with Great-Grammy, I didn't want a brand-new house with a manicured lawn, glistening hardwood floors, or perfectly coordinated furniture. I wanted *this* one.

I wanted Great-Grammy back. And—

I wanted Great-Grammy back.

TWENTY-FOUR°

I filled the garbage bags. Great-Grammy would have been proud of the way I decided what to keep and what to give away.

I did everything I thought I should. As in, everything I imagined Great-Grammy would have approved of. Like, shoving those flowered suitcases underneath my bed as far as I could.

Somewhere in the middle of sorting socks, folding shirts and sweaters, and hanging Sunday dresses, as Great-Grammy called them, it occurred to me that even if she *had* been having money problems, it wouldn't be Grim Hesper she'd want helping her.

It would be Aunt Tilly.

Baker stuck his head in my room around five. That was usually his time to be so ravenously hungry he couldn't think of anything but food. I expected him to ask about dinner, or the stuffed garbage bags, or my mountain, which was now a smallish hill, but he didn't.

"What is going on around here?" he said, gesturing toward the hall.

I let out a low grumble. "I've been staying out of the way. Grim Hesper's had tons of people cleaning and fixing the whole house. I'd check your bedroom. They've been everywhere."

"Rosie," he said slowly. "When was the last time you left this room?"

I was folding a pair of leggings, wondering if I should keep them or not. "Not for a few hours, why?"

"Everything's gone!"

"Yeah." I nodded. "She sent the chandeliers out to be cleaned. The rooms look naked."

"That's not what I mean," he said. "Get up. You need to see for yourself." The color was gone from Baker's face.

I jumped to my feet and followed him.

About midway down the stairs I noticed it wasn't just the foyer chandelier that was missing. The area rug, the bench we put our schoolbags on, the paintings and mirrors that had hung in the front hall since eighty years before I was born...they were gone, too.

My feet stepped double-time as we landed on the now-naked wood floor of the foyer, then ran into the living room. I couldn't believe what I wasn't seeing. It was bare. The couch, side tables, paintings, rugs, and even Great-Grammy's favorite chair, the one she died in— where was everything?

Baker took my arm and we held each other up as we sped across the house to the dining room, which was just as empty as the living room. I was about to scream when I noticed something else.

It was quiet.

No creaking footsteps, no hammering or scraping, no buzzing chain saws or rumbling diesel trucks.

"Where is she?"

I could barely shake my head. "I haven't seen her for hours."

My pulse started racing.

"Baker, c'mon!" I sprinted through the kitchen to the basement door.

We were too late.

As we rounded the corner, *dear* Grim Hesper appeared from below. That below. The *basement* below.

She was in a serious lather as she slammed the door, and when she saw us her eyes popped even bigger. "What on earth is Mother *doing* down there?"

We were doomed. My insides trembled as Grim Hesper kept on in a low, accusing tone. "I've noticed you two sneaking down to that god-awful tomb, but until now, I didn't know why."

Baker and I froze stiffer than Great-Grammy's dead body. Neither one of us could get words out of our mouths.

"What the devil is going on here?" Grim Hesper screeched and raised both hands to the ceiling, clutching her cell phone so hard her knuckles turned white. "There must be fifty thousand dollars' worth of supplies down there! Is she opening her own Walmart?"

I raised my eyebrows meaningfully at Baker while Grim Hesper rattled on. She'd discovered Great-Grammy's stash, not the stashed Great-Grammy.

"I had my suspicions Mother was going mad. Now I'm certain. Wait till Lou hears about this."

I squeezed Baker's arm. "I know, it's crazy, isn't it? She knew she'd be gone and really loaded us up with anything we'd need while she was away. We thought she was going overboard, but you know grand-mothers. Sometimes they do that, especially *great* ones."

That's when Baker decided to chime in. "And what kid would complain about a year's worth of Snickers bars? Not me."

Brilliant idea. Distract her!

"You've eaten half of them already," I complained, glaring and shaking my head.

Baker shrugged and smiled at Grim Hesper, which was pretty convincing, considering he hadn't touched a single Snickers. There were too many other desserts on hand to bother with candy that wouldn't expire until the year 2121.

"Well," Grim Hesper said, her eyes still squinted and lips still pursed, "I suppose we'll use some of it over the next week or so. I'll deal with the rest later. No one looking at the property will be considering the basement for anything serious. It's the land they'll want. For now, I'll simply pretend it's not there."

I almost whooped with relief. But then I remembered the furniture.

It was Baker who asked. And despite his smile, his tone wasn't friendly.

"Gram Hesper," he said. "Where did the furniture go? Great-Grammy's not going to be happy to walk in and find the house empty."

Grim Hesper's body tensed, but her lips slid into a smile that matched Baker's. "Oh, Baker, *dear,* she'll be thrilled to return to a clean house." She paused as though she was considering something important. "Actually, when we last discussed the value of the house, she told me that some of the furnishings, paintings, and such are worth quite a bit. So, as a surprise, I'm having it cleaned and appraised, down to the last chair and serving fork."

I remembered that argument. Grim Hesper insisted none of it

was doing anybody any good sitting here, gathering dust. And what Great-Grammy had *actually* said was that it was all worth quite a bit *to her*. It had nothing to do with money. Even if she had a chair from 1825, which I knew she did, Great-Grammy wouldn't sell it. She'd talk about its history, like who made it and who sat in it, until people got tired of hearing about it. (There's a strong possibility I was one of those people.)

After a long pause, Grim Hesper shrugged. "She needs the money, you know."

Baker's lips flattened. "Great-Grammy doesn't need the money. When will we get the stuff back?"

Grim Hesper was inching her way backward. "These things take time, *dears*. But don't worry, I'm watching over everything like a hawk. We'll be in fine shape before you know it."

I did an about-face and turned the oven on. I didn't know who I was angrier at, myself or Grim Hesper. I ripped the plastic wrap off the casserole labeled *Baked Ziti* and then pressed foil over it, sealing it tightly. For once I had no words.

"This is from Great-Grammy's friend Helen Brooks," I said, mostly to Baker. "She says it should take about forty-five minutes," I added, concentrating as hard as I could on the attached index card.

"Wonderful! I didn't know what you children did for food. But since you're taken care of"—Grim Hesper eyed the ziti suspiciously—"I believe I'll keep my dinner plans." With that, she swept out of the room.

I looked over at Baker, who had collapsed onto a chair at the kitchen table, one of the few remaining places to sit in the entire house.

We didn't have to wait long before Grim Hesper reappeared, wearing a flowing dress the color of the ocean and strappy silver shoes. She'd never looked like an actual grandmother—and never seemed to want to. Great-Grammy always joked about Grim Hesper's "friend," the plastic surgeon. However she kept looking so young, it was working.

When her driver arrived, she wrapped a silky ivory scarf around her neck twice and let its beaded fringe fall down in front of her. With a toss of her white-blond hair, she sailed out the front door with a "Ta-ta!" and a wave of her fingers.

We fumed as we watched the limousine cruise down the drive, Baker in his quiet way and me in my loud way. Baker returned to the kitchen table as I paced back and forth between the kitchen and the empty dining room, blurting out things like "How could she?" and "She knows there's nothing we can do!" and "But there's got to be *something* we can do."

Once, Baker chimed in, "I wish Great-Grammy *was* coming home. She'd fix everything."

"C'mon," I said, realizing we were stewing. "The ziti still has twenty minutes, let's go outside."

"Good idea. That's what Great-Grammy always did when she was mad," said Baker.

I headed out the door first. Something was different.

My eyes scanned the whole front yard. As far as I could see, Great-Grammy's yard art was gone.

I whirled around, my mouth open.

"I know. I guess *you're* happy, right?" Baker met my eyes. "When I came home, a truck was driving away, piled high."

It was like somebody had just slapped our great-grandmother across the face with her own things. The furniture and the yard art, and almost every single thing she treasured.

I bulleted across the lawn, past the line of trees, Baker at my heels the entire way to the road. The gator rock band was still by the mail-box, and there were a few flower windmills here and there, and the three pigs still sat together under Great-Grammy's favorite elm tree, but the rest was gone. Even the Home Sweet Home sign I used to think was so old-fashioned.

I'd gotten what I'd wanted for the whole three years we'd lived with Great-Grammy—a cleaned-up, normal-looking yard—but Baker was wrong. I definitely wasn't happy about it. We trudged silently up the driveway and across the lawn, to the far side of the house where the maple had fallen. There was no sign of the tree, and the roof where it had landed looked about the same as it did before it fell and started this whole disaster.

"Maybe the train room is back to normal, too," said Baker hopefully.

When we went back inside, I'm not sure what we expected to find. The train room smelled of paint, and there were a gray tarp and a stepladder in the corner. Other than that, the room was a blank slate.

We moved closer to inspect where the damage used to be. The walls and the ceiling had never looked so perfect.

Baker spun around. "Where are my trains?"

Oh, no. There was no reason for Grim Hesper to send *them* any-where. "Maybe Mr. King boxed them up?"

Baker let out a long sigh of exasperation. "Or Cruella sent them to be appraised with everything else. You don't think she'd—"

I grabbed Baker's arm to stop him. "She wouldn't."

"Well, I don't trust her. Especially with Dad's trains," he said. "She was always mad because he was so close to Great-Grammy."

"I wonder if Grim Hesper gets along with anybody," I said.

That's when I began to think about it. Maybe it wasn't the trains. Was it the fact that the trains were our great-grandfather's first, and then they skipped over Grim Hesper and went to our dad, her son, just because she was a girl? And now they were my brother's.

It was their history that made them so special to Baker, but I sort of got how being skipped over because you weren't the "right" sex could make a person mad. I mean, I didn't care about trains, but maybe when she was a girl, Grim Hesper did.

Family history was complicated. And it was everywhere in this house.

I usually squashed down my memories. They hurt too much. But Great-Grammy kept hers alive, not just with her stories, but with her things. I could practically hear her talking as we drifted back to the dining room: her father fixing this door, or her mother cooking chicken and dumplings in that pot, the way she looked into this mirror before that formal dance, or this hutch, filled with those everyday dishes, and that china cabinet for these fancy ones. Everything from the oak stairsteps made from a tree that had been struck by lightning, to the silver candlesticks that were a wedding present from the fiftieth secretary of state, was connected to a memory.

I looked out the window. Even the trees outside were linked to memories—like when they were planted, and by whom—and so was the teetering rock wall Great-Grammy's great-great-grandfather had built around the family graveyard.

I raised my eyes to the empty spot where the dining room chandelier used to hang and remembered the dinners we'd eaten with our parents and Great-Grammy when we were younger. Great-Grammy would run in and out of the kitchen carrying huge platters of food. Even then Baker was underfoot, helping with dinner rolls or following Great-Grammy's orders to spread the crumb topping on an apple crisp or weave the pastry strips into a crisscross pattern for her famous peach pie, which was now Baker's famous peach pie.

Except for Grim Hesper, Aunt Tilly, Baker, and me, and Great-Grammy's remaining friends, most of the people who ever sat around the dining table in this room had died. No wonder Great-Grammy said death was part of life and nobody could avoid it. There might have been a ton of death in our family, but so far, no one on earth had managed to live forever, either.

Baker must have slipped into the kitchen while I was distracted, because he was back with one of Helen Brooks's Russian tea cakes in his hand and another in his mouth. My brother hadn't stopped eating, but I was beginning to wonder if he would ever bake again.

I sighed as my eyes roamed the ceiling above the front windows, where an old stain streaked the plaster. It was from some long-ago blizzard when the snow melted and leaked inside. Once I asked Great-Grammy why she didn't paint it. She told me she liked the cracks and wrinkles here and there. They were the smile lines of a well-loved and happy home.

I'd never understood what she meant, but I was beginning to now. Too late.

Baker popped the second cookie into his mouth just as the timer for the ziti chimed, and we silently set the table and served ourselves. I needed to tell Baker about Great-Grammy's loan, but I couldn't. Not yet.

The baked ziti tasted amazing. So did the Russian tea cakes, which Baker treated like salad, bread, and dessert. He set the bag beside his plate and kept eating them between mouthfuls of ziti.

I knew I couldn't avoid it any longer. "Let's go downstairs after dinner. There's something you need to know."

I had to break it to my brother that Grim Hesper was going to get everything she wanted, and why we had to let her.

TWENTY-FIVE°

It might have been the cookies talking, but Baker was so cranky he sounded like me as he stomped down the basement stairs.

Baker was boiling over like a too-full pot of spaghetti. "This makes me so mad," he fumed as we settled on the blanket under the table. He opened his laptop. "There's got to be some way to stop her. Who sends furniture out to be cleaned?"

"And appraised," I added.

"Right," said Baker. "What's that about? Trying to say Great-Grammy needs money. She has plenty of money."

When I didn't respond fast enough Baker said, "This isn't what Great-Grammy wanted." He gestured upward. "Look what she's done in less than one day! The whole place is cleared out. And what about my trains? All we've got left is our clothes and the kitchen table. She'll have us moved out by next week."

I felt the same way, but I knew something Baker didn't. "Grim Hesper might not be our favorite person, but she's trying to help Great-Grammy get out of a mess."

"I'll say. She won't recognize the place, it's getting so clean."

I stared hard at my brother. He was going to have to face facts about verb tenses.

"What?" he said.

"Great-Grammy *won't* recognize the place? Baker, she's never going to see it again."

"Uh, I meant, you know. From above, or wherever she is. Don't you think she's still—with us?"

I felt Great-Grammy with me constantly, whenever I looked at something she loved, or when she talked in my head. But she wasn't here to answer actual questions, like why did she pretend she was so responsible and lecture us about counting every dollar we earned?

It didn't make sense. Great-Grammy shouldn't have taken out a loan and bought these supplies and filled the accounts. Instead of making everything better, the money just made things worse.

I felt tears streaming down my face.

Baker's arm came around my back and he squeezed my heaving shoulders. "Rosie, don't cry. I'm sorry for yelling."

"It's not you." I couldn't look at him between sniffs. "What's happening—it's because of *us*, Baker."

His arm stiffened around my shoulders and I felt him back away. "What do you mean?"

I needed to get control of myself, so I took a long deep breath. "I mean that Great-Grammy shouldn't have taken us in. She couldn't afford it. Plus, if she hadn't been working so hard, maybe she wouldn't have gotten sick—and this whole mess might not have happened."

Baker screwed up his face as if I were speaking a foreign language.

"Think about it," I said. "How on earth did she pay for everything?

Raising kids is expensive. She doesn't work. Do you ever remember her having a job? I mean, besides being a teacher a long, long time ago, before she worked with Great-Gramps doing whatever they did."

Baker shrugged. "She always saved as much money as she could, and she bargained for everything, even at yard sales. Remember? Besides, she had plenty of money, right? You looked at the checking account, and she told me there was a savings account, too. How could she order all this stuff if she was out of money?"

I looked straight into Baker's eyes and spoke slowly. "A loan for more than a million dollars, that's how. From the bank."

Baker's body deflated like a bad soufflé. "For real?"

I sighed. "That's not the worst part."

Baker waited for me to finish. And I waited a second before I did.

"The bank president knows Grim Hesper, and she called her about the loan Great-Grammy wanted. Grim Hesper cosigned it—I saw it with my own eyes—but she says Great-Grammy never knew she helped her borrow it. And Great-Grammy stopped paying a few months ago."

Baker was quiet as he let what I'd said sink in. "Stopped paying—you mean, she forgot?"

I shrugged. "I guess. And Grim Hesper says the only way to pay the bank is to sell this place. Now."

"But Aunt Tilly—"

"She's not here, Baker," I said. "Besides, Great-Grammy would never want Aunt Tilly to pay the loan for her. She always said people should be responsible for their own money."

We didn't say anything. We just sat under the table and stared at Great-Grammy's baskets, her cell phone, and her overflowing notebook.

Baker's gaze fell to his lap. "What's going to happen to us?"

"Nothing good." I tried to picture what life might look like without our home, even if Aunt Tilly came back. Stepping into our future was like stepping into one of Baker's train tunnels with no idea how long it was, or what we'd come across in the dark.

Since Grim Hesper was at dinner, we stayed in our "office" and went through the last basket and Great-Grammy's notebook again. There was a strange old key at the bottom of the basket, with a string around it and a worn tag that said *Ida*.

"Maybe this is the key to the lockbox," said Baker.

"No, she said she'd lost that," I said. "Plus, it's not locked, remember?"

"I'm going to keep it with me, in case."

Baker wrote a twentieth email to Aunt Tilly, which almost seemed like a waste of time, since none of it mattered anymore. Nobody could do anything about Great-Grammy's loan. Even if Tilly showed up and took charge, I was 99 percent sure she'd agree: the house needed to be sold.

I opened Great-Grammy's notebook, remembering when we'd first read it. At the time it seemed like there was a lot to do and keep track of, but as I reread her notes now, I realized that Great-Grammy hadn't left much for us to do besides taking care of ourselves and going to school. Most of the bills had been paid ahead six months.

If only we'd called Mr. Grooms back and had him take down the tree *before* it fell on the house and Grim Hesper fell on us.

Baker had finished the email and was shuffling through one of the baskets. "Look," he said, holding up two envelopes. One had his name, and the other had mine.

I reached out for the one with my name on it: *Rose Marigold Spreen, My Great-Granddaughter.*

A letter. From Great-Grammy.

I looked up to find Baker staring at me with his eyebrows raised. "What do you think they are?"

"I don't know." My hands tingled and my fingers shook. I dropped the envelope on the blanket. "I don't think I can open it right now. But you do what you want."

I bent my head back to the notebook, furiously turning page after page, tears dripping on each one and Post-it notes coming loose. Soon Baker was going to start calling *me* a crybaby. Then a random piece of paper escaped the notebook and floated to the blanket.

I picked it up and unfolded it. It was the phone messages I'd written down from *last* Saturday. I reread the one from the man from the National Association of Graveyard Preservation. "How far does our family graveyard go back?"

"I think the oldest one is 1903." Baker peered over my shoulder. "Why?"

"Well, if some important historic person was buried on our land, don't you think that would be important?"

"Yeah, but Great-Grammy would have known about it." Baker put the lid on the small box he'd been going through. "And she would have told us, like she told us about everything else." Then his eyes drooped. "Except the loan."

"She *was* getting forgetful," I said. "Remember the medicine she was taking?"

I closed her notebook, put it in the basket, then picked up the envelope with my name on it. Some part of Great-Grammy was tucked inside, and I wasn't ready to read what she had to say.

I walked up two flights of stairs, put the envelope on my dresser, then fell into bed without changing my clothes. I needed sleep.

A lot of sleep.

TWENTY-SIX°

For the second Sunday in a row, I woke up to the smell of nothing. No bacon, no oozy warm sugar and cinnamon caramelizing as sticky buns baked, no herbed egg and cheese casserole, and definitely no biscuits and sage-sausage gravy.

Smells drifting into my bedroom because Great-Grammy or Baker was up to something delicious were part of what made the house feel like home—another thing I'd realized too late. Not only was it an empty house now, it mostly smelled of things like dust, paint, and the worst: Grim Hesper's bold-as-she-was perfume.

I stared at Great-Grammy's envelope on my dresser. I hadn't opened it the night before because I was sad. And scared. The way Great-Grammy carefully wrote my name in long wispy letters that were way neater than her usual scribbles made me think that whatever was inside the envelope was important.

Once I read it, that was it. The last bit of her thoughts and words would be gone. Everything over. Just like eating the last chocolate tart from the freezer. Or the final forkful of noodle wiggle. Or anything she made.

I felt too rotten to read it now, anyway. We couldn't save her house from being sold, and Grim Hesper had taken over everything, just like Great-Grammy never wanted.

I sat up in bed. There was no breakfast to look forward to and no place to hang out except my bedroom or the kitchen. I was alone. Baker was working on his robot project at Will's house, Karleen was at church with her parents, and Grim Hesper was "brunching with a friend" after her "fellowship meeting," whatever that meant. I couldn't picture my grandmother doing much fellowshipping, but that's where she'd said she was headed at eight in the morning.

I decided to go back to sleep.

It was a little before 10 a.m. by the time I made it downstairs. I put my schoolbooks on the kitchen table and looked at the dwindling fruit bowl. There were no bananas, something old me would have been glad about, but I scanned the counters just to be sure, and then opened the fridge. A *Taco Casserole* was thawing, which told me that Baker was having one of his Mexican food cravings, but no pie plate of biscuits or egg casserole stood ready to go in the oven. I grabbed the milk and a bowl for cereal.

After my disappointing breakfast, I cleared the table and got to work. An hour later, I was hunched over my history assignment when the house started making noises again. And again. And again. Somebody had to be leaning on the doorbell.

There was no reason to dread opening the front door, since the story had changed: Great-Grammy was away and Grim Hesper was here "taking care of us." I just didn't feel like talking to anyone. But whoever it was, wasn't going away.

I opened the door to find a man in a sport jacket and dress pants standing on the porch.

He looked me up and down. "I'm looking for Hesper Spreen."

"She's not here," I said. "She'll be back sometime this afternoon."

The man shuffled side to side and then backed away. He stopped just short of the steps and let out an impatient breath. I could tell he didn't want to come back.

He reached inside his jacket for an envelope and held it in the air. "It's very important that she get this immediately."

I opened the screen door and took it. "Okay."

Then he whipped out his cell phone and spun it sideways, pointing at a line with an *X*. "Sign with your finger."

Once I signed, he took off down the steps and was gone.

I looked at the envelope with Grim Hesper's name on it and wondered why she was getting work deliveries on a Sunday.

There was no hall table anymore, so I climbed the stairs to the second floor and Grim Hesper's room. I opened the door and was about to put the envelope on the nightstand when I noticed two red folders sticking out from the covers on her unmade bed. Red was a strange color for file folders, so I looked closer.

One had my name on the tab, and the other had Baker's. I stood beside the bed staring at the folders. I might be a lot of things: grumpy, pushy, inquisitive in the not-polite-but-other way. But. *BUT.* I was not a snoop.

Still, one of those folders had my name on it. Then I remembered the envelope in my hand with Grim Hesper's name on it. Taking a long, deep breath, I put it on the nightstand.

I closed the bedroom door behind me and simultaneously congratulated and kicked myself for not being a snoop.

My hand was still on the doorknob when I asked myself: Wasn't any folder with my name on it basically mine?

So I marched back in the bedroom and picked up the folder that said *Rose Marigold Spreen.*

I pulled out three sets of printouts that were clasped together. There was also a yellow legal pad with tidy notes. I looked at the top printout, where a group of girls wearing oxford shirts, ties, and gray skirts stared back at me with vacant smiles. My stomach began to curdle and froth its way up my throat as I read the words at the bottom: *l'INSTITUT SUISSE: Offering internationally recognised programmes and personalized curriculum tailored to the most special of young women.*

The next was a similar packet for a school in France, except the photograph on the front was a graduation scene with caps being thrown in the air. And the next, a school in India, which showed a simple but enormous brick building with a mountain range in the distance.

I looked more closely at the notes on the yellow pad of paper. Columns of words and numbers that were so neat they could only have been written by a human calculator: Grim Hesper.

This time she wasn't even keeping me in the country. She wanted me an ocean away.

I laid the papers out on the bed, took my phone from my pocket, and pressed the camera icon, quickly taking pictures of each of them. I was about to pick up Baker's folder when there was a noise from downstairs.

My heart galloped as I stuffed the brochures and yellow pages back inside the folder and ran from the room. Even without looking, I could guess what the folder with Baker's name held: boys' boarding schools, probably in Siberia.

I'd barely closed Grim Hesper's door before the click-clack of her heels echoed from below. I moved so fast I almost fell down the last few stairs and into the foyer, coming face-to-face with my *dear* grand-mother as she appeared from the dining room, phone to her ear.

"Yes, yes, just do your job," she was saying. "And let me worry about getting the necessary signatures. We'll take care of this first thing in the morning."

She stared at me as we passed each other, and I stared right back, refusing to look away as she climbed the stairs. Maybe I couldn't do anything to stop her, but I had a strong feeling Grim Hesper was happy about the money Great-Grammy had borrowed and the trou-ble she was in.

She'd always wanted us to disappear, and Great-Grammy's prob-lem was the sort of gift only Grim Hesper would appreciate: the exact excuse she needed to get rid of me and Baker, and the house, and even Great-Grammy, so she could control it all.

"Grim Hesper," I said when she was about halfway up.

She turned slowly, her neck twisted. "*What* did you say?"

I spread my mouth into a wide smile. "*Gram Hesper,* I just wanted to tell you a man came by with an envelope. He said it was important that you get it right away." I looked at the empty foyer. "There was nowhere to put it, so I brought it to your room."

She stood straighter and continued up the stairs. "Thank you, Rosie."

I wanted to snarl a warning, like dogs do when they're dealing with a threat. Instead, I took my phone from my pocket and sprinted to the kitchen. Baker needed to know what our grandmother was planning.

Aunt Tilly remained our only hope. She would never in a million years let her mother send us to boarding schools across the ocean. We needed our aunt, and we needed her now.

I texted Baker pictures of the boarding school pamphlet covers and Grim Hesper's notes, then noticed the light blinking on the house phone. I thought back to the last time we'd checked messages. It had been days.

I picked up the handset. There was only one message, from the man who researched historic graves and cemeteries.

"Hello, Mrs. Spreen. Harry Mudd again, the researcher with the National Association of Graveyard Preservation? The grave I'm looking for is dated back to the Civil War, and I've narrowed its location down to five square miles, some of which falls within your property lines. I was hoping to walk the area tomorrow, and could be at your place around 11 a.m. You wouldn't need to be home. My cell number is 212-555-1776. Would you please call and let me know if I might come by?"

I didn't know why this grave, which nobody knew anything about, was so important to the National Association of Graveyard Preservation. But I did know that Great-Grammy would be curious. Besides, if Grim Hesper could invite people to look at our property, so could I.

I couldn't press Mr. Mudd's number into my cell phone fast enough. He didn't answer, so I left my message at the beep. "Mr. Mudd, my name is Rosie Spreen. My great-grandmother wanted me to let you know you can look at our property anytime. She's out of town right now, but you can call me if you need anything."

A text had come in while I was leaving the message. It was Baker.

She is the worst. We won't be done with our robot until 4 or 5. I'll try to hurry.

I spent the rest of the afternoon in my room, which turned out to be not so great an idea.

When Baker texted me he was on his way home, I headed downstairs to put the taco casserole into the oven. But when I entered the kitchen, I found Grim Hesper and Karleen standing together. Karleen was holding a large grocery bag, and I knew what that meant.

"That lovely Mrs. King has sent her *darling* daughter over with a pan of chicken—er, with a casserole. I was just saying you children have some sort of taco surprise planned for tonight." Grim Hesper's tone was singsongy, but her beady eyes told me she hadn't misheard me earlier. I was tangling with the wrong person.

Karleen was watching Grim Hesper wide-eyed, and I realized she'd never seen our grandmother before. I got it. The lady knew how to make a statement—her clothes, the way she spoke, even the way she walked. On the street, people would stop and stare as if Grim Hesper *had* to be someone important.

"Thanks, Karleen. That was nice of your mom." I reached for the bag and put it on the table. "This is my grandmother, Ms. Spreen."

"Yes," said Grim Hesper. "We just met."

I took the casserole out of the bag and headed to the basement. "I'll put this in the downstairs freezer—be right back."

I didn't expect Karleen to follow, but she was right beside me as I opened the upright freezer door. We looked at the jam-packed shelves. "Hold on a sec," I said, handing her the ceramic dish. "I've got to move a few things."

I took a bag of cookies and put it on a rack on the door and rearranged the casseroles on the top shelf to make room. I turned to grab Karleen's mom's casserole, but it wasn't there. Karleen wasn't there.

I swung around, thinking she must be behind me, when there was a loud crash and Karleen screamed at the top of her lungs.

She stood on the other side of the basement, her mouth open, the freezer door up and her mom's casserole down, exploded on the concrete floor.

I shot across the basement to Karleen and put one arm around her while using my other hand to close the freezer, silently saying hello and goodbye to Great-Grammy.

Karleen was heaving, gasping for air and trying to speak, but she couldn't. I heard footsteps and was about to start convulsing, myself. I knew who I would see when I looked.

Grim Hesper was halfway down the stairs, bending at her waist so she could see us—and the broken casserole dish and the glops and splatters of food—from across the room.

"What on earth?" She took one more step down and peered closely.

"Everything's okay," I said. "I told Karleen about the ghost last week. She thought she saw something and got spooked. Don't worry, I'll clean up the mess."

"Make sure you do," Grim Hesper said. "There will be people coming through here, and we don't need it to smell like spoiled chicken." She sighed as though we were hopeless and then, with a shudder, she turned and scuttled back up the stairs. I wondered if she honestly believed there was a ghost.

"I wa wa-was only tr-try-trying to to helelp," sputtered Karleen after Grim Hesper disappeared. "Rosie, what . . . There's a . . . Is tha-a-a-t . . ."

I gripped Karleen tightly and led her away from the mess, and the freezer, to the stairs. "Sit. It's not what you think. I'll tell you, but I need to take care of this first."

I prayed that Karleen would stay put and not run for the nearest grown-up, especially since that grown-up would be Grim Hesper. Or her mother. Neither would be good.

I hurried to the table and loaded up with paper towels, a garbage bag, and a bottle of cleaning spray. Then, with one eye on the stairs where Karleen sat, I filled a bucket with water at the work sink and added a few glops of soap. I put everything by the freezer, grabbed a handful of torn-up towels from Great-Grammy's rag basket, and got to work.

It was gross, but not animal-shelter-cleanup gross. At least Karleen's mom's casserole smelled good. I scooped up the big chunks of chicken, glops of rice, and jagged pieces of blue pottery, silently hoping the casserole dish wasn't special to Mrs. King, and dumped it in the garbage bag. Then I dipped a towel into the bucket and started scrubbing.

As I worked, I considered what to tell Karleen. Great-Grammy was wearing a ski mask, so her face wasn't showing. Still, she was also wearing an old-lady dress. Who could it be besides Great-Grammy, or *somebody's* grandmother?

Karleen was my only friend. After everything I'd been forced to give up, I didn't want to lose her, too. But I'd lied again and again—this time she wasn't going to buy anything but the real truth. Would she ever forgive me for doing something so awful? Who puts their great-grandmother in a freezer?

I finished cleaning and headed to the stairs with an inward grimace. Karleen had skipped a grade in math, so she wasn't an idiot. There was a pretty good chance she'd figured out the body in the freezer was Great-Grammy.

I sat beside Karleen on the almost-bottom step. She was staring straight ahead, as if she were in a trance. I turned to check that the upstairs door was closed. It wasn't, but I didn't hear any signs of Grim Hesper. "Are you okay?" I whispered.

Karleen shook her head the tiniest bit. Enough to tell me that first, she wasn't in a trance, and second, she wasn't okay.

"I'm sorry. I should have told you to stay with me on this side of the basement."

Karleen faced me, and she didn't whisper. "You mean, you should have told me not to go near that freezer, the one with the *dead body* inside?"

She put her hands on her cheeks, and her head swung back

and forth, faster and faster. Without warning, she was still. "Your great-grandmother doesn't have shingles, does she?"

"What do you mean? Of course she does!" Baker's voice startled us from the top of the stairs.

I angled my thumb toward the freezer as he got closer, and whispered, "Karleen opened it."

Baker's mouth dropped open. "How?"

"So it *is* your grandmother?"

"Great-grandmother," corrected Baker.

I narrowed my eyes at him, then faced Karleen. "Yes."

"There's only one reason a person ends up in a freezer," Karleen said. "Did you kill her?"

"Karleen!" I said. "No. Of course not!"

Her whole face scrunched and she pointed across the room. "Then why is she in there?"

"It's a super-long story," Baker responded. "You better stay for dinner so we can explain everything. I just put the taco casserole in the oven."

"Oh, sorry. I was going to do that," I said. "But what about Grim Hesper?"

"That's what I was coming to tell you. She said she needed to go to her house to find something, and that she wouldn't be back until late."

I looked at Karleen, who already had her phone to her ear.

"Mom, is it okay if I stay at Rosie's for dinner?" Then, a few seconds later, in a steady and weirdly sincere tone, she answered her mother. "Mrs. Spreen doesn't mind at all."

My heart started beating normally again. Maybe everything would be okay.

TWENTY-SEVEN°

We started from the beginning. I told Karleen about Great-Grammy's fainting spell, and Baker told her about the real visits to the specialists. I told how Great-Grammy measured herself on the driveway, and Baker told about her ordering the mountains of supplies in the basement. I told how Great-Grammy paid the bills months and months ahead, and Baker told about the new freezer, and her instructions to put her in it after she died.

After dinner, we brought Karleen back to the basement and showed her our office, and the notebook, and the baskets.

"So you've been waiting for your aunt Tilly to respond. But then I called 911 and the police came and your great-grandmother wasn't here, so they let Hesper take you. And now she's going to sell the house and send you to boarding school?"

"Yeah," said Baker, wagging his head.

Karleen spoke in a clipped tone. "And your grandmother living here is the exact opposite of what your great-grandmother wanted. Does that cover everything?"

Baker and I stared at each other. Was it even possible to cover everything? I looked back at Karleen. "Absolutely not."

Karleen scrunched her nose. "I don't understand. Your gram Hesper looks cool, and she seems, well, nice enough. What makes her so awful that your great-grandmother went to so much trouble?"

Baker sighed. "She's never been the daughter or grandmother type."

"Or the *person* type," I said.

"Remember what Great-Grammy told us about her seventh birthday?" said Baker. "After the party, Grim Hesper insisted on going straight to the store to return the presents her 'customers' gave her. She wanted the cash instead."

Karleen crinkled her forehead. "Customers?"

"Yeah." I laughed, even though it wasn't funny. "That's what she used to call anybody who brought gifts. She's always been that way, I guess. But this is worse."

Baker nodded. "Great-Grammy always told us this place is worth a lot because it's been in our family for a long, long time. Grim Hesper doesn't care about that. She only cares about dollar signs."

"My dad always says your great-grandmother is sitting on a gold mine. Or I guess, now, your gram Hesper is." Karleen looked up, her eyes growing wide. "She doesn't know her mother is dead!"

"Yes, it's awful, and Grim Hesper should know, but it's also the whole point." I took out my cell phone and pulled up the photos I'd taken. "I have proof she wants to send us away to other continents."

Karleen stared at the screen, her mouth dropping open. "Switzerland? I thought you were exaggerating."

"Nope," I said. "If it hadn't been for Great-Grammy, she'd have sent us away years ago."

"She can't do that! We're finally best friends!"

A tingly feeling went through me, and I reached out to give Karleen a hug. She hugged me back, and we were smiling at each other, probably looking like goofballs, when Baker put a hand on each of our shoulders.

"Yes, she *can* do that," he said. "If anybody finds out Great-Grammy's dead and our aunt isn't here, a judge will make Grim Hesper our guardian."

He let go of us and flipped open his laptop. "That's why we have to reach Aunt Tilly. She would never send us away."

"My parents constantly talk about who I'd go to if something happened to them. A few months ago my mom even showed me where they keep their wills. I hate it because I don't like to think anything bad would ever happen to them."

Baker caught my eye, and I knew we were thinking the same thing. Karleen had just hit on a problem we'd been ignoring.

The will. The one we hadn't found and had barely looked for.

"Great-Grammy made a new will and hid it so it'd be safe." Baker faced his screen again. "But she moved it so many times she forgot where."

"Forgot?" said Karleen.

Baker nodded as he typed. "She was taking medication that made her a little loopy."

I remembered the day we rescued Baker from the groundhog, the day Great-Grammy fainted. She was talking about her property and how she didn't want a bunch of houses built on it. She'd said she had a plan, not to disinherit Grim Hesper, but she was doing *something* that would make her mad. Was she talking about her new will?

"It's important that we find it," I said. "But that's only one problem. Great-Grammy didn't want to sell this property, and Aunt Tilly wouldn't want to, either, but it turns out Great-Grammy took out a loan and didn't pay it back. Now the bank wants the money."

"Okay, sent." Baker shut his laptop.

"Sent what?"

"Another email to our aunt," I said. "We send one every day and every night, so hopefully she'll see one the second she has Internet. Wherever she is."

Baker's whole face drooped. "Can Grim Hesper really sell the house without Great-Grammy here?"

None of us had an answer, so we sat there in the quiet.

"Wait a minute." Karleen slowly raised her hand. "Your great-grammy took out a loan? For what?"

"It had to be for the supplies and to pay the bills—to take care of us after she died."

Karleen scooted from under the table, then stood looking around the basement. "It doesn't make sense. She filled this house with everything you could need. She cooked. She wrote down every detail in her notebook and boxed up her important papers."

"Except her will," I said.

Karleen waved her hand like that didn't matter. "You said she forgot to pay the loan payments to the bank? But she paid everything else six months in advance—why not that loan?" She reached down and pulled me up to stand beside her. "Rosie, look at how organized everything is."

I looked. Every item on every table was in its place, in rows and stacks like soldiers in military formation. I knew what Karleen was saying: How would Great-Grammy have forgotten to pay the bank, when she wanted to save her home most of all?

But the fact was she'd forgotten some things, like the lockbox. Mr. Grooms and the tree—she never mentioned that whole disaster-waiting-to-happen. And if she knew about the Civil War dude, she forgot to tell us that, too.

But a loan? I pictured the papers with Great-Grammy's signature, the ones Grim Hesper showed me. How could Great-Grammy have forgotten to pay a loan for so much money? Wouldn't that have been on top of her to-pay list?

I didn't know what, precisely, but something was wrong. Great-Grammy wouldn't forget four months in a row. There had to be a mistake with the bank. And if that was true, Grim Hesper wasn't going to fix it, because she wanted to sell the property. It was the exact sort of thing Great-Grammy had been afraid of—Grim Hesper finding a way to swoop in and take over.

"Baker!" I said. "Karleen's right. It doesn't make sense. She wasn't forgetful until the last month, so she might have missed one payment, but definitely not four, like Grim Hesper said."

Baker poked his head out from under the table. "Even if that's true, what can we do?"

"We can do what Great-Grammy would've done: find the mistake, and fix it."

"How, Rosie? We're kids. Who'd listen to us? Not Grim Hesper."

"You're right. Grim Hesper doesn't want to fix this problem. But we do!"

Baker jumped to his feet. "Yeah, but how?"

"We check with where she got the loan in the first place: the bank. But first, we have to find the paperwork." I pointed under the table. "It's got to be buried in there somewhere."

Karleen and Baker stared at me.

"Don't just sit there," I said. "We've got work to do!"

For once I had a good reason to be bossy.

TWENTY-EIGHT°

It took us more than an hour to go through Great-Grammy's records.

Somewhere in the middle of our hunt, Karleen got a call from her mom saying it was time to head home. She hugged Baker, then turned to me.

"I'm sorry about your great-grammy," she said. "I liked her a lot." She gave me a super-big hug. As I watched her run up the basement stairs, I realized Karleen wasn't mad at me for lying to her, even though she could have been. Great-Grammy had always said it was important to have one true friend. Now that I understood what a true friend was, I agreed.

And Karleen was the truest friend ever.

After Karleen left, Baker and I kept going. We'd been through the receipts. We'd been through the list of monthly payments. We'd been through the list of computer accounts. We'd been through the password book. We'd read through the notebook twice, in case we'd missed some mention of a loan. We'd even pulled out Great-Grammy's old laptop and searched her history and files on that.

Next, we double-checked every stack and folder in the baskets.

There were records and receipts for everything from siding repairs, to each piece of Great-Grammy's yard art in alphabetical order, to the new upstairs toilet and bedroom closets she installed the year we moved in with her, but there were no million-dollar loan papers anywhere.

I was starting to see how Great-Grammy might have forgotten to pay it. Between repairs and everything else this house needed, it must have been hard to keep track. Only, it seemed like she did keep track. Of Every. Single. Detail. Great-Grammy might not have chased down every dust bunny, but she'd always watched her "pennies," and never spent them frivolously, as she put it. And though I griped about it, she'd taught us to do the same.

We signed into the bank account again and double-checked every payment made through the checking account. There was no loan payment to the bank anytime in the past twelve months.

Then I checked her savings. It turned out *that* account was loaded. Baker hung over my shoulder. "It *is* our fault. She borrowed the money so we wouldn't run out."

"I guess," I said. "But that doesn't explain why she didn't make the payments."

"Well, she shouldn't have missed them. She had enough to pay her bills. Look!" Baker jabbed the screen with his finger. "We should call Grim Hesper right now and say we don't have to sell the house."

"Are you crazy?" I said. "That would mean telling her everything. And she'd want to see Great-Grammy's papers. No way we're showing them to anybody but Aunt Tilly. Definitely not Grim Hesper . . . Great-Grammy would come back to life just to murder us."

We both stared at the computer screen. It seemed like a simple enough mistake to fix, if we could just find the loan and pay whatever Great-Grammy owed.

Baker pointed to a string of numbers, below the checking and savings accounts, in its own area. "What about that?"

"I don't think that's it," I said. "It says *Investments*."

"Well, click on it."

I pressed the link and waited for the page to load. And waited.

Then it appeared—a long list of companies and columns of numbers and symbols.

Baker leaned forward with his mouth open. "Do people borrow money to buy stocks?"

One thing was clear: this situation had gotten too complicated for Baker and me to figure out. We needed help.

We clicked on the Examine Bank home page and found a picture of a woman: Lou Fontaine, President. The same woman Grim Hesper had mentioned.

"That's the person who has the answers," I said. "But we have to be careful. She's friends with Grim Hesper."

"We don't have a choice, Rosie," said Baker. "Do we call? Or write an email, or what?"

"No, I think we need to see her in person." I peered closer at the main address of the bank. "She works in Washington, DC."

"We can use Byron's Car Service." Baker's fingers flew over me to the keyboard. "Here, let's map it."

According to Google, it would take twenty minutes to get there in current traffic. But it was Sunday night, so it would be worse any other time.

I stared at the map. "We should plan for forty-five minutes."

"Okay, but when? We've got school."

I raised my chin. "How's that app you've been playing with? Have you been able to get Great-Grammy's voice to say anything?"

Baker scratched his head. "It was slow at first, but I'm sort of getting the hang of it. Why?"

"This might be the perfect time to try it out." I faced Baker and pretended to sneeze. "I'm coming down with a very bad cold. How are *you* feeling?"

The corner of Baker's mouth rose. Then he fake-sneezed. "Dang. How did you give it to me so fast?"

"Nice. Hopefully, Grim Hesper has an early meeting."

"It doesn't matter," said Baker. "We'll tell her we always call Byron when we miss the bus."

"She'll be happy she doesn't have to drive us." I glanced back at the screen and looked at the photograph of the bank president. "Do you think Ms. Fontaine will help us?"

Baker shrugged. "Why not? We'll say Great-Grammy sent us. Even if she talks to Grim Hesper, everybody knows Great-Grammy's sick and is out of town."

"I don't know," I said. "I wish Aunt Tilly were here."

Footsteps sounded from above. We jumped out from under the table and started throwing the stacks of papers and files into the baskets.

"You go upstairs," Baker said. "Just tell her I'm looking for something for dinner for tomorrow."

"Okay." I pointed to the basket where we put the money stuff. "Get one of the signed checks, so we can pay what Great-Grammy owes."

"You want me to bring a signed check upstairs *now*?" said Baker. "What if Grim Hesper searches me?"

"Baker, don't be idiotic," I said. "She snoops around the house, not our pockets. We can't keep popping down here—nobody eats that many casseroles. It's suspicious."

The door creaked open. "Are you children down *there*?"

I ran toward the stairs. "Coming!"

Grim Hesper was leaning against the kitchen counter reading her phone. She looked up when I entered the room. "Where's your brother?"

"He'll be up in a minute. He can't decide between pot roast or noodle wiggle for tomorrow's dinner." I needed to throw her off the track. "There's leftover taco casserole if you want some."

"My *dear* Rose Marigold, I don't eat leftovers." Then she cleared her throat. "Now, I might as well tell you. There's a group of potential buyers coming to see the property tomorrow afternoon, and I want this place shipshape. I assume you cleaned the mess your friend made earlier?"

"Yes." I took a quick look at the basement door, but my eyes caught something else. Brightly colored brochures on the kitchen table, and two stacks of forms.

Grim Hesper kept talking. "Good. I had Mother's bedroom boxed up and sent to my house. I spent the evening going through all of it"—she paused before continuing—"trying to find a way to reach her friend Priscilla. But there wasn't a single record, not even an address book. That's odd, isn't it? Do you have any idea where she kept her, ah, important papers?"

I swallowed. "No idea." Then I pointed to the table. "Gram Hesper, what are those?"

Her head rattled as she followed my gaze. "Oh, yes, that's the other thing I need to speak with you about. Assuming Mother has not yet made plans for your summer, I've found the perfect preparatory programs to get you ready for next year. You and your brother need to fill out the information to complete the applications. They need the names of your doctors, and those sorts of things."

"We don't usually have summer plans. Great-Grammy takes us—"

"You must realize, dear, that everything will be different now. Mother's ill. I'm sure this shingles of hers is only the beginning. She's mismanaged her money, and I've told the bank we're putting the property up for sale so the loan will be paid soon. We're lucky they aren't foreclosing!"

Baker came bounding into the kitchen, a foil-covered pan in his hands. "Hi!" he said with a way-too-friendly-and-trying-to-be-innocent expression on his face.

I pointed to the kitchen table. "Summer school."

Baker's smile disappeared instantly. He looked from the forms to Grim Hesper. I thought he was going to object, but he just shrugged. "Summer school sounds great. *Doesn't it,* Rosie?"

My whole head twisted, hard left. Was he nuts? I inhaled, about to argue, until I realized my brother was sometimes, *sometimes,* smart in a people sort of way.

I exhaled. "Yes, Baker. I think summer school might be good for us this year." I gathered up my sweetest expression and delivered it to our grandmother. "Is it okay if we fill out those forms after school tomorrow?"

Grim Hesper smiled. "Of course." Her eyes dropped to her phone again, as if we didn't exist. She thought she'd won us over and solved her summer problem.

What she didn't know was that for the last three summers I'd complained to Great-Grammy there was nothing to do here. Nothing to do but dig holes, and transplant vegetables, and nibble fresh-picked strawberries, and cucumbers and tomatoes, and belt golf balls into the trees, and run barefoot, and catch lightning bugs, and examine anthills, and sit on blankets and eat Great-Grammy's fried chicken and snickerdoodles, and wait for the deer to cross from one side of the property to the other at the same time every morning and every evening, and watch paper lanterns fly, glowing, into the night sky. Even worse, I always grumbled that there was no place to go. No place but parks, and outdoor movies, and national monuments, and Fourth of July fireworks, and the garden center, and the summer festivals Great-Grammy loved.

I felt tears coming and sniffed them back as I climbed the stairs beside Baker. At the top we pledged that we'd go to the bank in the morning and find a way save Great-Grammy's house from Grim Hesper's plans.

There was something else our *dear* Grim Hesper didn't know.

Somehow, some way, Baker and I were going to have another summer here. Not just because that was what Great-Grammy wanted, but because that was what we wanted—what *I* wanted.

I shut my bedroom door and threw myself onto my bed. Great-Grammy had made this place, her not-brand-new-or-perfectly-dusted-and-polished place, our home.

I pulled the covers over me. But it was impossible to hide from what hurt my heart the most.

If only I'd told Great-Grammy that her house, our home, was exactly where I wanted to be all along.

TWENTY-NINE°

Morning came fast and it was weird. Grim Hesper didn't make sure we got up on time, or that we ate breakfast, or ask if we'd done our homework. Nothing but her own hot shower and coffee seemed to matter to her.

She walked out of the house, never asking about school or how we would get there.

At the slam of the front door, Baker waved his cereal spoon in the air. "I can't believe Dad and Aunt Tilly had her as a mother."

I kept buttering my English muffin. "Grim Hesper didn't do any mothering. It was either Great-Grammy or nannies who raised them whenever they weren't away at school."

"Good point." Baker pulled his phone from his pocket, eating with one hand and swiping with the other.

I plopped a spoonful of strawberry jam onto my muffin. "Did you finish the recording?"

"I was up till after midnight working on it—I got it as close as I could to what you wrote down." He stuck the phone in my face. "Listen."

I knew I'd hear her voice, but when Baker hit Play, it was like listening to Great-Grammy herself. The hairs on my arm prickled as a chill ran through my whole body. I couldn't speak, not even to tell Baker to turn it off.

"What's wrong?" he said.

My lip quivered as I tried to tell him, but even without words he knew. He swatted at the screen and put the phone on the table. Then he put his hand on mine. "It took me an hour to listen to her without crying the way I always do."

I stared across the kitchen table at my younger brother, and for some reason more tears streamed down my face. What was wrong with me? Where were the tears coming from?

"Here." Baker handed me his napkin.

I sniffled into the napkin and pushed my plate away. The thought of swallowing sweet strawberry jam made my stomach woozy.

Baker kept his hand on mine as he finished his cereal. When he was done, he picked up his bowl and my plate and brought them to the sink. I watched as he rinsed them, then loaded the dishwasher. He was being nice, the way he always was.

What could I say to be nice back?

"I know you were putting random pieces of her words together, but it was amazing. It sounded just like her." I paused for a moment, and Baker turned to look at me. "Good job, Baker. Great-Grammy would be proud. Just like I am."

The corner of his mouth rose. "I didn't mean to make you upset."

"It's not your fault," I said. "I miss her, and she sounded so—alive."

I cleared my throat and stood. We had an important day ahead. "Are you ready?"

Baker returned to the table and looked at me closely. "Are you?"

"Yeah, I think I'm okay now."

Baker's eyes dropped to his phone screen. "Okay, hold on a sec."

While he was restarting Great-Grammy's recording, I picked up her phone and scrolled to the school's number.

Our eyes met. It was time. "Here goes," I said.

I dialed and, when it began to ring, held the phone so Baker could listen. There was a special line for absences, and all we had to do was leave a message. A good thing, since Great-Grammy couldn't exactly answer questions.

We listened to the secretary's instructions, and at the beep, Baker quickly hit Play and we put the phones face-to-face. It was easier hearing her voice now that I was prepared.

"This is Ida Spreen. I am calling for my great-grandchildren, Baker and Rosie Spreen. They are sick and will not be in school today. My phone number is 301-555-1601 if you need to reach me. I will send a note with them when they return to school. Thank you."

I pressed End Call.

"We did it!" said Baker, a grin spread across his face.

Maybe I should have felt happy, but I didn't. "I have to finish getting dressed. What time is Byron coming?"

"The bank opens at nine a.m., so I said eight-fifteen."

"Okay." I looked Baker up and down. "We should wear our dress-up clothes."

Baker inspected his beat-up sneakers. "I guess."

Byron arrived an hour later. When he saw us, I could tell he was surprised. We did look more respectable than usual, Baker in his long pants and dress shoes and me in my favorite dress. I hated dresses, but this one had pockets, so I didn't mind it as much.

"You two are going to Examine Bank in DC, without Ida?"

"Yes, sir," said Baker.

I didn't think that was enough information. "She told you she was sick with shingles, right? She needs us to deliver some important papers." And in case he was wondering, I added, "It's a teacher work-day, and I guess she wants us out of the house. It was a long weekend."

Byron peered at us. "Yeah, she told me. Hop in. She left her card on file." He turned and faced the steering wheel, and we were on our way.

A few minutes later my phone vibrated and I took it out of my pocket. I'd texted Karleen and told her about going to the bank and that we were "sick" and wouldn't be in school. She'd texted back two words:

Good luck

Forty-five minutes later, we pulled up to the bank. Byron said he'd wait at the diner on the corner, and we stepped onto the crowded sidewalk, people rushing in every direction.

The building was six floors of splotchy gray marble. We approached the entrance, cars and trucks and buses burping clouds of exhaust as they rumbled, vroomed, and screeched behind us.

I inhaled deeply, but there was absolutely zero fresh air.

Baker reached for the heavy door handle and opened it wide, letting me through first, and we moved quickly past the security officer at the entrance.

The aroma of coffee was strong as I scanned the elegant room. It was huge, with columns and marble floors and planters filled with trees and flowers. If it hadn't been a bank headquarters, it could have been a ballroom. In the middle, there were tall tables where people stood filling out forms. Beyond them, tellers sat behind glass, waiting for customers to approach. Couches and doors to offices lined opposite sides of the room.

There was a large directory on the wall near the entrance with rows and rows of names. "Do you see Lou Fontaine?"

It took Baker three seconds to point to the bank president's name. We headed to the elevator.

The fourth floor was thickly carpeted in a blue-and-gold geometric pattern with a solid border along the walls. Right in front of us was a ship's worth of polished wood built into a long desk where two women sat, ready to greet us. The one wearing purple glasses and a red scarf tied around her neck cleared her throat.

"May I help you?" she said.

I nudged Baker, but his mouth just hung open. So I stepped closer. "Our great-grandmother's name is Ida Spreen, and she's sick with shingles. But there's a problem with her loan, and she sent us to see Ms. Fontaine to get it fixed."

The lady smiled in a forced-patience kind of way. "Do you have an appointment with Ms. Fontaine?"

Baker and I exchanged worried glances. He'd worked all night on Great-Grammy's message, and texted Byron for the ride, and brought the signed check. I'd made sure we dressed "suitably," just like Great-Grammy would have insisted.

Obviously one of us had forgotten something.

"No," I said.

The lady raised her chin. "I'm afraid Ms. Fontaine's schedule is full today. Perhaps your great-grandmother can call and schedule an appointment when she's feeling better."

Baker gripped my arm. "But we have to get this fixed today. It's important. She's been sick awhile, and somehow she forgot to pay her loan. Our grandmother, Hesper Spreen, told us Ms. Fontaine says if she doesn't pay, we need to sell the house."

I was glad Baker had found some courage and spoken up, but *why* did he mention Grim Hesper?

Scarf Lady tipped her head. "Hesper Spreen? The attorney?"

"Yes, ma'am."

Her smile was gone in an instant and she stood. "Wait here." She sailed around the back of the large work area and marched down the hall, out of sight.

"What just happened?" Baker whispered.

I glanced sideways and muttered out the corner of my mouth. "We weren't going to mention Grim Hesper, remember? She's friends with Ms. Fontaine."

Before he could respond, Scarf Lady reappeared and gestured toward the hallway. "Come with me."

She led us down a long corridor, making several turns, until we came to a massive door. She knocked softly, then entered the room, waving us in behind her.

The office had floor-to-ceiling windows overlooking treetops and a grayish sky.

There were a seating area with a long couch and coffee table by the windows and a small conference table near the wall on the far right. On the far left was the same person pictured on the bank website, Ms. Fontaine. She had short brown hair and lightish skin, her nose and cheeks covered with freckles. She sat behind an ornately carved wooden desk, with a large, colorful painting hanging on the wall behind her and two enormous computer screens angled in front of her.

"Ms. Fontaine," said Scarf Lady, "these are the Spreen children."

The bank president raised her eyes from her work and motioned at two empty chairs in front of her desk. "Come have a seat."

We dropped in the chairs as Scarf Lady left and the office door clicked shut. The bank president seemed far away as she stared at us from between the computer screens and across the wide desk.

I wanted to leave right that second. Coming to see her had been a mistake.

"So," said Ms. Fontaine, her face crinkling into a curious smile, "you are Hesper's grandchildren."

Baker and I nodded.

"She told me her mother, your great-grandmother, has been very ill. I'm sorry. However, I'm glad to hear that Hesper's convinced her to move. That house must be a terrible burden for a woman her age to keep up with, especially in her condition."

I clutched the arms of my chair and held my breath. One, two, three...

Baker seemed to know I shouldn't be the one to talk, and he jumped in. "Great-Grammy wants to keep the house. It's getting hard for her, so our aunt Tilly is coming home to help."

I didn't dare look at Baker.

Ms. Fontaine leaned back in her seat. "Your aunt Tilly. Hesper's daughter, the author? I'm surprised to hear she's coming home. Hesper misses her dreadfully but says she's far too busy to even visit."

If Baker could flat-out lie, I could talk without getting mad. We were here for one reason.

"That's her," I said. "She's coming, but she's not home yet. That's why we're here. Grandmother Hesper told us about the loan payments."

Ms. Fontaine clasped her hands and leaned forward again. "She did?"

"Yeah," said Baker. "Great-Grammy, well, she would have paid them if she hadn't been sick and busy doing other things for us. It's sort of our fault it got so bad. The last thing Great-Grammy wants is for the house to be sold."

"And she's off seeing a specialist about her shingles, so—"

Ms. Fontaine held up her hand. "Shingles? I thought there were . . . other problems."

What lie was Grim Hesper spreading? We had to stop explaining things and get to the point.

"Great-Grammy doesn't want to sell the house to pay off the loan just because she missed some payments. She says she has plenty of money and tons of stocks. She signed a check and told us to pay you whatever you want so that the house doesn't have to be sold."

"Oh?" said Ms. Fontaine. "That's very generous of Ida. Of course, she *did* secure Hesper's loan with her property." She faced the larger computer screen. "Let me pull up the accounts and look at the paperwork and we'll start from there."

My shoulders dropped as I sighed in relief. Ms. Fontaine was going to help us.

Baker nudged my arm and leaned into me. "What did she say?" he whispered.

"What?"

"Is she getting them mixed up? Ida and Hesper?"

I swatted Baker away from me. He needed to be quiet. We were finally getting somewhere.

But he leaned closer. "Rosie. She just said Great-Grammy secured *Hesper's* loan. What does she mean?"

I whipped my head around to face him as I rewound Ms. Fontaine's words: *That's very generous of Ida. Of course, she* did *secure Hesper's loan with her property.*

I closed my eyes and tried to picture the loan papers Grim Hesper had shown me. I remembered seeing both their signatures. But did we have it backward? Was the loan Grim Hesper's? What would she need money for? Not only had she been hoarding money since she was seven, she was also a successful attorney. She had plenty!

Something was a lot more not-right than we'd thought.

"Ms. Fontaine," I said, "Great-Grammy's accounts are up-to-date, right?"

"Ida's?" Her eyes flitted between us and the computer screen as she typed. "Of course they are. She's always been very good with her money. But I did just notice that sometime in the last few months she added a cosigner to her accounts."

"Who?"

"There are rules about these things, so I can't say." She squinted at the screen and shrugged. "No worries, though. It looks like she was just putting her affairs in order. I'm sure Sherman was encouraging her. That's what good attorneys do."

I remembered that name. It was the person we were supposed to go to when Aunt Tilly came home.

"Sherman Ashwick? Her attorney?"

Ms. Fontaine was still tapping the keyboard. "Yes. He's represented Ida forever. As a matter of fact, I was surprised he wasn't involved in the paperwork concerning her property. But Hesper said he was retiring soon, so she had someone from her firm look it over."

Ms. Fontaine faced us again. "Does your grandmother know you're here, taking care of this, ah, legality?"

"Grandmother Hesper, you mean?" said Baker.

Ms. Fontaine nodded. "Yes."

"No, ma'am," I said. "And please don't tell her. Great-Grammy wants it to be a surprise."

The bank president raised her eyebrows for a moment, as though she was thinking hard. Then she stood. "Let's go to the table so I can see what you've brought. You say Ida sent you with a signed check?"

We nodded as Ms. Fontaine walked around her desk, talking as she crossed the office. "It's too bad that commercial building Hesper bought has been slow to attract leases. But's that's how real estate works. I'm sure she'll appreciate her mother stepping in to help."

Baker and I exchanged fast wide-eyes as the bank president moved past us. Grim Hesper bought a whole building? *That* was what the loan was for?

We followed Ms. Fontaine, and when we sat, Baker dug into his pocket for the check and pushed it across the table. "The reason Gram Hesper doesn't know we're here is 'cause she and Great-Grammy are sort of in a fight."

"Yeah," I said. "To make up, Great-Grammy is going to pay the loan, and we're not supposed to tell Gram Hesper until Great-Grammy comes home."

Baker leaned forward. "So could you not say anything about this whole thing to Gram Hesper?"

"Or even that we came to see you?"

Ms. Fontaine listened expressionless as Baker and I talked over each other. I was getting a horrible feeling that we'd made everything worse, but the bank president smiled.

"I know about family members not getting along, especially when money is involved. And Ida and Hesper certainly have different ways of looking at finances," she said. "Don't you worry, I'll keep this between the four of us: you two, me, and Ida." She paused and picked up the check, studying it. Then she broke the bad news. "I'll need to confirm the transaction with her before I apply the payment to the loan. I understand she's out of town, but since it's a substantial amount of money, I'd like to talk to her personally. I don't see any problem beyond that. Perhaps I'll even stop by the house. Will she be returning soon?"

I barely heard Ms. Fontaine as she continued. "The first thing we need to do is fill out the check with the amount owed and the loan number."

"Uh—" I was still back where she said she might stop by our house for a visit.

It was a good thing Baker was thinking. "That would be great."

I knew for a fact that nothing was great. This was so much worse than I'd thought. If Ms. Fontaine came to see us, we wouldn't just have to fake Great-Grammy's voice. We'd have to figure out how to convince the bank president that Great-Grammy was alive in our house.

And this time, somehow, Great-Grammy was going to have to answer questions.

THIRTY°

As usual, trouble made Baker think he was starving to death.

We'd been in the car thirty seconds when Baker exclaimed, "Are you as hungry as I am?"

I glared at him, took out my phone, and started texting. "Seriously, Baker. We'll be home soon. The traffic's better."

I pointed to my phone and then to his pocket.

He exhaled and reached into his pocket. "We could do a drive-thru."

Me: NO DRIVE-THRU. We need to talk. Not in front of Byron. + How can you think about food after everything Ms. Fontaine told us?

He twisted to face me. "What do you mean?"

I pointed back to his phone as I spoke. "I mean, there are other things more important than food."

Me: She wants to talk to Great-Grammy. Also, Grim Hesper? Seriously? Do you think GG used the property to help GH get

that building? NO WAY. She's pulling something. Trying to sell
the house while GG's away.

    Me: !!!!!!!

It was taking Baker too long to read, so I poked him.

"Hold on." He shoved me away but started to type.

Baker: I have no clue what you just said.

    Me: This is a mess. I don't think we should wait for Aunt Tilly
        to go see Great-Grammy's lawyer.

Baker: But I'm hungry.

I elbowed him. Hard.

Baker: Fine.

"His last name is Ashwick. Google him," I said.

Half a block later, Baker held the screen in front of me. "There's
only one lawyer named Ashwick nearby: Sherman. His office is close
to our house."

"Sherman. That's him." I leaned as far forward as my shoulder belt
let me. "Uh, Byron? Would it be possible to make a stop before we go
home?"

Byron nodded. "No problem. What's the address?"

Baker read it aloud. Minutes later we pulled up to a building nothing like Examine Bank headquarters. It was basically a giant white

box sticking out of the middle of a parking lot. Except for the string of chrome elevators, the lobby was wall-to-wall white, too.

There were three large directories that listed the name of each office by floor. "This is going to take forever," I said.

Baker looked up from his phone, already heading to press the circular Up button between the elevators. "It's suite 702."

Life before search engines must have been one long, annoying scavenger hunt.

"Remember," I said as we stepped off the elevator, "Mr. Ashwick probably knows Great-Grammy's sick, but not that she's you-know-what. So we have to tell him everything without telling him anything. If we let it slip . . ."

Baker nodded gravely. "He'd have to call the police."

Mr. Ashwick's building was nothing like the bank's, and neither was his office, starting with the receptionist. No sooner had we opened the door than a miniature dog came bounding toward us, loudly yip-yapping his welcome.

"Zeus!" said a short, robust woman, chasing after the dog. "You must behave while we're at work, you silly dog." With one hand she scooped Zeus from where he was attached to Baker's leg, and with her free arm she hugged me first, then Baker.

"It's so lovely to see you children." The lady's accent was Spanish and her smile was brighter than Karleen's. "I imagine there's trouble brewing if you're visiting on a school day."

There was a piece of light blue construction paper taped to her desk, announcing her name in colorful crayon: MRS. SARA RODRIGUEZ.

She cuddled Zeus and reached for my hand. "Come get settled in our meeting room. I'll let Sherman know you're here. Just in time for our morning snack!"

She escorted us down a narrow hallway and into a room overcrowded with furniture and books. "Have a seat on that couch and we'll be right in."

I opened my mouth to speak, but Mrs. Rodriguez put a finger to her lips. "Not a word, child. Not yet." Then she backed out of the room and closed the door.

Baker faced me. "That was weird, right?"

I nodded. "Totally different than the bank."

Baker leaned close to me and kept his voice low. "She's acting like she knows us, or something."

"How would she? We've never met her."

Baker closed his eyes and sniffed the air. "Do you smell something?"

At that moment the door swung open and Mrs. Rodriguez appeared again, this time carrying a large platter that held a dish of cookies, a ceramic pitcher, and four glasses. She put the platter down on the table in front of us. "I hope you like sugar cookies," she said as she poured milk. "They're straight from our toaster oven."

Baker's mouth was already full, so he just nodded.

Mrs. Rodriguez went in and out of the room carrying pads of paper, pens, and folders, and kept our glasses of milk filled.

A few minutes later, there was a clunk, slide, clunk, slide, clunk, slide noise from outside the room. We looked toward the hall. When the man appeared, he took up the whole doorway. It could only be Great-Grammy's attorney, Mr. Sherman Ashwick.

He was old. Not Great-Grammy old, more like Grim Hesper old, and basketball player tall. He wore a gray sweatshirt and a pair of navy-blue gym shorts, and his long legs practically glowed, they were so chalky white. What kind of lawyer dressed like he was relaxing at home on a Saturday afternoon?

Mr. Ashwick maneuvered his way into the room, leaning haphazardly on his cane, and landed with a thump and a skid in the armchair across from us. Mrs. Rodriguez sat in the chair beside him.

His cane fell on the floor, and Mr. Ashwick kicked it out of the way as he fingered the hair he hadn't had for a whole lot of years. Then he took a good long look at Baker and me.

"Sara makes the most delicious goodies, doesn't she?" He reached for a cookie and took a big bite.

He continued to study us as he ate the entire cookie. Then, after a long gulp of milk, he shifted forward in the chair. "I had a feeling we'd see you two soon. You must be Baker, and you"—he chortled—"must be the notorious Rosie."

I swallowed the last of my cookie. They *did* know us. Wait—I was notorious?

"How did you recognize us so fast?"

"Oh, sweetheart, how could I *not* recognize you?" said Mrs. Rodriguez. "Why, we've known every member of your family and have been hearing about the two of you since before you were born. Your great-grandmother was one of Sherman's first clients. She and your great-grandfather owned several successful businesses in their day, and we handled their legal papers."

"I could have picked you kids out anywhere," agreed Mr. Ashwick with a laugh. "Ida showed us photographs over the years, but never the usual ones, with the smiles. No sir, they were shots of Baker screaming with fright, nose to nose with some snake, or you, Rosie, your arms folded and an obstinate look on your face, refusing to get in the car just because."

Mrs. Rodriguez giggled. "Remember the one—"

Mr. Ashwick waved her off. "We've gone on enough, Sara. I'm sure the children have more important things on their minds, or they wouldn't be here."

It was quiet. I don't think either Baker or I knew where to begin.

We didn't need to. It was Mr. Ashwick who broke the silence. He spoke slowly, as if each word was important. "We are aware that Ida has been sick and is working with specialists. We also know about her plans to preserve herself so researchers can study her brain sometime in the future."

Baker and I looked at each other. *That* was new information. And very helpful at this moment, so I nodded as if we already knew.

"Great-Grammy left to visit those specialists," I said.

"And then she got a sore throat, so she hasn't been able to talk on the phone," said Baker, scooting forward in his chair. "Plus, she's busy—"

I nudged Baker's knee to stop him. "—with the specialists," I finished. Each word we said, and didn't say, was important.

I spoke as carefully as I could. "She wants Aunt Tilly to come home to help take care of us, but she's not back yet. When our grandmother Hesper found out Great-Grammy was gone, she moved in. Nothing is happening the way Great-Grammy wants."

"Yeah," Baker agreed. "She gave us a list—"

"Anyway," I interrupted again. "It's sort of a disaster."

Baker leapt to his feet and waved his arms. "A total disaster!"

I took a deep breath. "See, Grandmother Hesper is trying to sell the house while Great-Grammy is, um, out of town."

"And she's going to send us to boarding schools!"

"In different countries." I squeezed my eyes shut, but I couldn't block the image of the girls in white shirts on the brochure in Grim Hesper's bedroom. "Grandmother Hesper said the bank would force us to sell the house because Great-Grammy forgot the loan payments, but we went to the bank and Ms. Fontaine said—"

Mr. Ashwick frowned and held up his hand. "Loan?"

Baker tipped forward, his eyes wide. "More than a million dollars!"

"Oh, my," said Mrs. Rodriguez.

Mr. Ashwick cleared his throat. "Before we go on, I need one dollar from each of you."

I was confused, and besides, I didn't have any money. "A dollar?"

"A retainer," said Mr. Ashwick. "We should make you my official clients."

Baker stood and reached into his pocket. He pulled out a wad of cash and handed Mr. Ashwick a dollar. I elbowed him as he sat. "Seriously, Baker? You shouldn't be carrying that much money." I paused before adding, "But can you give him a dollar for me?"

Mr. Ashwick took another dollar from Baker, then gestured to

Mrs. Rodriguez. "Sara, please write the children a receipt and begin a file. Miss Rose Marigold Spreen and Master Baker Alexander Spreen are now my clients."

He turned back to us. "Now we can proceed. Let's start at the beginning, shall we?"

And skipping over the fact that Great-Grammy was lying dead in a freezer dressed like an old-lady burglar, that's what we did.

THIRTY-ONE°

First, I explained to Mr. Ashwick that the place to start was before the beginning.

I told him about the spring day Great-Grammy, Baker, and I were cleaning the yard and she fainted, which must have been when she decided to visit the doctor.

Baker explained that almost a month later, he was home sick from school and noticed Great-Grammy doing weird things. She confessed that she'd been to the hospital for tests and was very sick, but insisted she had a big plan and made him promise to keep it secret from me until she was ready.

Best we could, we described receiving texts from Great-Grammy asking us to come straight home from school on Wednesday, twelve days ago. Then we got to the part where we walked into the house and found her in her chair with her notebook. I couldn't tell them she was dead, so I just said Great-Grammy had instructions for us and we argued about what to do. Baker wanted to follow the instructions and, at first, I didn't.

"Instructions?" said Mrs. Rodriguez.

"Obviously she had come to realize how sick she was." Mr. Ashwick cleared his throat. "Ida has always been a planner. And I know she wants to make sure you two will be okay in the event of her death. Rather than dwell on the instructions, as I'm sure they are hard to think about, tell me about the trouble that's happened since she left town."

Neither of us wanted to talk about the freezer, so it was a relief to keep pretending Great-Grammy was alive. All we had to explain was that we'd had one problem after another. No luck finding Aunt Tilly; too many casseroles; the tree falling; the visit to the police station; and the worst... Grim Hesper moving in and claiming Great-Grammy was too old and forgetful to keep the house, or us.

The more we explained, the madder I got. "The whole house is *empty*, and she wants to clear Baker and me out, too—to boarding schools across the Atlantic Ocean!"

"Well." Mrs. Rodriguez harrumphed. "None of this surprises me. Hesper has always been fixated on the best cars, the biggest houses, the most exotic travel, expensive jewelry, and of course the wealthiest *people*..." Mrs. Rodriguez's face turned bright pink and her pleasant voice grew harsh and impatient. "It wasn't enough to send her children away before they were even teenagers, she chose the most elite boarding schools in the country—oh, how she boasted about those schools. And when those darlings came home for visits? Where did they stay? With Ida!"

"Now, now," said Mr. Ashwick. "Hesper's also endured her own pain over the years. Her husband left her with two small children, and then her son, the only person who could halfway manage her, died."

Mrs. Rodriguez raised her chin and spoke to the air in a high-pitched, singsong voice. "It seems to me a person with such a loving family would lean on them to get through pain, not turn on them every chance she had."

Mr. Ashwick shifted in his chair. "Sara."

It was as though Mrs. Rodriguez woke up. "Oh, dear. I'm so sorry. She is your grandmother, and of course this is hard for you."

"It's okay," said Baker. "We're afraid of her, just like everybody else."

"Yeah," I agreed. "And you haven't even heard the worst."

Mr. Ashwick snorted. "The loan?"

Baker and I spoke at once. "Yeah, the loan."

We proceeded to tell them what we'd discovered. How when we arrived at Examine Bank headquarters that morning thinking *Great-Grammy* owed money, we found out it was Grim Hesper who'd borrowed so she could buy an office building and Great-Grammy who had guaranteed it with her own house. And we—or Great-Grammy—wrote a check to save the house. But that wasn't the end of it, because now Ms. Fontaine, the bank president, needed to speak with Great-Grammy personally.

Mr. Ashwick's eyes got wider, and wider, and wider. "So Hesper took out a loan for a building? Do you know when?"

I shrugged. "In the past year or two maybe? Right, Baker?"

Baker screwed up his eyebrows like he was thinking back. "Yeah, it was something like that."

"Hmmmm," said Mr. Ashwick. "As her attorney for more than forty years, I'm concerned that Ida signed a document I know nothing about. Ida was never against helping anyone, but she and Hesper had a volatile relationship when it came to money. There was an incident concerning Hesper's law school loans quite some time ago, and Ida did her best to forgive that, not that she ever forgot." He chuckled as he leaned forward and took another cookie. "She figured out how to set that to rights, though. Brilliantly, if I do say so." He was about to take a bite when he shook his head. "Something about this loan isn't right. I think I should have a chat with Ms. Fontaine." Then he looked at his watch. "It's getting well past lunchtime."

As if by some secret cue, Mrs. Rodriguez reached for the silver platter. "If you will excuse me, I'll clear up."

After she'd closed the door behind her, Mr. Ashwick grimaced. "None of this makes sense. I doubt Ida would have signed anything that put her property at risk. I'm not sure how—or if—Hesper managed to get Ida to guarantee this loan, but I don't want to wait until your great-grandmother returns to begin investigating. I need your help to find out what Hesper's been up to." He looked pointedly at each of us and added, "Do you understand what I'm saying?"

I thought back to Saturday, when I found the boarding school brochures in Grim Hesper's room. "You want us to spy?"

"I'm not encouraging anything specific, but, *for example*, it might be helpful to obtain pieces of writing or signature samples from your grandmother Hesper. Perhaps something lying about the house that you happen to see." He waved his hand at the piles on the table. "I have plenty of examples of Ida's, but I need both so I can have an expert compare them."

Baker let out a long *Whooaaa*. "You think Grim Hesper has been forging Great-Grammy's signature!"

"Like she did with the law school loans?" I wouldn't be surprised, except for one thing. "But she's a lawyer now, and that's against the law."

Baker threw up his hands. "It's Grim Hesper!"

"We don't know for certain," said Mr. Ashwick, reaching to the floor for his cane. "If it's true, it would be hard to prove, especially since Hesper is telling everyone that Ida's become 'forgetful.' I suggest we take this one step at a time."

Then I remembered the most important thing *we* kept forgetting. "Um, I'm not sure if we're supposed to talk about this with you, but before Great-Grammy, er, left, she lost her will—"

"—to live," interrupted Baker. "She lost her will to live."

Mr. Ashwick dropped his cane. "Are you referring to the will that she recently changed? She's lost it?"

I nodded. "That was one of the instructions on her list. She wanted us to look for it while she was . . . away."

Mr. Ashwick sighed. "Well then, she's likely lost our copy, too, because she mistakenly took it with her the last time she was here. I left her a message, because we still have to register it with the state . . ."

"What happens if we can't find it?"

Mr. Ashwick paused. "It would only be a problem if Ida were to pass away before she returned from her trip and her most recent will could not be located. In that case, if someone presented the court with an older, signed will—"

I got what he was saying. "Someone like our grandmother Hesper."

"Yes. Originally she was the sole beneficiary." Mr. Ashwick turned both his palms up and shrugged. "Well, I suppose Ida needs to stay healthy, and we'll draw up another one for her signature as soon as she returns home." He reached for his cane again and got to his feet. "But considering her medical condition, I advise you two to do your very best to locate that will."

We followed Mr. Ashwick as he clip-clopped out of the room and down the hallway to the reception area. After we exchanged cell phone numbers and said goodbye to Mrs. Rodriguez and Zeus, the lawyer held the door open for us.

"I'm going to contact my best investigator—perhaps he can help locate your aunt Tilly as well. Her presence would make a big difference." He tapped his cane on the floor. "As for you two," he said, "I need you to text me as many samples of your grandmother's handwriting as possible. Most importantly, find that will. If Hesper is capable of forging Ida's signature, she may be capable of much worse."

Baker and I didn't talk the whole way home, and not just because of Byron. We were both tired, and besides, there was a lot to think about. By the time Byron turned up our driveway it was almost two-thirty in the afternoon. He let us out halfway up the drive because there was a white pickup truck blocking the way.

What was Grim Hesper doing now?

We ran up the walkway and took the porch steps two by two. Just as I held the key to unlock the front door, there was a movement out the corner of my eye. I turned to see a shadowed figure come around the house and step into the sunlight. I nudged Baker. "Who's that?"

It was a tall, skinny man wearing a long-sleeved khaki-colored shirt, and pants stuck inside his boots. A backpack hung from his shoulder, bouncing against his side as he ambled along the front yard. His eyes were on a large piece of paper as he walked, and he was headed straight for a large groundhog hole when Baker called to him.

"Watch out!"

The man stopped, adjusted his glasses, and peered closely at the grass in front of him.

"Thanks!" he said, looking up and waving. He sidestepped the hole and hurried toward the front porch. As he got closer I noticed that despite his wide-brimmed hat, his face was a coppery-red tan, like he usually forgot to wear it. "Harry Mudd, from the National Association of Graveyard Preservation. Thanks for letting me look around."

How could I have forgotten the historic grave dude?

"Right," I said. "I'm Rosie, and this is my brother, Baker."

"A pleasure." He climbed the porch steps and held out his hand.

"Did you find the grave you're looking for?"

He shook his head. "Nope. I've been traipsing around here for over two hours using every gadget I've got, and there's not a marker or clue to be seen. Would it be possible to speak with your grandmother?"

Baker shrugged. "She's away right now."

"And she's our *great-grandmother*," I added. "Is there something you want us to tell her?"

"Oh, no, I'd just like to explain what I'm doing and apologize for the trouble. I think I must have gotten the coordinates wrong." Then he laughed. "Maybe I recorded a number backward."

Baker tilted his head. "You're looking for a specific person?"

Mr. Mudd grinned. "Yep. He's an important scout who warned the Union Army that the Confederates were coming. Later, he was ambushed and buried with four other men. They were moved, but he was overlooked. By the time the mistake was discovered, the area was overgrown and nobody could locate him."

"That's sad," I said. "Do you want to move him so he's with the other four?"

"That's the idea." Mr. Mudd made his way down the steps. "Please thank Mrs. Spreen for giving me access to her property. I appreciate it." With a wave, he was off.

I didn't put the key in the front door until Mr. Mudd drove down the driveway and turned onto the road. "All clear," said Baker. "Hopefully, Grim Hesper won't be home anytime soon. We need to *find the will*."

"Don't forget what Mr. Ashwick told us," I said as we entered the foyer and I watched Baker bolt the door. "Now would be the perfect time to look in her room."

Just as the words came out of my mouth, the sound of tires crackling on blacktop sounded from outside. My heart sank as we scrambled to the dining room window. Sure enough, a parade of fancy black sedans was speeding up the driveway. That could only mean one thing: Grim Hesper was back, along with whatever posse she'd roped into her evil plan.

THIRTY-TWO°

A bunch of men and women wearing flashy outfits strode down the walkway in groups of twos and threes. It was obvious which person mattered most, because Grim Hesper stuck to his side as she waved for the rest of them to follow her to the middle of the front yard.

Walking across the grass, Grim Hesper clutched Important Man's elbow and steered him around one of the groundhog holes.

"She's never going to let go of his arm, is she?" I said to Baker as we watched from the dining room window.

"Not a chance," said Baker. "He's probably the guy she's after to buy the place. He looks rich."

"What do you mean? He's the only one wearing jeans and a T-shirt. And his hair is long and scruffy."

"Duh," said Baker. "Megarich dudes don't have to dress up because they don't care what anybody thinks."

The group gathered around our grandmother as she reached into her briefcase and started handing out booklets that looked like the appraisal she'd dropped off for Great-Grammy. She gestured as she spoke, pointing first toward the greenhouse, then beyond where the tree fell, and finally toward the house.

"What if they come inside?" said Baker.

The whole group was looking at something above the house. The roof?

"It doesn't matter. We can't search for the lockbox or anything else until they leave."

Baker put his hand on my shoulder. "It does matter. *Great-Grammy* is in here."

"Grim Hesper said nobody cares about a cruddy old basement, remember?"

Baker didn't say anything.

"Okay, what if I sit at the top of the stairs to make it harder for anybody to get by?"

Baker twisted his head. "You're just going to sit there?"

He was right...that might look strange. "I'll bring a book."

I was trying to think of a better idea when we heard the dead bolt turn and the front door creak open. With that warning, Grim Hesper whisked around the corner and into the dining room. She stopped cold when she saw us.

"Oh." She glanced at the trail of potential buyers in her wake. "I didn't realize you two would be home from school already." Her tone was lighthearted, but her eyes said otherwise as they narrowed, inspecting us from head to toe. "Why are you dressed up? Did I miss a special event at school?"

I caught the laugh in my throat. As if she cared one iota about any special event of ours! "No, we just felt like looking nice today."

"Well," she said slowly, probably wondering how to deal with us in front of her *friends*. "Well," she repeated. "You look very nice. But we are conducting business, so I suggest you remove yourselves and work on, er, homework."

Then she twirled in place, reached for Important Man's arm, and led the entire crew across the foyer and into the living room, gushing awfulness as she went. "The house needs a tremendous amount of work, so it would be an easy decision to tear it down and separate the property into quarter-acre lots, or even build clusters of luxury townhomes. It's hard to tell because of the dense woods, but there's a full ten acres to work with. Or, if one was willing to endure the challenge of an extensive renovation, the house could be preserved. The options are limitless."

She was giving them a tour. Of the whole house. "You were right," I said to Baker under my breath.

Baker's ears turned bright red—a sure sign he was panicking. "Go get your book," he said as he headed across the room toward the kitchen. "I need a snack."

Leave it to my brother to think of food at a time like this. Newsflash: he needed to help, too.

I followed him to the kitchen and watched him open the refrigerator and pull back the foil on one of the casserole dishes. A cover! People don't think about what's underneath a cover unless they're looking for something specific.

Baker lifted a single, cold enchilada out of the pan and stuffed half of it in his mouth.

"I have an idea," I said, reaching around him to shut the refrigerator. "We need to put something on top of the freezer."

He raised his eyebrows and inhaled the rest of the enchilada.

"Like a tablecloth," I said as he chewed. "Or maybe some of the supplies."

It took three swallows before he could speak. "Why?"

I shoved him toward the basement door. "So they won't open it."

"But—that's nuts, Rosie."

"Then you come up with a better idea!"

Baker grumbled as he opened the basement door. "I don't understand why I have to do it!"

"Do *you* want to sit here and talk to people?" I hissed.

When he disappeared down the stairs, I ran to the back hall and snatched a book from my backpack. As I returned to the kitchen, I heard footsteps noisily echoing down the stairs from the second floor.

In the nick of time, I sat on the top step and opened *Mockingjay* to where I'd left off at chapter eighteen.

The clunk-clunk-clunk of shoes on hardwood floors and what sounded like a hundred conversations at once bounced off the walls of empty rooms and hallways. Grim Hesper must have let them loose to look around on their own. A few voices came closer and I shouted down the stairway to remind Baker to return with an alibi. "Don't forget to bring up something for dessert!"

But after a few minutes, it became clear that our grandmother didn't want anyone going down to the basement, either. She swept from the side hallway to the kitchen, discouraging anyone interested by guiding them toward the rear door, saying that her mother had quite the mess of supplies down there and until she cleaned it up it would be much more useful to look at the rest of the property instead. Then she opened the back door and ushered them outside to the massive backyard.

That strategy didn't work with the dude dressed in jeans.

"Hesper, you must understand. If I buy this property, I want my project manager to live here with his family. It makes it so much more convenient to have someone on-site from planning to permit, and through the construction period. He and his wife have small children and I promised to inspect every inch so that I can assure them there are no infestations." Then he laughed and added, "Or dead bodies."

My mouth dropped open. I peered around the corner to look at the two of them standing alone in the kitchen. Grim Hesper looked, well, *grim*.

"Archie, the basement is a mess right now. Give me two days to empty it, and then you can inspect to your heart's delight. My mother has so many supplies down there, you wouldn't be able to see anything properly."

Something cold poked my knee and I turned. Baker held a casserole dish and a loaf cake wrapped in cellophane and was attempting to squeeze past. "C'mon, move, I—"

I held up my hand to shush him and pointed to the kitchen.

Baker craned his head around me so he could see, too. Then he stood and set the casserole on a lower step. "Get your phone out. They might say something we can use."

Duh. I should have thought of that. I dug my phone out of my pocket and pressed the video app.

As inconspicuously as possible, Baker and I peeked around the corner again. It was like a game of Twister, but I managed to hit Record in time to catch Archie let out a long, frustrated sigh.

"I have a crew prepared to begin work in ten days, and I'm ready with a cash offer so we can finish this deal by the end of the week. Are you sure your mother is willing to move that quickly?"

Grim Hesper was working hard to keep her smile, but the furrow lines on her forehead showed she knew she was losing this battle. "Of course she's ready. In fact, she just overnighted me her power of attorney. We can proceed while she's out of town."

I couldn't believe what I was hearing. The only good thing about her outright lie was that Grim Hesper still thought Great-Grammy was visiting her friend Priscilla.

And then I realized something else. It didn't matter if we had Grim Hesper's lie on video, because we couldn't prove anything without opening the freezer. I stopped recording and stuffed the phone in my pocket.

"That's terrific news," Archie was saying. "Now that I've seen the rest of the house, once I look at the basement, if everything's in order, I'll have an offer drawn up this evening."

"Perfect," said Grim Hesper. "Right this way."

Baker and I scrambled upright. "Quick!" I whispered. "Grab the food and go back downstairs."

Baker reached for the casserole and scurried down the stairs while I stood and blocked the doorway.

"Excuse us, Rosie," said Grim Hesper. "I need to show this gentleman the basement."

There was no plan, and no way to predict what might happen, but I figured Baker shouldn't go it alone. So instead of scooting aside, I turned and led the way, one leisurely step at a time.

"Baker," I called. "Did you find something for dinner?"

He was standing beside the upright freezer, holding the casserole and the loaf cake. "What about noodle wiggle? And a pound cake?"

I headed straight for him. "I think I'd rather have Great-Grammy's chocolate tarts instead of cake. They're probably buried way in the back." I snuck a look at the other freezer. What on earth had Baker done?

I scrunched my eyebrows as we stuck our heads together, pretending to search deep in the "food" freezer, and aimed my thumb at the other one.

He grinned back at me. "I made a sign on one of the Scrabble racks. It says: KEEP OUT."

OMG. OMG. OMG.

"That's what you wanted, right? To keep people from opening it?"

My brother. I wanted to throw him into the freezer next to Great-Grammy, but there was nothing I could do now except start counting to a bazillion.

I'd made it to twenty when I remembered the tour that was happening somewhere behind us. I angled my head so I could see.

Archie was circling *our* supply table, while Grim Hesper waited in the middle of the room, her arms folded.

"There's a lot of toilet paper." Archie looked from Grim Hesper to us with his eyebrows raised. "One might think a disaster was imminent."

"Oh, yes, that's my mother." Grim Hesper laughed, then added, "I warned you, she's a bit eccentric. She's headed to a new condominium for seniors, and the move will do her good."

"I hope it has big closets." Archie chuckled, heading to the stairs. "I've seen enough. Hesper, I think we can put this deal to bed."

I elbowed Baker. Did he hear that? Grim Hesper already had a condominium for Great-Grammy! As if Great-Grammy were just one more thing to remove from the house. Like the furniture and the yard art—and us.

Baker and I watched them climb the stairs, forgetting about noodle wiggle and chocolate tarts. Grim Hesper was way ahead of us. If she was successful, and she usually was, Archie was going to buy the house.

There was something else. Sooner or later Great-Grammy was going to have to come out of the freezer. I had figured we could wait until Aunt Tilly was here and we had Mr. Ashwick and Mrs. Rodriguez to help us figure that out, too.

But now it was a matter of days before some mover, or Archie, or even Grim Hesper opened the freezer. Nobody on earth could help us if that happened.

We had to do something to stop our grandmother from selling. If we ended up back in the police station, this time they'd put Baker and me behind bars.

THIRTY-THREE°

After she hurried the rest of her guests away, Grim Hesper went out to "celebrate" with Archie, and I've been writing this email since—

I glanced at the upper right corner of my laptop. They'd been gone since five o'clock and it was almost seven-thirty. I'd been in our cave office working on the email to Aunt Tilly for more than two hours.

At first Baker argued that I shouldn't tell Aunt Tilly *everything*, but he finally gave up and left me alone. Not long after, he came back with a giant carrot and his own update. Apparently he couldn't find a scrap of paper with Grim Hesper's handwriting anywhere—though he admitted he was too scared to go in her bedroom by himself.

I bit off the top of the carrot he'd handed me and might have glared at him. But I didn't call him a baby.

The next time he showed up, he set a bowl of chips by the laptop and told me he was searching for the will but it wasn't going very well. We'd already scoured Great-Grammy's laptop hard drive and had come up with exactly zilch. The only actual clue she'd left was in her notebook.

So I reminded him that Great-Grammy's hint was *Under the house*, and he should be double- and triple-checking here in the basement.

Then Karleen came over and they *both* brought me food. They made a salad and Baker taught her how to make his "emergency dressing" from mayonnaise, ketchup, and relish. Karleen smiled ear to ear as she handed me a bowl and a fork.

"I'm learning to cook!" she said.

Twenty minutes after that, it was a giant hunk of noodle wiggle and a glass of water. Then came one of Great-Grammy's delicious chocolate tarts.

I said, "I'm so full I'm going to throw up if I eat one more bite. Go away and no more food. I have to concentrate on this email to Aunt Tilly."

But after their dessert, Baker and Karleen decided to search the basement together. Very loudly.

There was a long creak, like a door opening. "Not in the metal cabinet," said Baker. Then the sound of toppling containers. "Nope, not under the sink," said Karleen.

Baker let out a long exhale. "Well, we know she didn't put it in the freezer." There was silence for a few seconds, and then he said, "Or did she?"

I was about to holler that Great-Grammy said she'd already checked the "food" freezer and he better keep that door closed, when I remembered *another* door: the Door to Nowhere. Maybe that was where she put the lockbox. It was under the house... "Hey, Baker," I called. "Do you still have that old key we found in one of Great-Grammy's baskets?"

He poked his head under the table. "Yeah, why?"

"Try it on the Door to Nowhere," I said.

Baker stared at me as if I'd told him to capture a tarantula with his bare hands. "No way."

"Fine." I held out my hand. "Give it to me."

He slid the ancient-looking key from his pocket and handed it over. I walked across the basement into the shadows beyond the stairs. "I can't see a thing. Where's a flashlight?"

Baker ran to the second table. "Is a lantern okay?"

"Sure."

He turned it on and when he reached me, stretched out his arm.

"Nope," I said. "You hold it."

Karleen popped between us. "What are you guys doing?"

"I think Great-Grammy might have hidden the lockbox behind the old root cellar door." I inched forward with my hands in front of me. Even with the lantern, it was difficult to see. "This key had to be in the basket for a reason, right?"

Baker held the lantern out ahead of us, and step by step, we crossed the crumbly floor. The farther we got, the more crumbly it was. I glanced down and scraped the floor with my shoe. It was pure dirt.

Baker moved the lantern higher so the wall was lit. "There it is," I said.

It was a heavy iron door, like to an old-fashioned furnace, about four feet tall. There was a thick coat of grainy crud over the keyhole.

I lifted the key and poked at the hole—or where it looked like the hole should be. It was the right size, like it *should* fit, but the key wouldn't go in. I wiggled it and pushed harder. "It's crusted over. I can't get it."

"Let me," said Baker, more confident now that we were here.

I moved over and handed him the key. "Go ahead."

Karleen craned her head around my shoulder. "Have you ever been inside?"

I shook my head. "Never."

Baker stabbed the key at the door, but it was no use. "It's not crust as in dirt, it's crust as in rust. I can't get it to go in at all."

I snatched the key from him. We were wasting our time.

Karleen leaned forward and squinted at the lock. "My dad has a lot of tools in our garage. Maybe he could open it."

"We can't tell your dad," said Baker. "Besides, if we can't get it open, there's no way Great-Grammy did."

I backed away. The normal side of our basement was creepy enough, and I had an email to finish. "I'm going to put the key back in the basket. Why don't you guys go look upstairs again?"

"But that's not *under the house*," said Baker.

"What about the storage shed? Or the green*house*," I said. "Just go away. I'm almost done!"

They went.

I kept writing until there was nothing more to say. I stared at my computer screen and the longest email in history. Aunt Tilly was bound to get here sooner or later, but would it be soon enough to make a difference? At least by the time she showed up she'd know *why* we were somewhere across the Atlantic, or in handcuffs.

I typed *Love, Rosie and Baker*. After a deep breath, I hit Send.

It was quiet. Too quiet. What were Baker and Karleen doing?

The answer was up the stairs and to the left, where I found them hovering over the kitchen table. Baker scooped liquidy vanilla ice cream onto two servings of chocolate tarts while Karleen stood beside him, ready to swoop in with a can of whipped cream and a bag of Reese's Pieces.

"If you're having a second dessert, you better have found the lockbox."

Neither looked at me. Karleen said, "No, we forgot about this box of ice cream sitting out. We didn't want it to go to waste."

"Baker! We don't have time for this!" I'd gotten good at *not* shouting lately, but this was ridiculous. "I've been writing Aunt Tilly a very important email, and you guys were supposed to be looking for that lockbox until you found it! And what about the pictures we were supposed to text Mr. Ashwick? Did you find something with Grim Hesper's writing on it?"

Baker put down the scoop, shoved the bowls in front of Karleen, and barely looked at me. I knew guilt when I saw it. "I forgot?"

I stomped out of the kitchen and hoped Grim Hesper would celebrate a little longer.

I took the stairs to the second floor two by two, Baker and Karleen scrambling behind me. I kept my hand on the railing as I rounded the banister at the top of the landing and ran to Grim Hesper's room.

I clutched the door handle and twisted, halfway expecting Grim Hesper to have figured out a way to lock it. Thankfully it opened, and the three of us burst into her room. There were papers and clothes everywhere, and the bed wasn't made. It was sort of unbelievable.

Grim Hesper didn't want people to see the piles of supplies in the basement, but her own mess was so much worse. Great-Grammy always said, people are quick to point out somebody else's mess while they stood knee deep in their own. And she was right.

"This is—your grandmother's room?" said Karleen.

"Uh, yeah," I said. "The good news is she won't be able to tell we looked around."

Baker raised his eyebrows. "Now I know why she needs two maids. It's worse than my room."

He was right. It was as if a tornado had blown through.

I waved my hands in the air. "Take out your phones and get as many pictures as possible. We're looking for Grim Hesper's signature, or anything with her handwriting."

We split up. I went to the dresser, while Baker and Karleen divided the rest of the room. There on the dresser was a single page: the power of attorney. I scanned it. It gave Hesper Marigold Spreen authority to act on behalf of Ida Marigold Spreen with regard to the house and property.

Mr. Sherman would want a photo of that!

I was digging into my pocket for my phone when Baker let out a loud whoop. Karleen and I were beside him in an instant.

"It's Great-Grammy's will," said Baker. "She had it all along!"

"It can't be." I peered closer at the blue-covered document.

But it was.

LAST WILL AND TESTAMENT
IDA MARIGOLD SPREEN

I snatched it out of Baker's hands and turned to the first page. We scanned the document as I flipped page after page. The only name mentioned stood out in bold: **Hesper Marigold Spreen**.

Baker dropped to the bed. "Well, even though she's lying to Archie, it doesn't matter. The house, and everything...it's hers anyway."

"No, Baker," I said. "This can't be the will Great-Grammy wrote with Mr. Ashwick this spring. Remember what he told us?"

"Yeah, I remember. He said a judge would use the latest *signed* will."

I turned to the last page. Sure enough, it was dated almost thirty years ago. "Darn." I pointed to show Baker and Karleen. "It's signed."

Baker gave his head a vigorous shake. "This is ancient! There's no way—"

"You're right, it isn't the one Great-Grammy hid. But what do you think will happen when Great-Grammy's daughter, the lawyer who knows every judge in town, brings this to court? We don't have another signed will."

I closed my eyes.

There was a dewdrop sound.

"Oh, no. My mom just texted. I have to go home." Karleen looked from her phone to the page with the signatures. "The judge needs a signed will?"

"Yeah," said Baker.

"Well, I can solve that problem right now." Karleen plucked the will from my hands and headed to the door. As she got to the hallway, she turned. "Until further notice, there are now *two* missing wills."

That was the exact moment Karleen Elizabeth King became not only my true and best friend. She also became my hero.

THIRTY-FOUR°

Baker and I were still staring at each other as we heard the front door shut behind Karleen.

"That was the most brilliant idea ever," said Baker, with a huge grin. "I can't believe Karleen thought of it. Grim Hesper can't do anything if she doesn't have that will. Right?"

I pulled Baker to the dresser. "Don't get too excited. Remember, Great-Grammy's not officially dead yet. And until she is..." I held up the power of attorney I'd found. It gave Grim Hesper the authority to act on Great-Grammy's behalf. "...she's got *this*. She can sell the property."

Baker studied the document more closely and pointed to the date beside Great-Grammy's signature. "Great-Grammy didn't sign this. She was dead yesterday!"

"Duh." I rolled my eyes at Baker. "Let's call a meeting and announce that to everyone. While we're at it we can take them to the basement and give them a nice surprise."

My phone buzzed. It was a text from Karleen. I read it aloud to Baker.

Forgot to tell you. Look on bedside table. See you tomorrow!! ☺

We couldn't get to the bedside table fast enough. There was no mistaking what Karleen meant. Baker picked up a yellow legal pad with page after page of Great-Grammy's signature, again and again and again.

"Grim Hesper's been practicing, and she wasn't any good at first." I angled my cell phone and clicked photos of each page. Then I went to the dresser, where we'd left the power of attorney that Great-Grammy most definitely did not sign, and took a photo of that, too.

"I thought Mr. Ashwick said we needed something with Grim Hesper's signature," said Baker.

"Don't these count?" I was only half joking.

"Of course not," said Baker. "She's trying to write like Great-Grammy."

We searched the room again just to be sure we didn't miss anything. Baker was bending to the floor by the tiny writing desk in the corner, butt in the air, when he popped upright holding a stack of papers in his hands.

"This looks important," he said. "It was behind her heap of shoes." He made his way across the room and handed me the top half of the papers.

We sat on the bed and shuffled through our stacks, which were mostly receipts for everything Grim Hesper had been doing to Great-Grammy's house. Deliveries, cleaning services, repairs.

"Wow," said Baker. "We have the signatures Mr. Ashwick wanted, that's for sure. She had to sign for all of it." Baker was holding a thick stapled booklet. "Look, this one's for the furniture and..."

"Baker, what is it?"

Baker's mouth was open, but he'd stopped talking. I peered over his shoulder. It was an agreement with Wells Antiques Appraisals and Sales for the appraisal and auction of the "listed goods." Every chair, every mirror, every table . . . everything Grim Hesper sent away!

They were auctioning Great-Grammy's furniture.

Baker kept turning, page after page. Then, halfway through the packet, he froze. It was a long itemized list of his trains: the engines, cars, houses, pieces of track—even the tiny people and trees.

I put my arm around my brother. "Don't worry, Baker. We're going to stop her. Look, right there in that box. It says the auction isn't until Saturday."

Baker was silent as I took the receipts from him and laid them across the bed. "This is more proof," I said, snapping pictures of each one. "We'll send these photos to Mr. Ashwick, and somehow we're going to find Great-Grammy's real will, and everything is going to get fixed. Your train room will be back together by next week. You'll see."

"Maybe, but in what house?" Baker's eyes were welling up, ready to spill.

I restacked the receipts and returned them to the floor where Baker had found them. "C'mon, we better get out of here before Cruella comes home."

Baker followed me from the bedroom. As I closed the door, he stared at me. "I need to tell you something." He inhaled deeply. "It's important."

So much for curling up under my covers and going to sleep. "Okay. Come to my room."

I was used to bossing Baker around, but lately things between us had changed. If he had something important to tell me, it was important to me, too.

I sat on my bed, propped against the pillows, and watched Baker pace the room. The expression on his face was strange.

"Ever since Great-Grammy told me she was dying, I've felt like two different people."

Silence. Back and forth he went.

I pinched my thumb and counted to ten.

More silence. Back and forth.

So I asked, "What do you mean?"

Baker cleared his throat. "I mean, I've been a person who keeps secrets and does every single thing she asked me to do, and another person on the inside, who feels horrible because of the lying. I can't do any of the things I used to. Just thinking about baking something—measuring flour, or melting butter—reminds me—I can't."

I nodded. "I get it."

Baker kept his eyes on the floor. "No, you don't," he said. "Because if Great-Grammy had told *you* she was sick instead of telling me, you would have argued with her and talked her out of this plan. Maybe we would have found another way to deal with Grim Hesper. Or, if I'd told you myself, even though she told me not to . . ." Baker covered his face with his hands. "It's my fault we're in this mess. I want to do what Great-Grammy wants—wanted—but I don't want our lives to be ruined. Maybe I deserve it, but you don't, Rosie."

"That's not even close to being true, Baker."

Baker squinted. "What do you mean?"

"Think about it. No one on this planet could talk Great-Grammy out of something once she set her mind to it." I stood and put my hand on his shoulder, looking straight in his eyes. In that moment I realized something else. "Baker, this isn't your fault, or my fault. We loved Great-Grammy and we're just doing what she asked us to do. She'd be very proud of us, even if things don't turn out like she planned. She always was."

"Even if we end up at boarding schools—or worse?"

I smiled. For the first time in a very long time, I felt like I was being a really good older sister. "Yes. Even then."

At that, a voice came echoing up the stairs. "You children better get downstairs and clean the mess in this kitchen! There's melted ice cream *everywhere*! I'm conducting business here tomorrow, and this house needs to be spotless!"

"I guess her celebration's over," Baker said as we headed out of my room.

I knew he was wrong, though. Unless a miracle happened, Grim Hesper had only begun to celebrate.

THIRTY-FIVE°

Tuesday morning we were waiting for the bus at the bottom of the driveway when we heard her voice. "I'm coming! I'm coming!"

I turned to see Karleen running across the field between our houses. She looked like she should be in a fashion show in her flowered skirt, jean jacket, and matching sneakers, but it was her woven white, blue, and yellow hat that slouched over her tiny swinging braids that made her look so "Karleen."

I looked past Karleen to the kitchen window where her mother was watching. Mrs. King waved and smiled. At me? Just in case, I waved back.

Mrs. King's pork enchiladas were delicious, and she'd been giving me rides to the shelter. And she let Karleen ride the bus to school with us. I was beginning to think she liked Karleen and me being friends.

Karleen let her backpack drop to the ground and melodramatically sat on top of it. "I thought I was going to be late. I'm glad I learned how to climb the fence," she said between huffs and puffs. "Oh, and did you send the pictures to your Mr. Lawyer guy?"

I nodded and checked my phone to see if Mr. Ashwick had replied.

"Not until pretty late last night. Grim Hesper came home and I had to help *somebody* clean up the ice cream mess in the kitchen."

Karleen's head drew into her shoulders like a turtle. "Sorry."

The bus arrived and we followed Baker up the steps. As we walked single file down the aisle, Karleen whispered, "What happens after your lawyer gets the pictures?"

I shrugged. I had no idea what happened next, besides surviving school without getting in trouble for missing homework, or for letting something suspicious slip from my mouth, while simultaneously praying that nothing bad happened at home—as in, somebody looking inside a certain freezer.

I began to add up everything that could go wrong in eight hours. By the time the bus dropped us at school, I'd counted more than fifty-three ways we were absolutely, positively doomed. Starting with #1: handing in a real-fake note excusing Baker and me from school the day before.

Was it possible for a twelve-year-old to have a heart attack?

Somehow the day got better, and so did my zooming pulse. It started with English class, when I got my short story back with an A+ at the top and a note from Mr. Davis telling me how imaginative and well written it was, and that he hoped I'd make it an even longer story. I couldn't wait to tell Aunt Tilly, if she ever got here.

At lunch they served my favorite doughnut holes for dessert. And then, at the end of the day, Karleen and I sat beside each other in math. It was the exact opposite of two weeks ago when she drove me nuts. We passed notes about school being over soon, and summer, and which trees and bushes would have fruit and when. And then she invited me for a sleepover after school was out. She'd already asked her mom!

For the first time since my parents died and we moved in with Great-Grammy, I had a friend who didn't stop liking me when I was grumpy, or even when she found out I'd done something awful like put my dead great-grandmother in a freezer. I knew 1,000 percent that Karleen would be my friend no matter what, and it made me happy, even though there were tons of reasons to be scared—and sad.

For a while, I forgot about Grim Hesper and Great-Grammy and the trouble Baker and I were in. But when the bus pulled up to our house that afternoon, I remembered.

As Baker and I waved goodbye to Karleen, I realized that if Grim Hesper had her way, I wouldn't pick apples, or strawberries, or *anything* this summer. There wouldn't be sleepovers. There wouldn't be Saturday mornings at the shelter, petting the cats and dogs, or taking care of kittens and puppies.

Grim Hesper was lying, forging, and every bad-person thing she could do to get what she wanted. Was it because she was desperate to keep the office building she'd bought, or because she hated Great-Grammy's house and loved money? She was acting like she didn't care about anything *but* money. Could that be true?

When I was being awful, my awful usually covered up my sad. Was it the same way for Grim Hesper? What was her sad? Did losing her husband so long ago make her this way? Or had she just been born greedy, thinking the whole world only existed to please her?

Whatever it was, would it ever get better?

I shook the possibility away. Grim Hesper was determined to sell our home, and unless Aunt Tilly showed up to stop her, she'd send Baker and me packing, and the boring, simple life I had, in the house I'd thought I hated, with the people I'd thought made me crazy, would be over.

I checked my phone for the twentieth time and wondered why Mr. Ashwick hadn't texted back. We needed him. Didn't he realize it was an emergency?

Out of habit, I walked to the mailbox, around the mound of dirt where the Home Sweet Home sign used to be. I tapped Gator Guitar Dude's tail hello as I passed, and opened the mailbox.

It was empty.

"Rosie, hurry up!" Baker was walking backward, already halfway up the driveway.

When I caught up with him, I noticed a black sedan parked in front of the garage, beside Grim Hesper's red sports car.

Baker eyed the car. "That can't be good."

He was right. My stomach started spinning like a washing machine. Those doughnut holes might not have been such a good idea.

"What do you think she's doing now?" I said as we climbed the porch steps.

"She doesn't have much left to do." Baker opened the screen door and abruptly stopped. "Unless she packed the suitcases she bought us and that car's here to take us away."

"Don't worry, Baker. Grim Hesper would make us pack our own bags."

We walked into the house and heard voices coming from the kitchen, so that's where we headed.

Grim Hesper was at the table, her back to us. Archie sat beside her, and between them there were a stack of documents and several pens.

Grim Hesper spun in her seat as we entered the kitchen and leapt to her feet. She was wearing fire-engine red from lips to heels. "Oh, my darling grandchildren! Home from school already?"

I dodged her incoming fake hug, maneuvering around her, but Baker didn't escape as easily.

I gestured toward the table. "What's going on?"

Grim Hesper turned and smiled. "You will be happy to know that we've finalized everything. Mother will be so pleased!"

Baker stepped closer to me. "You sold the house. Already?"

"Just about," Archie laughed. "Your grandmother is a tough nego-tiator, but all's fair in business!" He stood and offered his hand to Baker, and then me. "We didn't officially meet yesterday. I'm Archie Zimmerman." His eyes shot around the kitchen before returning to us. "I imagine it will be hard to leave the family home, but I hear you two have quite the adventures ahead."

Grim Hesper breezed across the room and opened the refrigera-tor. "I've been chilling this since last night, hoping we'd come to an agreement soon," she said, raising an oversized bottle of champagne in the air.

In an instant Archie was beside Grim Hesper as she reached inside a nearby cabinet for Great-Grammy's special glasses. "Let me help you," he said.

Baker grabbed my arm and tugged me through the dining room and out the side door. "She's the rottenest, worst, no-good person in the entire world!" he said as we stepped onto the grass. "What are we going to do?"

I put my hand on Baker's shoulder. "I have an idea."

Baker calmed down. "You do?"

"No," I said. "But you need to get a grip, otherwise we're going to end up in Switzerland."

"You're right."

We turned at the sound of a white pickup grumbling up the driveway, and Baker frowned. "Who now?"

I strained to see who was behind the wheel. "It's Harry Mudd. Remember? The graveyard guy."

"Huh," said Baker. "Wonder what he wants."

We headed to where Mr. Mudd parked. He was scouring the bed of his truck, picking through tools.

He waved as we got close. "Hey! I rechecked my coordinates, and I'm almost positive the grave I'm looking for is on this property. It's either down there"—he pointed somewhere around the gator rock band—"or back there." He arched his arm and vaguely motioned at the backyard. "Do you think Mrs. Spreen would mind if I kept looking?"

Just then, a small SUV turned up the driveway.

"She won't mind," I said, staring at the SUV. This day was officially a circus.

Harry Mudd headed toward the gator rock band with a shovel and a tool bag as the SUV came to a stop a few feet from us. The passenger door opened and Mr. Ashwick appeared, wearing a suit and tie and looking more like a typical lawyer than he had the day before. He held his cane in the air in a greeting. "Hello," he called. "Ms. Fontaine was good enough to give me a ride."

And there she was, the bank president, walking across our driveway.

She was smiling, looking at Baker and me curiously. "I've had no luck contacting Ida and was hoping she'd returned."

I briefly caught Mr. Ashwick's eye, but he looked at the sky.

"Uh, she's still away," I said.

"Sherman tells me Hesper is living here with you two." Ms. Fontaine glanced past me, at the red sports car. "She's here now?"

"She's in the kitchen, selling the house," said Baker. "They're signing the papers now."

Ms. Fontaine raised her eyebrows. "She found a buyer that quickly?"

Baker and I nodded.

Ms. Fontaine turned to Mr. Ashwick. "You were right to call me, Sherman. The bank needs to get to the bottom of this." She quickly walked to her car and returned with her briefcase. She reached inside and brought out a thick stack of paper, fanning it so we could see.

"I believe you sent these to Sherman?"

They were printouts of the photos we'd texted Mr. Ashwick, the ones from Grim Hesper's room. Right on top was the picture of the legal pad. The one with dozens of *Ida Marigold Spreen* signatures.

"Yes," I said.

She thumbed through the pages and held up the image of the power of attorney. "I'm especially interested in how Ida signed this document when no one has been able to reach her. I have questions for Hesper, but I think these photos are enough for the bank to begin an inquiry into Hesper's original loan."

"You don't understand," I said, wishing we could show them the video we took of Grim Hesper in the kitchen with Archie. "The man inside is rich. He's buying the house with cash. It's going to be over soon."

"I'm afraid investigations like this take time," said Ms. Fontaine. "Our only hope is—"

"She stole my trains!" Baker took the stack and shuffled through it. "Look! They're going to be auctioned this Saturday. And the Archie guy is going to dig up Great-Grammy's land..."

I stopped listening to Baker because he'd hit on something. Grim Hesper had stolen his trains and she was stealing Great-Grammy's home—our home. What do you do when somebody's stealing? I took my phone from my pocket.

Karleen wasn't the only one who could call 911.

The bank president marched up the walkway, telling Baker not to worry, Mr. Ashwick plodding behind them. And then there was me, the caboose.

"Is this an emergency?" the woman on the line asked.

I thought for half a second. "Yes."

"Describe your emergency."

"Well, it's a long story, but—our grandmother is robbing our house."

THIRTY-SIX°

By the time I caught up with everybody in the kitchen, I had no idea if the police were on their way. The operator told me 911 was for life-threatening emergencies and transferred me. The next person thought I was pranking them but said they'd send a patrol car.

Mrs. Fontaine and Grim Hesper were eyeing each other, while everyone else—Archie, Mr. Ashwick, and Baker—watched and waited. Nobody was sipping champagne.

Ms. Fontaine shook her head. "I can't get in touch with your mother, and I've left several messages for you, too, Hesper," she was saying. "I have questions about your loan, the one she guaranteed with her property."

"Oh, Lou," said Grim Hesper through tight lips. "Please don't worry. As I said, my mother is away, visiting a friend, and has been impossible to reach. But you'll be glad to know we've come to an agreement on the sale of the house. It's going through! Can you believe it?" Grim Hesper raised her eyebrow.

"That's a surprise. So soon?" said Ms. Fontaine. "Are you saying that Ida's agreed to pay your entire loan with the proceeds from this house?"

Grim Hesper recoiled as if Ms. Fontaine had struck her. "That is between my mother and me, but yes, that's the idea. I am her only child, after all."

The two women's eyes locked in a staredown. It was beginning to appear as if Ms. Fontaine and our grandmother weren't as friendly as we'd thought.

Ms. Fontaine reached into her briefcase, pulled out an envelope, and held it between them. Just as Grim Hesper grasped it, though, the bank president pulled it back.

"Hesper," she said, "there's another issue, and I need to speak with Ida about it personally." Ms. Fontaine let a moment pass before she added, "As soon as possible."

Grim Hesper raised her chin. "As soon as possible?" She eyed the envelope in the bank president's hand. "What could be so important?"

Ms. Fontaine took a deep breath. "We were looking more closely at the loan papers, specifically the guarantee, and there are questions only she can answer."

"Why on earth would you be looking at those?" Grim Hesper screeched. She wasn't even pretending to be friendly anymore. "I told you, the loan will be paid off in a matter of days. It's a complete nonissue."

Mr. Ashwick cleared his throat. "No, Hesper, I respectfully disagree. This is not a nonissue. As Ida's attorney, I have some concerns."

Grim Hesper's eyes landed on Mr. Ashwick. "I haven't seen you in forever, Sherman," she said with a satisfied purr, as if she were holding four aces in a game of cards against him.

Mr. Ashwick offered his hand and they shook.

"I suppose you're worried about the loan, too, Sherman? As I keep saying, there is no need—"

"Hesper," said Mr. Ashwick, cutting her off. "I have a difficult time believing that Ida would have risked the home she loved in that way, or that she would even sell it at all."

"Sherman, I promise you, there is no need to worry about my mother or her risk. As you heard me tell Lou, we're selling the property to Mr. Zimmerman for a great price. The loan will be paid by next week, and Mother will have plenty left over for years to come. You recognize Mr. Archie Zimmerman, don't you?" Grim Hesper glanced at Archie. "You should. His business dealings are in the *Post* every week."

Archie Zimmerman stood and shook Mr. Ashwick's hand.

"A pleasure," said Archie.

"Likewise," said Mr. Ashwick, immediately turning back to Grim Hesper.

"I've handled your mother's legal business for decades. You know that. But she never brought papers concerning any of these transactions to me. If Ida gave you a power of attorney to sell this property, I'd like to see it."

Grim Hesper's lip twitched. "Things have changed. She's not been herself, and we decided she can no longer live alone. And recently, since I'm an attorney, she's relied on me and my firm—" Before she could finish her sentence, there was a loud pounding on the front door.

Grim Hesper leapt from the kitchen to the dining room, past Mr. Ashwick, and all but shoved Ms. Fontaine out of the way. "Excuse me," she called behind her. "I must answer the door."

I bolted after her through the dining room, just in time to see Grim Hesper open the screen door. "Officers?" she said, stepping onto the porch. "Is there a problem?"

I stood in the foyer, a tumble of bodies suddenly beside me. We inched forward together until our faces were almost pressed against the screen.

"I'm afraid I have no idea what you're talking about," Grim Hesper was saying. "I am Hesper Spreen, the owner of this house."

The officer's tone changed, probably because he recognized her from the courthouse. "Ms. Spreen, I'm sorry, ma'am. I'm Officer Valdez, and this is my partner, Officer Shipman." He gestured to a female police officer observing from the walkway. "We received a call about some sort of property disagreement and fraudulent behavior? Were you aware of this complaint?"

Grim Hesper briefly turned and glared at Mr. Ashwick through the screen, and then the rest of us, before returning her eyes to the officers.

"Oh, it was a misunderstanding." She laughed and fanned the air with her fingers. "You see, there was some paperwork and we are selling the house, and well, it's settled now."

"Yes, ma'am." Officer Valdez pulled a small notebook from his pocket. "But according to our records, approximately four days ago, there was an incident at this address involving minors, a tree, and a missing guardian, so there are boxes we need to check off before we can leave." He turned a couple of pages, and when he looked up again, he crooked his head so he could see through the screen door to five faces staring back at him.

He returned his gaze to Grim Hesper. "You understand that it's our job, ma'am?"

"Of course." Grim Hesper's tone was not one bit understanding.

"Is one of you Rosie Spreen?" Officer Valdez said, peering around Grim Hesper again.

"Rosie? Why on earth do you need Rosie?" said Grim Hesper, standing three inches taller, blood flushing her neck.

"That's me," I said.

"Since you called, I'll need a formal statement," said Officer Valdez.

Grim Hesper's hands rose into tight fists. "I am her guardian and she will provide no such thing, not unless I'm present acting as her attorney."

"That's okay, Gram Hesper. Mr. Ashwick is my lawyer," I said in my most agreeable tone. Then I pointed. "And he's here, so I can talk to you."

The officer nodded and waved at the screen door. "Mr. Ashwick? Why don't you and Rosie come outside," said Officer Valdez. "Officer Shipman will speak with the rest of you inside, if it's okay."

Grim Hesper held up a hand. "It is absolutely not—"

I pushed the screen door wide open, scraping it against Grim Hesper's scarlet sleeve. "C'mon in." I smiled and held the door the way Karleen would.

I doubted inviting police officers into a house with a dead person in the basement was a good idea, but if Grim Hesper was against it—and it was easy to tell she was by the daggers shooting from her eyes—then I was all for it.

THIRTY-SEVEN°

I held the door for Officer Shipman and Grim Hesper, then followed Mr. Ashwick down the porch steps to speak with Officer Valdez. He kept asking if I felt safe. When I said I'd feel much safer if someone would stop my grandmother from selling my great-grandmother's home and her furniture, he said that would be a matter for an attorney such as Mr. Ashwick to handle.

While Officer Valdez droned on and on about what his actual job was, I watched Grave Hunter Dude shoveling around our gator rock band. He must have dug ten holes already.

I felt Mr. Ashwick's hand on my shoulder. "I'll keep an eye on Rosie and Baker and their custody, Officer. We've been trying to reach their aunt Tilly, since Ida's been called out of town."

When we went inside, the argument that had been happening in the kitchen was happening again in the foyer. Only this time, Officer Shipman was in the middle, looking like it was the last place in Montgomery County she wanted to be.

Ms. Fontaine was standing close to Grim Hesper. "If you refuse to cooperate, Hesper, I will be forced to get the Examine Bank legal team involved."

"This is ridiculous," said Grim Hesper. "The bank will have its money as soon as the sale goes through. By the end of the week, isn't that right, Archie?"

Archie Zimmerman was about to speak when Mr. Ashwick walked straight up to him and said, "I'm sorry to inform you, Mr. Zimmerman, but you won't be able to close the deal with Hesper until we reach her mother."

My heart skipped a beat. What was Mr. Ashwick doing?

Grim Hesper let out a nervous laugh. I knew she didn't want Great-Grammy to come home in time to ruin her plans. "My mother, she's quite the adventurer. She's off with a friend and barely has time to text. I have no idea where she is, to be honest, but I promise this deal is sound. I can show you the power of attorney she signed. We even have a lovely retirement condominium picked out. It's furnished and ready for her when she returns, with a staff to provide any service she might need." She looked around for Ms. Fontaine, trying to be pleasant again. "As I've said to Lou many times, this land and these children are too much for an eighty-eight-year-old woman to handle."

For a moment it was quiet, and then there was a rap on the screen door. Baker opened it and Mr. King and Karleen entered the crowded foyer.

"Hello," said Mr. King, scanning the room. "I hope I'm not interrupting something, but I'm afraid I need to speak with Mrs. Spreen Senior."

Karleen hurried to my side, shooting me a guilty *I'm sorry* look.

Archie Zimmerman started maneuvering around Mr. Ashwick, who was sort of, maybe purposely, getting between Archie and the door with his cane.

Mr. King stepped farther inside and angled his head at Karleen while he waved a familiar set of papers with a light blue cover page. "My wife found this in Karleen's bedroom, and we're wondering why on earth our daughter has an important document of Mrs. Spreen's."

Every person in the foyer seemed to stop breathing. Most of us knew what that important document was: Great-Grammy's will.

The old one. From thirty years ago.

Mr. Ashwick stuck out his hand. "I'm Sherman Ashwick, Ida's attorney. May I see that?"

"Of course," said Mr. King.

Just as he was handing the will to Mr. Ashwick, Grim Hesper swooped in from where she'd been standing by the stairs and snatched it from Mr. King's hands. "Wait just a minute," she said. "I've been looking for that."

"Hesper." Mr. Ashwick's voice dropped two octaves. "I need to confirm that that's Ida's most recent will."

Grim Hesper flicked page after page, then met Mr. Ashwick's eyes. She held out the will to him. "As you can see, I am the sole beneficiary. So regardless of anything you might be concerned about, in the end"—she stretched out her arms—"all of this is mine."

"Mr. Ashwick," said Officer Valdez. "I'd like to take a look at that."

"Of course, Officer," said Mr. Ashwick. "But I should tell you that this document is not Ida's most recent will."

Officer Valdez scanned the will, then looked up. "There is a more recent one?"

Grim Hesper's eyes widened. "Why are we talking about wills when nobody is dead? What matters is the power of attorney."

"True," said Officer Valdez, returning the document to her. "But I do have a question regarding the children. They were released to your care, is that correct?"

"Yes, Officer."

"Be advised that you need to inform the court where the children are living." He gestured to the empty rooms. "Since you obviously don't plan to stay here."

"Of course, Officer," said Grim Hesper. "I am making plans as we speak."

Officer Valdez whipped his finger around in a *wrap it up* signal to his partner. "Okay, then," he said, turning to Mr. Ashwick. "I think it's best if you find a way to contact Mrs. Spreen Senior. If there are any complaints to be made, come down to the station. You lawyers should know how to do that." He took business cards from his pocket and passed them around.

It looked like the party was over as the police officers started for the door and the foyer stirred with movement and chatter. Mr. Zimmerman was trying to escape Grim Hesper and her assurances, Karleen's dad was telling her it was time to leave, and Mr. Ashwick and Ms. Fontaine were huddled together whispering about what to do next.

Then, through a pane of glass, I saw Harry Mudd charging across the front walkway. Just as Officer Valdez was reaching for the door, the doorbell rang.

Valdez held the door and Mr. Mudd swept excitedly inside, not noticing the officers in uniform as he barged by them. The cops shook their heads at his bumbling entrance, then continued out the screen door.

When Mr. Mudd saw Baker and me, he grinned so wide it seemed his whole face would burst. He landed with a thump directly in front of us and exploded with his news.

"I think I know where the body is!" he shouted so that he could be heard above the clamor. And he was.

Instantly, there was quiet. Nobody moved, breathed, or spoke—until Officer Valdez and Officer Shipman shot back into the house.

"What did you say?" said Officer Shipman.

"The body!" said Mr. Mudd gleefully. "I'm ninety-seven percent positive it's underneath this house. Is there a basement?

Officer Valdez's hand went to his gun holster. "A body. In the basement of this house?"

"I knew something wasn't right here," said Officer Shipman.

Every eye was on Harry Mudd.

"Why, yes." He turned to face Baker and me again. "Do you think your great-grandmother would mind me taking a look?"

I glanced at Baker. The last place we wanted to go was the basement, especially with police in the house. But with everyone staring at Mr. Mudd, and now us, there wasn't much of a choice.

We had to make the crowd go away. I scooched between Mr. King and Karleen to the staircase and hopped to the third step so I could see everybody at once. "It's okay," I said, even though it wasn't. "This is Harry Mudd, and he's looking for a grave from the Civil War. C'mon, Mr. Mudd, we'll show you the basement."

Then I jumped down, grabbed Baker and Karleen by their arms, and pulled them toward the back hall, whispering, "We have to make sure he doesn't go near *you-know-where*."

Mr. Mudd followed us. Just behind him, I heard Grim Hesper exclaiming, "I most certainly would mind!" and Archie Zimmerman saying, "I don't understand. A dead body in your basement, Hesper? What does this mean?"

It turned out that everyone else had the same question. Both police officers, Archie Zimmerman, Grim Hesper, Mr. King, Mr. Ashwick, and Ms. Fontaine clomped down the wooden stairs after us.

"It means nothing," said Grim Hesper. "You don't need to be part of this. Let's just talk tomorrow after you've had a chance to—"

"Oh, it means something, if it's true," Mr. Ashwick called loudly enough for Mr. Zimmerman to hear. "It could take months—years—to decide how to proceed with the sale if there's a historically significant burial site in this basement. And what if there are others?"

Mr. King looked shocked. "Selling? No, it can't be. Mrs. Spreen would never give up this place. It's her home. Why, just two months ago she told me she wanted to keel over on her tomato plants and be buried in the family plot."

I looked up and saw him send a hard look to Grim Hesper before adding, "For a while she thought I was interested in tearing down her splendid home and developing the land. I assured her I had no such plans. Our corner of the world would never be the same without her, or this beautiful piece of property."

The eleven of us came in for a landing on the basement floor, not knowing quite where to go or what to do. Great-Grammy's supplies were heaped everywhere, and the two places we didn't want anybody to look—the enormous freezer with the Scrabble tiles spelling KEEP OUT on top, and the toilet paper castle that camouflaged our office— were screaming *Look! Look! Over here!*

Mr. Mudd rummaged through his knapsack, pulled out a flashlight, and purposefully strode to the shadows of the far right corner, opposite where the freezer stood. We were quiet as he got down on his knees and searched through his knapsack again, this time coming up with a large magnifying glass. Then he stooped and began examining every inch of the floor and walls.

Grim Hesper marched across the basement and hovered behind him. "What, may I ask, are you looking for?"

"A grave marker, perhaps. Or part of one?" Harry Mudd didn't turn around as he answered. "The soldier I'm trying to find was a scout buried after a Civil War battle, along with four of his comrades. Their commander wanted them moved to a more formal memorial site, but somehow this young man was overlooked. By the time the mistake was realized, the area had become so overgrown it was impossible."

"Interesting," said Mr. Ashwick. "What about his descendants?"

"Interesting?" snapped Grim Hesper. "This is a complete waste of time. We are talking about someone who died over a hundred and fifty years ago. What does it matter?"

This time Harry Mudd turned and looked Grim Hesper in the eyes. "It matters a lot."

She put her hands on her hips and spun around. "Well, I'm going back upstairs. Archie, are you coming?"

"Actually, I'd like to stay and see how this turns out," he said. "Since it may impact how we proceed with the development."

Grim Hesper let out a deep breath. "As you wish. But if Mr. Mudd finds a body, I will personally have the unfortunate fellow moved wherever he likes."

Harry Mudd was inching farther and farther down the wall. "It's more complicated than that, I'm afraid. This young man is considered a national hero, and if I find him, it's not up to me what happens. The process could take months, depending on how many organizations get involved. And of course the body would need to be properly cared for in order to preserve his remains."

Both officers pulled out their flashlights and turned them on. "What would a marker look like?" asked Officer Shipman as she and Officer Valdez split up and aimed their beams of light from corner to corner of the basement. When their lights crisscrossed over Great-Grammy's freezer, Karleen, Baker, and I exchanged looks.

Two police officers and a grave expert were in our basement looking for a dead body. Not good.

I tugged on Karleen's and Baker's arms, whispering, "We need to split up."

Baker grabbed a lantern from the table and gestured toward Officer Valdez. "I'll go with him."

That meant I should stay close to Officer Shipman.

Karleen put a hand on my shoulder. "I'll try to get my father to go home. I have to go to the shelter anyway."

I didn't want Karleen to leave, but maybe others would follow. I nodded.

"Would you look at how much Ida's got here?" said Mr. Ashwick, who'd been circling the tables, inspecting Great-Grammy's stash. "It's been such a busy day, I forgot to have lunch. I'm sure she wouldn't mind if I snagged a snack. What do you think, Hesper?"

"Perhaps you should get a proper meal," said Grim Hesper. "I highly recommend the Slotted Spoon. It's only ten minutes away."

I agreed with Grim Hesper. *Everybody should leave.*

"Oh, I wouldn't miss this for anything. I'm very interested to see if Mr. Mudd finds his grave." Mr. Ashwick leaned his cane against the table and rubbed his hands together. "This bag of Snickers seems to have my name on it."

As though there'd been some sort of snack-time announcement, Ms. Fontaine began sorting packages of candy. "Ooooh, Almond Joys are my favorite." She looked across the table at me. "Would you like one, Rosie?"

I was standing in front of the "entrance" to our "office" so Grim Hesper wouldn't notice it, keeping an eye on Officer Shipman and making sure nobody wandered anywhere near the freezer.

The thought of food made me gag. "No thank you."

Mr. Ashwick struggled to open his second candy bar. "You know, Harry," he called across the room, "I remember a story about this basement being haunted." He chuckled. "Who was it that refused to come down here for years?"

"Oh, that was Gram Hesper," said Baker, who was shadowing Officer Valdez, holding his lantern high.

Grim Hesper didn't say anything, but her face changed, and she took a few nervous steps backward, as if she wanted to get away from something. And then I realized, she *did*.

The Door to Nowhere!

"Ummmmm," I said. "What about the Door to Nowhere? We tried to open it last night, but the key wouldn't go in. It's rusted shut."

The next thing I knew, Harry Mudd was in my face and there were six sets of eyes closing in behind him, waiting for me to explain. Grim Hesper stayed where she was and kept looking toward the dark side of the basement, beyond the stairs.

"Door to Nowhere?" Mr. Mudd's eyes were like magnified marbles behind his glasses. "Here? In the basement?"

Baker beamed his lantern toward the far wall, opposite where they'd been looking, behind the back of the stairs. "It's right there, to the left," he said. "Close to the ground."

I nodded. "Yeah, Great-Grammy said, er says, her family used to store root vegetables there."

Baker laughed. "She always joked about a ghost living behind it because it was the only thing that made Gram Hesper behave, even when she was a teenager."

"It wasn't funny in the least," Grim Hesper said indignantly. "Very strange noises came from this basement at night."

Harry Mudd disappeared into the shadows on the other side of the stairs, only visible because of his flashlight.

"This could be it." There was a jerking noise, and then he said, "Yes, the lock is rusted shut, but I think I can clean it out. Is there a key?"

"Maybe," I said.

I didn't want to give our hideout away, but everything in the basement was going to be gone when the donation truck came, anyway. And if Harry Mudd found what he was looking for, everybody would be distracted by *that* dead body and hopefully get the heck out of our house.

I scooted underneath the table and rummaged around the basket where I'd put the key the day before.

"Mother used to keep a box of spare keys in the freezer," Grim Hesper was saying.

Mr. Ashwick asked, "Which one?"

"How should I know?"

Just as my fingertips felt the key at the bottom of the basket, I heard the familiar tug and whoosh of a freezer door opening.

My hand froze. *All* of me froze.

What were they doing?

"This one is chock-full," said Grim Hesper. "My mother and I have our differences, but everyone agrees she's a wonderful cook. A shame it will all go to waste."

Wrong freezer. Or right freezer. I started breathing again.

That was too close.

As fast as I could, I scrambled from underneath the table, holding the key up high. But nobody paid attention to me.

Ms. Fontaine was opening her third or fourth Almond Joy. Harry Mudd, Baker, and the two police officers were putting on a light show, shining their flashlights on and around the Door to Nowhere so Mr. Mudd could work on the lock, and Karleen was pulling her dad toward the stairs.

Away from the commotion, Grim Hesper stood in front of the

upright freezer, peering inside with Mr. Ashwick beside her, eyeing the stacks of casseroles. It wasn't enough to sell everything Great-Grammy loved, she wanted to ditch the last meals she'd made, too.

I was holding the key higher, about to announce that I'd found it, when someone behind me chuckled. I turned to see Archie Zimmerman.

"That's cute," he said, smiling at the Scrabble rack in his hand. " 'Keep out.' "

And then he reached down with his free hand—

"This one looks brand-new," he said.

Gripping.

The.

Freezer.

Lid.

My stomach dropped as I watched Mr. Zimmerman lift it wide open. For a millionth of a second he was quiet. Then he took a step backward.

"Mr. Mudd," he squeaked. "I don't suppose you're looking for two bodies?"

It was another stampede. Mr. Mudd, the officers, Mr. Ashwick, Ms. Fontaine, and Mr. King surrounded Mr. Zimmerman and the freezer, while Baker, Karleen, and I traded wide-eyed *What do we do now?* looks.

"Oh, no!" cried Ms. Fontaine. "Is that—"

"Everyone, stand back," said Officer Valdez. "It appears we have a crime scene on our hands."

"I knew it," Officer Shipman said under her breath, but loud enough for everyone to hear. She raised her voice, telling Officer Valdez, "I'll call for backup."

As everyone else inched back, I moved closer.

I peered between the two officers as Officer Valdez spread his arms wide to keep us away. And even though he was blocking my view, I saw her.

Great-Grammy.

There was nothing left to do. Nothing I *could* do.

The biggest lie was—over.

THIRTY-EIGHT°

Within minutes, more police officers came tromping down the basement steps. Cameras flashed. "Evidence," like the ski mask and the gloves, was carefully removed and put in clear bags. The perimeter of the freezer was taped off; details were discussed and observations made, then written down.

Next was a pair of paramedics, who confirmed that the elderly woman in the freezer was, as already had been determined, dead.

Then the forensic investigator arrived and agreed that the police and paramedics were correct. There was a woman in the freezer. She was elderly. And she was dead.

Now they just had to figure out when it happened, why it happened, how it happened, and most importantly, who had put her in the freezer. She was presumed to be Ida Marigold Spreen, the owner of the house.

"Yes," said Grim Hesper in a dull tone. "That is my mother."

Officer Shipman moved closer to Grim Hesper. "Ms. Spreen, come with me, please? We have some questions."

Grim Hesper looked from Officer Shipman to Officer Valdez. *"Now?"*

"I'm not a detective," the forensic investigator was saying to one of the other officers, "but I'd lay bets that when you discover who put Mrs. Spreen in the freezer, you'll find out how she died."

That's when Grim Hesper must have understood, because she spun around and glared at Baker and me, her face as red as the dress she was wearing and her eyebrows narrowed. "It's not me you need to question. It's these children. They've been living in this house for three years."

"Be assured, Ms. Spreen, we will speak with everyone," said Officer Shipman. "Would you like to call your attorney?"

Grim Hesper twisted to face the officer and screeched, "You can't possibly think *I* had anything to do with this?"

Mr. Ashwick stepped out of the shadows, with Mr. Zimmerman right beside him. They'd been talking privately.

"Hesper," said Mr. Ashwick. "I have some questions, too. Like how on earth did Ida sign the power of attorney you needed to sell her property to Mr. Zimmerman *yesterday*?" He waved a hand at Great-Grammy. "Since it appears that she was in no condition to do such a thing."

Grim Hesper pressed her lips into a long, thin line. Then she glanced down, and a tiny smirk rose at the corner of her mouth. She was still holding Great-Grammy's old will.

Oh, no. Once the police found out Great-Grammy hadn't been murdered and it was Baker and me who'd followed her orders and put her in the freezer, none of the other stuff mattered. Because according to the will in Grim Hesper's hands, she'd be able to do whatever she wanted with this house and everything of Great-Grammy's.

Grim Hesper might not win this battle, today, but she would win the war. Everything we'd done for Great-Grammy to protect what she'd built and loved—the lies and pretending—would be wasted.

There were loud clomp, clomp, clomps, and I reached for Baker as two paramedics walked a stretcher down the stairs.

I wanted to run away. Great-Grammy was leaving her home, our home, forever. I squeezed my brother's hand. He was the only person in the world who could possibly understand what I was feeling.

There was a tap on my shoulder: Mr. Mudd.

"Under the circumstances," he said, "I think it's best if I return another time."

I looked past him, toward the dark side of the basement and the Door to Nowhere.

The key was still in my hand! I held it out to him.

"No, no," said Mr. Mudd. "Now that I'm satisfied the grave is somewhere behind your Door to Nowhere, we can hold the rest for later."

"What about—" Baker started to speak, but Mr. Mudd interrupted, gesturing at the freezer and Great-Grammy. "I'm very sorry for your loss." As he walked away, he glanced back. "Take care of yourselves, and don't worry, I'll be in touch. Our soldier isn't going anywhere."

His soldier wasn't going anywhere, but Great-Grammy was. I let my eyes drift across the basement. Over by the stairs, Officer Shipman was trying to question Grim Hesper, but she had her arms folded and her mouth sealed shut. Closer to me, Ms. Fontaine and Mr. Ashwick were telling Mr. Zimmerman things he didn't want to hear. Mr. King and Karleen had disappeared. I'd need to apologize to Karleen's parents for getting their daughter involved in our problems, but that would have to wait.

Baker tugged at my arm. Without looking, I knew what he was telling me. I took a deep breath and faced what I didn't want to see. The paramedics were lifting Great-Grammy out of the freezer. When they set her on the stretcher, one of them removed a white sheet from a gear bag on the floor and began to cover her.

"Wait," I said.

Both paramedics looked up.

"Can we—" I started, but my throat was stuck and my lips puckered. I squeezed my eyes closed. This would probably be the last time I'd ever see Great-Grammy. I had to get a grip. But my whole body was trembling, and try as I might, I couldn't force the words out.

Baker put his arm across my back and cleared his throat. "Please, can we say goodbye?"

The paramedic nearest Great-Grammy's face glanced over his shoulder. "Of course." He lifted the police tape and they pushed the gurney toward us.

I put my hand onto Great-Grammy's arm. Her eyes were closed, and she might have spent thirteen days below zero, but she still looked like Great-Grammy. I bent and kissed her cheek, and then Baker did the same.

I felt better, like she'd somehow kissed us back, even though that was impossible.

"We love you, Great-Grammy, and we'll miss you forever," I whispered through a long sniffle. "And even though you're not here, I'm going to be a better great-granddaughter, I promise."

"Me too," said Baker. "Great-grandson, I mean."

We backed up and watched the paramedics cover her with the

sheet, then wheel her across the basement floor. I stood, unable to move as they carried her up the stairs. At the same time, I felt almost...free. It was over, or one part was over. Great-Grammy was finally out of the freezer.

"I guess Grim Hesper was right," said Baker.

If Baker was trying to distract me, it worked. "What are you talking about?"

He was looking across the basement, past the stairs. "There's been a ghost haunting the basement this whole time."

I shivered. "Not for much longer, I hope."

"At least when Mr. Mudd comes back he'll know where to dig."

Baker's comment triggered my memory of something...but what?

The Door to Nowhere? The ghost haunting the basement? Mr. Mudd?

"Baker, say that again."

"What? About Mr. Mudd digging for the soldier?"

Digging for the soldier. *Under the house.* That was Great-Grammy's clue.

But we'd always known that.

Something about the digging. Harry Mudd had been digging around the gator rock band this afternoon, down by the mailbox, and yesterday he'd left mounds of dirt scattered across the yard. But when we got off the school bus today, there was a mound of dirt he couldn't have dug. He hadn't been there yet.

A mound of dirt that *could* have been weeks old.

Had Great-Grammy done the digging?

Maybe the lockbox wasn't under *this* house. Maybe it was under

Great-Grammy's favorite piece of yard art that was *shaped* like a house: the Home Sweet Home sculpture.

How could we have missed something so obvious?

I grinned at Baker and took hold of his arm. "We might not lose the war after all."

I ran, pulling my amazing little brother along with me, past the police officers, past Grim Hesper, past Mr. Ashwick and Ms. Fontaine, and past Mr. Zimmerman, the man who was never going to buy our Home Sweet Home.

Because if I was right and Great-Grammy's will was where I thought it was, I'd found the real key. The one we needed to get our lives back on track.

Home Sweet Home had never meant so much.

THIRTY-NINE°

We didn't stop to ask the people in uniforms why they were carrying Grim Hesper's laptops and papers out of the house. Baker and I just ran past them into the front yard.

"Hey! You two!" Officer Valdez called after us. "Where do you think you're going?"

It was probably a good idea to have a witness, so I waved him along. "Hurry up!"

We went at full speed until we hit the tree line. "You figured out where the will is, didn't you?" said Baker as we slowed down.

I nodded, panting. Then I cranked my neck and checked for Officer Valdez, but he wasn't the only one interested in us. When two kids ran for their lives from a crime scene, people followed.

Officer Valdez and two other cops were closing in, and Mr. Ash-wick was doing his best speed-walk across the grass, holding tight to his cane. When he saw me, he waved the cane in the air with a smile. He knew what we were after.

And there it was: the mound of dirt we must have passed fifty times.

I knelt on the ground, right where Great-Grammy's Home Sweet

Home decoration used to be...before Grim Hesper began "cleaning up."

Baker dropped beside me, his whole forehead furrowed. "Here?"

"Remember what Great-Grammy kept here?"

Baker's mouth dropped open. "It makes total sense!"

I squatted over the dirt and dug into it with my fingers, scooping as fast as I could. Baker did the same.

"Kids," said Officer Valdez as he stood a few feet away, panting. "I was about to talk to you about something when you ran off. You can't just disappear like that." He took deep breaths while the other two officers caught up.

Baker and I kept digging as Officer Valdez continued what sounded like an official speech. "I just spoke with my chief. You were released to your grandmother's custody last week, but in light of the current situation, we need to make different arrangements. We'll have to call Social Services."

"Social Services?" shouted Mr. Ashwick as he hobbled over the uneven ground toward us. "Nonsense. There's no need for that."

Officer Valdez raised an eyebrow. "Are you a family member?"

Mr. Ashwick planted his cane defiantly in front of Officer Valdez. "Their rightful guardian will be returning any day now. I'm sure of it."

"Oh?" said Officer Valdez.

"Yes," said Mr. Ashwick. "You may remember I represent the deceased, Ida Spreen, and I am also the children's attorney."

"That's good to hear, but without a family guardian present, the decision about who will care for them until the official guardian is present will need to go through appropriate channels."

Baker and I sat up and locked eyes.

We'd hit something hard.

We hunched over, frantically scraping and carving the dirt until the whole top of a metal box was visible.

We kept digging, nudging at its edges.

"What are they doing?" asked one of the officers.

"I believe they're digging up Ida Spreen's most recent will and testament," said Mr. Ashwick.

With one final wrench, the box was free. I lifted it from the ground, a lockbox with no lock.

"Open it." I held it out to Baker. "I'm afraid to."

Baker reached out and squeezed my shoulder. "Both of us."

He put his fingers on one side, and I put mine on the other, and we raised the lid together. There it was, sealed inside a plastic storage bag, the Final Will and Testament of Ida Marigold Spreen, our great-grandmother.

The sun was sinking, and the birds chitter-chattered their evening songs. My eyes swept the tree line, from one side of Great-Grammy's property to the other.

I took the plastic bag out of the box, unsealed it, and handed the thick documents—the will and its copy—to Mr. Ashwick. It didn't matter what Great-Grammy had decided. Whether Grim Hesper was in the will or not. Whether Great-Grammy legally named Aunt Tilly as our guardian or not. What mattered was that Great-Grammy's wishes would be heard. There would be no secrets or lies—not anymore.

I faced Officer Valdez. "Is it okay if we go back to the house?"

He glanced at the other officers. "Sure. But no running off again. Someone from Social Services will be here soon."

Mr. Ashwick was turning the pages of the will as we started up the lawn. "Yes, yes, this is Ida's most recent will, signed and witnessed," he said to nobody in particular. "The property and her assets are divided... first and foremost, to her daughter, Hesper, the exact amount of her law school tuition, including expenses and interest. And in Hesper's name a scholarship will be set up so a worthy young person can attend law school at her alma mater. Yes, yes. A generous donation to the animal rescue society, and another to the homeless shelter, mmm-hmm, very good, and Tilly, of course... oh, yes, here's what I was looking for... Tilly will be named guardian, and then"—his voice grew fainter as Baker and I walked arm in arm—"'the remainder of my estate shall be put in a trust for my great-grandchildren, Rose Marigold Spreen and Baker Alexander Spreen...'"

Baker and I kept walking. We might have to wait a few days or a few weeks for things to start getting back to normal, but our futures would not involve boarding schools across the Atlantic Ocean, or being separated.

I turned to my brother. "I'm starving."

Baker grinned. "Me too! Want to make some snickerdoodles?"

We were laughing as we approached the walkway, so at first we didn't hear the crackling asphalt of a car zooming up our long driveway. It was the honking horn that got our attention.

It was a regular old car, nothing special. But when it came to a stop at the top of the driveway, my heart stopped, too. After so much time hoping, it felt almost impossible. Was it? Could it be?

The back door opened. A second later, Karleen charged out of the car, her whole face beaming rays of sunshine as she ran, waving her arms and screaming things we couldn't understand.

When she reached us, she was so excited she ran around us in a large circle. "You'll never believe! You'll never believe!" she said again and again.

Baker grabbed her arm. "What, Karleen? What's happening?"

I looked past Karleen, at the car. The driver had opened the door and there was a funny cry. "No!" said the voice. "You rascal, you come back here!"

That's when Aunt Tilly's head popped up, her eyes wide. She shot around the car and ran toward us in a zany zigzag. But she wasn't running toward us. She was chasing after a very familiar and energetic ball of fluff that *was* running toward us.

Daisy!!!!

Suddenly the puppy was in my arms, licking the happy tears from my cheeks that I hadn't even known were falling. Daisy knew me!

Aunt Tilly flittered across the lawn, laughing. "Oh, dear, well there goes the surprise," she said, coming for us with wide arms.

The three of us hugged for a full minute. "I'm so sorry," Aunt Tilly whispered between sniffs. "We've lost the best member of our family, haven't we? And you two had to deal with it alone. I deserve to be flogged, but I promise everything will be okay now. I'll make sure of it."

Then Karleen was in the middle of us, and after another long, tight squeeze, Aunt Tilly stepped back and gestured to the police cars. "I would have been here an hour ago, but when I read your email I wanted to bring you two a present. So I stopped by the shelter and met your dear friend Karleen. And Daisy, of course." She petted Daisy, who was still frantically licking every bit of me she could reach. "I thought a brand-new puppy would help us start our lives together. What do you think?"

"As if you'll stay around for longer than a week," said Grim Hesper, coming fast down the walkway, tucked between Officer Shipman and another police officer.

"Oh, don't worry, Mother." Aunt Tilly tousled Baker's hair as Grim Hesper walked by. "Now I have the best kind of reason to work from home."

Grim Hesper didn't answer, and it wasn't till she passed us that we saw she was handcuffed.

Aunt Tilly was quiet, as though she was thinking. After a second she turned and took a few steps toward the driveway. "Mother, is there something you'd like me to do? How can I help?"

The officers were waiting for Grim Hesper to step into the back of the patrol car. "Help me?" She snickered. "Don't concern yourself with me, Tilly. I will help myself."

And then she disappeared from view.

Maybe one day Grim Hesper would understand she didn't have to be alone in this world. But today was not that day.

I felt an arm around me, then another, then another. It was my family hugging me.

And today was *our* day.

FORTY°

I didn't open my eyes. I didn't have to. Whiffs of salty bacon and the warm scent of sugar and cinnamon drifted into my bedroom—my bedroom with the lavender walls and wavy windows and nicked-with-memories furniture—whispering the kitchen's invitation.

It was morning, and for the first Sunday in weeks I felt cozy and safe. The furniture was back, Baker's trains were set up, and life was good again.

I snuggled the cotton blanket around my shoulders and inhaled deeply. As I let out a long breath, I looked at the dresser. I couldn't see the envelope from my bed, but I knew it was there. It was time.

The floorboards were cool to the touch of my bare feet. I didn't curse them now. Someone in our family had laid them across other unseen beams of wood, building this house piece by piece. Great-Grammy had told me that many times, but I'd only started listening after she stopped talking.

I took the envelope from the dresser, and instead of returning to bed, I went to the window and looked outside. The bright green grass, the flowering bushes, the bluebird vigorously shaking itself in Great-Grammy's seahorse birdbath—all of it.

Summer was here, and life was everywhere I looked. Even, surprisingly, the envelope in my hand. The handwriting was shaky but distinct. Great-Grammy's. *Rose Marigold Spreen, My Great-Granddaughter*, it said on the front.

I tore the seal, then removed the thick folded paper. It was two pages, written in blue ink.

Part of me didn't want to begin. It was like standing at the edge of a pool on the first day of summer. I knew the water would send a cold shock through my body, but I had to dive in if I wanted to swim.

So with a quick shudder, I dove headfirst into Great-Grammy's letter.

My Dearest Rosie,

If you're reading this, we both know what happened. After years of joking about it, I've finally keeled over! You probably don't think it's too funny right now, especially since what I'm asking of you and Baker is going to be difficult. Believe me, if I have any say, I'll haunt Tilly till she hurries home to help you two. And don't worry, she'll come. Tilly would give up traveling in an instant to give you a real home. And I know the three of you will be very happy together.

That brings me to what I want to say. I know how difficult the past few years have been for you. Losing your parents was a nightmare no child should have to endure. It broke my heart to watch you and Baker suffer the way you did. Sometimes you were angry at the world, and since I was around, you lashed out at me. I want you to know I understand that the things you said were said out of grief.

Don't waste one second feeling bad about that, or being angry that I'm gone, too. I'm still here, perched on your shoulder, helping you every step of the way. I promise.

Rosie, I love you. If I could stay on earth forever, watching you grow into the intelligent, hardworking, and loving young woman I already see inside you, I would. But all things end. Storms pass, one season turns into the next, happy turns to sad and then back again. It's probably why I value our home and the memories we've made here so much.

We pass down the pieces of ourselves that matter to the next generation in many ways. You and your brother are the best pieces of myself that I'm leaving here.

So, Rosie, I am sending you forward into the years ahead with the memories of our time together and all my love. When you need me, just look around, especially in the mirror. You will find me there.

A million hugs and kisses,
Great-Grammy

I looked out the window again. It was blurry through my tears. She'd known everything I'd been going through and understood me before I understood myself.

I didn't feel angry that she was gone, but I felt sad. Very, very sad.

Carefully, I folded her letter and returned it to the envelope, then held it to my heart as I opened my dresser drawer. I tucked it underneath my rolled-up socks, knowing I would read it again soon.

There was a scratch at the door, and then a knock. "Rosie?"

It was Baker.

"Come in," I said, wiping my eyes.

The door opened and Daisy burst in, her tail wagging even as she skidded across the wood floor.

Baker poked his head into the room. "Karleen just got here, and Aunt Tilly says after we eat, we can go to the garden store and find another Home Sweet Home sign for the yard. Yes?"

I felt a huge, down-deep, sunshiny smile spread across my face. I couldn't think of anything I'd rather do.

"Yes!" I said, picking up Daisy and snuggling her to my neck. "Yes! Yes! Yes!"

It turned out smiling was pretty easy once a person got the hang of it.

SPREEN FAMILY RECIPES

Always get a parent or guardian's permission before working in the kitchen.

Baker's Emergency Salad Dressing

Yield: ½ cup dressing

Ingredients:

- ½ cup mayonnaise
- 3 tablespoons ketchup
- 2 teaspoons sweet (pickle) relish

Directions:

- Combine all ingredients in a small bowl and whisk together. Keep chilled.
- Use as dip for vegetables or as salad dressing.

Great-Grammy's Noodle Wiggle Casserole

Serves 8

Ingredients:

- 1 pound bulk Italian sausage
- 1 cup chopped onion
- 1 clove garlic, minced
- Two 15-ounce cans of tomato sauce
- ½ teaspoon salt

- 1 teaspoon dried oregano
- One 10-ounce package chopped, frozen spinach, thawed and drained
- One 15-ounce container of ricotta cheese
- 4 cups shredded low-moisture mozzarella, divided. (Two 8-ounce blocks of cheese, shredded.)
- ¼ cup Parmesan cheese
- ¼ teaspoon pepper
- Half of a 15-ounce package of egg noodles (use approximately 8 ounces, but a little more is fine)

Directions:
- Preheat oven to 375 degrees.
- In large skillet, on medium heat, sauté sausage, onion, and garlic together, until sausage is cooked through. (Using wooden spoon, break sausage into small bits.)
- Then add tomato sauce, salt, and oregano. Simmer this mixture for 15 minutes, stirring as necessary.
- In a medium bowl, combine thawed and drained spinach (patted dry), ricotta cheese, 2 cups shredded mozzarella, Parmesan cheese, and pepper. Mix well.
- Cook egg noodles in boiling water according to package directions. Drain.
- In a 13x9-inch baking dish, layer noodles, meat sauce, and spinach mixture: First layer half of the cooked noodles, then spoon half of meat sauce over noodles, then half of the spinach/cheese mixture. You can spoon the cheese in dollops as evenly as you can, and then do your best to spread it over the sauce. This will not be perfect!

Then layer the remaining noodles, sauce, and cheese mixture in the same way.

- Top with the remaining two cups of shredded mozzarella.
- Cover with aluminum foil and bake at 375 degrees for 40 minutes. Then remove the foil and increase the oven temperature to 425 degrees and bake for an additional 10–15 minutes, or until top is bubbly and golden.
- Let stand for 5 minutes, then serve.

Baker's Malted Chocolate Chip Cookies

Yield: 12–24 cookies, depending on size of cookies

Ingredients:

- 1 cup plus 2 tablespoons all-purpose flour
- 1 tablespoon malted milk powder (usually found in baking aisle)
- ½ teaspoon baking soda
- ½ teaspoon salt
- ½ cup butter, softened (one stick)
- ½ cup granulated sugar
- ¼ cup light or dark brown sugar
- ½ teaspoon vanilla extract
- 1 large egg
- 1 cup semisweet chocolate pieces
- ½ cup quartered chocolate-covered malt balls, plus more for decoration. If parent isn't present to supervise use of paring knife, seal malt balls in plastic storage bag and whack with wooden spoon a couple of times.

Directions:

- Preheat oven to 375 degrees.
- Whisk together flour, malted milk powder, baking soda, and salt in a small bowl.
- In a large mixing bowl, beat softened butter. Then add granulated and brown sugar and vanilla, and beat until creamy.
- Add egg and beat until well combined.
- Mix in semisweet chocolate pieces and chocolate-covered malt ball pieces.
- To bake, prepare baking sheet with rectangle of parchment paper. Drop dough on parchment paper by heaping teaspoons or heaping tablespoons, and press down and shape a bit, leaving at least two inches between cookies. Decorate with halved maltball in center of cookie, up or down.
- Bake for 9–13 minutes, or until light golden brown, depending on size of cookies. Remove from oven and let cookies set for 2 minutes. Using spatula, transfer cookies to wire rack and let cool.

Great-Grammy's Refrigerator Strawberry Jam

Yield: 1 cup of jam

Ingredients:

- 1 pound fresh strawberries, washed and stems and white part removed, diced.
- ¼ cup sugar
- 1 tablespoon lemon juice

- 1 tablespoon tapioca flour (also called tapioca starch)

Directions:

- In a heavy medium-sized pot, combine diced strawberries, sugar, and lemon juice, and mash slightly with potato masher.
- Cook over medium heat until sugar is dissolved, then increase heat until mixture comes to a light boil. Continue cooking for 10–12 minutes, stirring frequently. For thickening, at the 10-minute mark, whisk in tapioca flour. This isn't necessary, but you will need to cook another 5–10 minutes if you don't. Allow strawberry mixture to cool and then transfer to a container with a tight lid and refrigerate. Use within 1–2 weeks.
- Slather on toast or English muffin, or spoon over ice cream or waffles.

ACKNOWLEDGMENTS

Sally Morgridge is an editor to her bones and, beyond that, passionate, open-minded, helpful, and wise. I feel like a more capable writer and storyteller knowing she has my back. I'm grateful to her and those at Holiday House who, when Sally passed the first pages of *Six Feet Below Zero* on to them, reacted so enthusiastically.

I'd also like to thank everyone at Holiday House who helped put this book together, especially Mary Cash, Terry Borzumato-Greenberg, Michelle Montague, Cheryl Lew, Hannah Finne, Jessica Dartnell, Raina Putter, and Kerry Martin. Thanks also to the Penguin Random House team who handled all things sales and distribution.

Agents help writers figure out which projects might be worth developing. When I sent Ginger Knowlton the first four nonsensical chapters of *SFBZ*, I braced myself for a "this story is a little too crazy to sell" email. Instead, she encouraged me to finish the book. If it weren't for Ginger cheering me onward, the *SFBZ* manuscript would likely still be four chapters on my hard drive. Thank you, Ginger!

A special thanks to cover artist Maeve Norton for creating such a wonderful jacket cover for *SFBZ*, and to copyeditor Barbara Perris, whose laser-sharp skills have now helped usher three of my books into the world.

The kid-lit community is large and full of supportive fellow creators, many of whom have become like family to me. I would not have enjoyed my writing journey a fraction as much without these special people in my life.

Rebecca Barnhouse is the best critique partner a person could ask for and one of my closest friends. When I came up with the idea for *SFBZ* and sent her the rough synopsis and first couple of chapters, I included a list of reasons why I shouldn't write the story. Her response was a list of reasons why I should. What would I do without Rebecca? I don't know. She always reads whatever I send, whenever I need her to, and mostly, she's one of the best human beings on the planet.

I also showed *Six Feet Below Zero* to a few other writing buds along the way, and whether they read ten pages, fifty, or the entire manuscript, I am grateful to each of them for their insights and encouragement: Anne Bingham, Vonna Carter, Katie Kennedy, and Rebecca Petruck. And a special shout-out to the members of my NC SCBWI workshop group, who read an early version of the first ten pages and urged me to keep going: Teresa Fannin, Eileen Heyes, Helen Rapoport, Bradley Scheel, Karen Staman, and Lori Tussey.

To my writers' groups, past and present, even if we're not exchanging work, you're always with me. The members of: Hoggtowne Scribblers & Doodlers, Secrets & Shenanigans, The Inkygirl Cabin, Loose Change critique group, Greensboro SCBWI critique group, and the SCBWI Blueboard, especially my former mod and admin buds.

To my children, who read when I ask and cheer me on when I don't:

Blake, Kevin, Ena Marie, and Thomas. Each of you is my favorite in your own way, and even though you're all grown, I'm still writing for the children you were. Thanks especially to Thomas, who proofed many stacks of pages during semester breaks, when I know he'd rather have been sleeping.

And with all my heart, I thank my husband, Jeff. It was his grandmother who inspired the character of Great-Grammy, and her property that I walked through in my mind as I wrote. In its way, this book is a love letter to both of them.